THE
GARDEN
PARTY

BOOKS BY WENDY CLARKE

What She Saw

We Were Sisters

The Bride

His Hidden Wife

Blind Date

Childhood Sweetheart

The Night Out

THE
GARDEN PARTY

WENDY CLARKE

bookouture

Published by Bookouture in 2024

An imprint of Storyfire Ltd.
Carmelite House
50 Victoria Embankment
London EC4Y 0DZ

www.bookouture.com

ISBN: 978-1-83790-978-0
eBook ISBN: 978-1-83790-977-3

For Laura

PROLOGUE

The silent death... that's what they call drowning. The person in the water unable to shout for help. Their energy reserved for the fight to keep their head above water, saving what little oxygen is left in their body. And by the time the water enters their lungs, it's too late anyway. The desire to cry out a memory.

It's what we all want, isn't it? A silent death. An easy death.

Take my hand, little girl. Hold it tight. I'll take you to see the tadpoles and the moon reflected on the water like a gold coin. Your mother needn't know. It will be our secret. Just yours and mine because you can't trust anyone... especially a neighbour.

But you trust *me*, don't you? I can see it in your eyes. In the way your fingers wrap around my own.

Drowning. *The silent death*. Because no one will ever know how you came to be there. What it feels like to lie below the surface of the pond, under your shroud of drifting birch leaves.

An accurate name. Because you'll never be able to tell.

Never.

ONE

RACHEL

A new start, I tell myself. *It's all we need.*

Beside me, sitting straight-backed in the driving seat, my husband Owen is a study in tension. Evidence of it in the angle of his chin. The rigid set of his shoulders.

I put a hand on his knee. 'You okay?'

Owen stares in front of him. Slows down to let a car enter our lane of traffic. 'Of course. Why wouldn't I be?'

There are many answers I could give: because we've given up our old life, because your last book didn't make any of the book charts, because you've lost your confidence, because of the state of our marriage. But I say none of these things. Instead, I place my hands over my stomach, trying to disguise the sound of its rumbling. Even though we've only been on the road for a few hours, the lunch we'd snatched – sandwiches in cardboard and cellophane wrap eaten at an empty breakfast bar surrounded by packing cases – seems a lifetime ago.

'We'll need to stop at a supermarket. Get something for later.'

Owen gives a heavy sigh, scratches at his beard. 'It can wait.

We've got enough to get by this evening. Anyway, we're nearly there.'

The town we've just driven through, a sprawling mass of pale-stone houses, had done nothing to excite me the one and only time we came up to view the house. And now, as we edge towards its outskirts, I feel the same. I sit up straighter in my seat, force myself to be more positive, because soon we'll be there. Our new home. Our new start.

'Not long now. I recognise the garage. How exciting!' The effort it takes to sound convincing is giving me a headache.

We drive for another few miles, then Owen indicates and turns left at a road sign that says Pond Close. It's not unpleasant, I tell myself as the cul-de-sac opens up in front of us. In fact, the estate agent hadn't been lying when he'd called the sweeping semicircle of houses desirable. As Owen slows, skirts the edge of the large, circular pond area that the houses encircle, I take in the properties: five of them in total, built of Cotswold stone. Their shiny front doors, all painted a dark blue, shaded by tiled porches. The outside space divided equally between a manicured front lawn and a wide gravelled driveway. Each property identical to the one next door as though there is some rule against individuality.

Our house is Number 2, and the removal van has got here before us. We pull up behind it, and I press my hand to the small of my back. Stretch legs marked red from the bag that's been wedged between my knees. I don't get out of the car immediately but take a moment, aware that neither of us feels the need to rush to the front door and embrace our new lives.

But we're here now and someone has to make an effort. I turn to my husband and smile brightly. 'We did it. We're here. We're actually here.'

And that in itself deserves a pat on the back, for the last few weeks, months even, have tested us to the limit. Everything that could have gone wrong has – problems with our buyer's mortgage, issues with the survey, the chain breaking due to the death of someone's mother. All at a time when we *needed* to move, to escape.

Owen replies, 'Yes, we did it.' He's making an effort too, but I can tell the enthusiasm is forced. Our old house was much nicer.

Despite the empty street, I have the distinct sensation of eyes upon me. A prickling of the scalp. A need to scan the windows of our neighbours' houses.

'Look at that, Owen. Did you see the curtain twitch?' I flick my finger in the direction of the house across the road from ours. 'I didn't know people actually did that except in bad films.'

Owen looks up but doesn't turn his head in the direction I'm pointing. 'You're imagining things.' He smiles at me.

'I'm not. I saw it clearly. Look, it's moving again. Haven't people got better things to do than gawp? You'd think they'd never seen a removal van before.'

'It's not the removal van they're interested in,' Owen says. 'They want to know what their new neighbours are like... what value we'll add to the close. They'll be wondering whether our lawnmower will be worth borrowing if theirs breaks down. What type of car we have. If we have a child old enough to babysit their kids.'

He stops. Sucks in his top lip. I know he didn't mean anything by it, but it's there all the same. The elephant in the room... or rather the car.

There's a rap on the window that makes me jump. One of the removal guys is pointing to the front door. He's making key-turning gestures, reminding me of a game of charades we played one Christmas when we were younger. Happier.

I open the door, lift my leg over the bag of essentials and get out. 'Sorry. Sorry. Let me find my key.'

My fingers feel thick and slow as I fumble inside my bag.

Eventually, I find what I'm looking for and pull it out, the cardboard tag from the estate agent's still attached.

'Owen?' My husband is still sitting there as if under some kind of spell. 'Come on. We need to get this stuff inside. Decide what we want to unpack tonight and what can wait until morning.'

Owen coughs. Pulls himself together. ''Course. Right with you.' He gets out and slams the door shut. Takes the key that's dangling from my finger by the string on the estate agent's label and palms it. 'Let's do this thing.'

He makes it sound as though we're about to embark on a marathon or a new business venture rather than let ourselves into our new home, but I let it ride. Despite my earlier reservations as we'd driven into Pond Close, I'm excited to reacquaint myself with the large kitchen with its wooden cupboards that are asking to be painted white or grey. The bedroom with its en suite and walk-in wardrobes. A property so different from the rambling seventeenth-century house which we'd bought with the royalties from Owen's third novel, *Dead Air*, that you'd think someone else had chosen it.

The grass in front of our house is long, unruly, and as I follow Owen down the path to the front door, I make a mental note to move grass cutting to the top of my to-do list. I just hope the back isn't as bad, though I know it will be. *That lawn is big enough for the largest trampoline*, the agent had said, his hand on the sliding patio doors that led onto the raised patio. *Perfect for kids to play footie on. No flower beds to worry about.*

He'd stopped then, realising he was preaching to the wrong people. There'd been no child seat in the back of the car. No belligerent teenager in tow as he'd shown us the large en suite and the two other bedrooms, one of which Owen had already earmarked as his writing space. We were a couple viewing a family home, and I'd felt his eyes slide down to my stomach as he wondered if he'd missed something.

I watch as my husband slips the key into the lock and turns it. Behind us, the younger of the three removal men lets out a breath. The box he's holding is full of our crockery, and I quickly stand back so he can take it inside. I use the opportunity to get acquainted with my surroundings.

The close is something you'd see advertised in an upmarket magazine or in the opening scene of a soap opera – each house standing equidistant from the one next to it like square beads on a necklace. The only thing setting Pond Close apart from similar developments being the circle of mown grass that the houses look onto. The pond of reed-fringed water in the middle, just visible through the bars of the low metal fence that encloses it.

'Where do you want this?'

I drag my eyes away from the pond's sunlit surface. One of the removal men is backing towards me, forehead glistening with sweat. When he reaches the step to the front porch, he hefts the heavy settee further up his arms so he can get a better grip.

'The large room to the right. The living room,' I say, though it's actually a combined living and dining area that runs from the front of the house to the back. 'The sideboard and coffee table will need to go in there too. Oh, and the dining table.'

For the umpteenth time since we saw the asking price, I think about what we paid for this house. Still questioning. As we'd driven away on the day of the viewing, I'd turned to Owen, wondering if there'd been some mistake. *It's too cheap. You don't think something will crop up in the survey, do you?* But it hadn't. The offer we'd made had been accepted without quibble, and I wonder now if we should have been more curious. Less eager to grab our bargain while we could.

As the sun starts to go down, painting the sky behind the houses opposite in a palette of tangerine and ochre, the doors of the removal van slam for the last time. The vehicle, its company name emblazoned in red capitals on its side, drives away and we're left alone.

I look up. See Owen at the window of the room that will be his writing room. When I wave, he raises his hand in return, then leans forward on the sill, his eyes scanning the close. What is he thinking? Is he really happy to be here?

There's a movement to my left; a light has come on in the front room of the house next to ours. Before it slips away, the yellow gaps between the slats of the white plantation shutters narrowing then disappearing, I see a woman's face. A child's.

I step back inside the house and close the door, wondering what our new neighbours will think of me... of us.

On the floor, kicked out of the way by the feet of the removal men, is a pile of junk mail: leaflets for Indian takeaways in the town, adverts for blinds and double glazing, someone offering gutter cleaning services. I'm bending to pick them up, thinking I'll take them out to the recycling bin, when in amongst them all I see an envelope.

Leaving the junk mail on the side, I turn the envelope over in my hands. It looks like a card, its flap sealed shut, but there's no name on the front. Could it be a welcome card? From one of the neighbours maybe?

I tear it open. Slide out the card. The picture on the front is old-fashioned, a baby in a rocking crib, reminding me of an illustration in a nursery rhyme book I'd once owned. The one about the bough breaking. The baby falling.

I'd expected it to be a welcome card, but the words printed on the front in curled silver script make my insides knit tight. *Congratulations on the birth of your daughter!*

With Owen upstairs and nothing unpacked, the house feels cold, empty – as though the life has been sucked out of it. I stare at the baby's sweet face and run my finger over the curled writing. Without realising it, my hand strays to my belly and, to my dismay, my eyes fill with tears. Who put this through our door?

Something creaks behind me, and I turn around, my heart quickening, half expecting to see someone there, but there's nobody. It's the house settling. This is not the time to start imagining things. I can't let something as ordinary as a card make me hover on the brink of dark despair as I did once before.

I know I should throw the card away, but I can't. Instead, a force I'm powerless to resist makes me open it. I want to know who wrote the card even though the act of knowing scares me. Whoever posted this through the letterbox is cruel. Heartless. I make myself look, my ribcage tightening around my lungs. It's signed from Lynne and Bob... no one I've heard of.

Wishing I'd never opened the damn thing, I drop the card onto the pile of circulars, hating where my mind is going. There's only one person who knows about our heartache all those years ago. Only one person who knew what I went through and how hard it was to stop myself from going under. But the card is not from them. How could it be?

There's the sound of a throat being cleared, and I look up. Owen is at the top of the stairs, a bottle of Cava in his hand. 'I wondered whether you might like some bubbly, Rachel. To celebrate.'

He comes down and my instinct is to hide the card from him, but there's no point – I don't want there to be any secrets between us.

'This came through the door. I found it on the floor with the junk mail.' I pick the card up and hold it out to him, nervous, but trying to act the opposite. 'It doesn't say who it's to and there's no name on the envelope.'

Owen puts the bottle of Cava on the floor and takes it from me. 'Who's it from?'

'Lynne and Bob. What do you make of it?'

He pushes his glasses up his nose with his finger and studies the crib with the baby. The italic silver writing with its message.

As he reads the names inside, my heart skips. Is that recognition I see in his eyes?

But I'm wrong. Owen's face breaks into a smile. 'Well, it's clearly not for us, put through the wrong door I imagine, but I think we should see it as a sign, don't you?'

'A sign?'

'That things will be different now we're here. That, maybe...' Seeing my face, he stops. 'Anyway, we don't need to think about that now.'

He tosses the card back onto the pile of junk mail, and I fight my frustration at what my husband said. Because if he means what I think he means, it's not just the person who sent the card who is unfeeling.

But we're here now and not wanting resentment to over-shadow our first evening, I pull myself together and point to the Cava. 'I'll see if I can find the glasses. Let's get this bottle opened.'

Leaving Owen in the hall, I pick my way between the boxes in the kitchen, reading their labels: *books, kitchenware, random stuff*. I take a chance on one, ripping Sellotape from the flaps and delving in, pleased when I see the kitchen light reflecting off glass.

I lift two champagne glasses from the box and as I place them on the worktop, my eyes move to the window where the sky is darkening. Squares of light show where our neighbours' houses are, and I wonder what they're doing. Tomorrow will be a new day... the start of our new lives. It's exciting. Or that's what I tell myself as I draw the curtains, blocking out the houses, the gardens, the pond with its metal fence. But if that's so, why is my hand shaking as I take the bottle of Cava from Owen and twist the metal cage from the cork? And why, when there is so much to think about, does my mind keep returning to that baby in its crib? And the little girl I saw at the window next door.

Owen watches as I press my thumbs to the cork and ease it out with a satisfying pop. Foam spills down the neck of the bottle, and I quickly pour the golden liquid into our glasses. Shaping my lips into a smile, I wipe my hand down my jeans, then hold Owen's glass out to him. Pick up my own.

'To our fresh new start,' Owen says.

Our glasses clink.

'To our fresh new start,' I repeat, then point to the vinyl wallpaper that I'd thought were tiles. 'Starting with this. It has to go.'

'Whatever makes you happy.'

I take a sip of my drink, the bubbles tickling my nose, and try not to think how Owen had said that once before. That time, I'd done exactly what made me happy, but someone else had paid the price.

I look around me at my new home. That's why we are here. So no one else can get hurt.

TWO

OWEN

Owen turns from the window, presses the palms of his hands against his cheeks and rubs them. He has to make an effort. Prove to Rachel that they've done the right thing. The room he's standing in is inoffensive, the walls an oatmeal colour, the carpet one shade darker. A room that's empty except for the boxes that stand waiting to be unpacked and the writing desk he's had since university.

This time it will be different, he tells himself. This time they will make it work. He can feel it. Felt it the day he'd seen the house on the website. That driveway. Those wide windows and blue painted door. Every description, every cliché, *quiet cul-de-sac, stylish and impressive home, fashionable neighbourhood*, pulling him in. Making him pick up the phone and book in a viewing.

If only Rachel could see the place through his eyes, but he's not convinced she will. He's not stupid, saw the way her smile slipped as they'd turned the corner into Pond Close. Noticed how she'd drawn in a breath before saying how exciting it was. Words that were not for her but for him. Designed to stop him feeling bad for having moved her here. For uprooting her from the house she'd loved and the garden she'd nurtured as tenderly as a mother with her baby. Thinking he didn't see it. Believing him to be unaware of her selfless act.

The box next to him is labelled *Novels*. Owen strips away the Sellotape, lifts the flaps and takes out the book that lies on top. Smiling as he might at a gift from a lucky dip. It's *Night Deepens*, his second thriller and the one he'd found most difficult to write. Not a bad one but not his best. Reaching up, he slides it onto the middle shelf of his bookcase. The others will join it soon.

Unless Rachel's happy here, he'll never have the success he once had. Will never be financially stable again. He needs to make it work for her... for them both. Give her the stable life she needs to remain well, for it can't be coincidence that her decline started when his sales did.

The door is open, and he hears Rachel downstairs: the clink of their empty glasses on the worktop, the burst of a song – she must have found the radio – and he's heartened. They'll get used to their new house, he'll start a new book, and everything will be fine.

He sinks into the swivel chair, rakes fingers through his fine, fair hair. Suddenly weary. Because if it's not, he doesn't want to think about what could happen. His thoughts turn to the little girl she got too close to. Tries to make sense of it, as he has many times before, and fails.

Downstairs, Rachel is still singing, moving things around in their new kitchen. It should put him at ease, but it doesn't. For, despite everything, he's still worried about his wife. Very worried indeed.

THREE

RACHEL

For a moment, when I wake the next morning, I think I'm in my old house. But as my eyes focus and I see, at the end of the bed, the sleek white doors of the walk-in wardrobe rather than the oak dressing table, I remember.

'Owen?' I reach out a hand, slide it across the covers, but Owen isn't there. I look at my phone. See it's a few minutes after seven. Owen never gets up this early. Not any more.

I slide my legs out of the bed and feel for my slippers, the carpet feeling strange to feet more used to polished oak boards. I slip my dressing gown on, knowing it's one of many new things I'll have to get used to.

'Owen?' I say again, louder this time. 'Where are you?'

'In here.'

I pad along the empty landing, stopping at the door of the smaller bedroom. The one that will be Owen's study. He's in there, a black hoodie zipped up to his chin. His feet pale against the navy of his pyjama bottoms. He's sitting on the office chair he uses when he writes, his forehead resting against the heels of his hands.

'What are you doing?' I say, smiling. It's good to see him in here.

He lifts his head. Looks at me through tired eyes. 'Thinking.'

'About what?' I catch sight of myself in the full-length mirror the removal men propped against the wall – pale face, slight figure, fair hair messed from sleep – and sigh. A lot of work will need to be done before I'm ready to meet our neighbours.

'My new project.'

'Yes?' My eyebrows lift in hope. 'Has something come to you?'

He shakes his head. 'Not yet, but I'm sure it will.'

I reach out a hand and rest it on my husband's shoulder, feeling the sharp ridge of bones beneath his pale, freckled flesh. I give a half-hearted squeeze, the slight shift of his body away from my fingers making me draw my hand away again.

'You're right. It will come.' I swallow back my disappointment. Force a confidence I don't feel. 'When you least expect it probably. I believe in you, Owen. You have more talent in your little finger than the authors of most of the books I've read. You'll find another publisher. I know you will. You're in a much better place now.' I shove my hands deep into my pockets. 'But it's not enough *my* believing in you. You have to start believing in yourself. You're a wonderful, talented writer.'

He doesn't reply, just bows his head, the knobs of his vertebrae pressing against the skin at the base of his neck. And I can't help thinking that the man in front of me is a world away from the one he once was.

Before the book reading, where we'd first met, I hadn't heard of Owen Packard. Or maybe I had, but it was a name that had left little impression on me as I'd traced my finger across it on the flyer in the library – thrillers weren't really my thing, you see, I was more of a romance reader. But there was something about the man's face that had spoken to me. Made me get out my phone, click on Eventbrite and book my place at the event the following weekend.

It might have been the pale eyes behind their glasses that had intrigued me or perhaps it was the thin, sensitive line of his lips. It could have been something else entirely – I can't remember now. Whatever it was, I found myself counting down the days until I could see this man I'd never heard of talk about a book I'd never read.

On the day itself, my initial impression as I'd sat in the packed room and watched Owen walk across the stage to his chair, was of a quiet, serious man. Yet, as he'd started to talk about his new book, the spotlight on him, he'd changed. Come alive – a moth emerging from its chrysalis. The emotion in his words, in his eyes, as he'd talked, conveying how much his writing meant to him. It had been seductive. Drawing me in. Making me wish there was something I could feel half as passionate about. Not knowing that, one day, there would be.

And, when I'd gone up to him after, told him how much I'd enjoyed the talk and that I was looking forward to reading *Deep Breaths*, his cheeks had flushed. His pale serious eyes, behind his glasses, lighting with pleasure at my words.

Deep Breaths wasn't to be a runaway bestseller, it would take another two thrillers to reach that status, but it would be enough of a success to make his agent rub her hands in glee. For Owen's life to change for the better.

That evening, he hadn't let me pay for the book, said it was his present to me. It was only when I'd got home after the book event, that I'd seen the handwritten note he'd slipped inside the cover of the hardback along with his mobile number. *I'd like to take you out for dinner if you'd let me.*

I smile at the memory, picturing the scrap of paper that's now in my bedside drawer, the creases in it wearing soft from the number of times I've unfolded it to read his words. My eyes slip to the box on the other side of the room, wondering when Owen will unpack the rest of his books. Looking forward to seeing them lined up on the bookshelf next to his desk as they had in our old house. Knowing I'll find any excuse to come into his study so I can let my fingers linger over the covers. Proud of him.

'We're in our new house,' I say. 'Things will be different now.'

Owen raises his head, blinks and smiles at me as though I've said something he's been waiting an age to hear. 'You're right, Rachel. This house... this close. We'll be happy here. I feel it in my waters.'

I laugh at his expression and am relieved when he laughs too. The old Owen is back, if only for now. I step closer to my husband, surprised when I feel his hand slide around my waist. But my surprise turns to disappointment when, just as quickly, his hand drops back to his side as mine had earlier.

Not wanting him to see how wretched this show of affection, so quickly taken away, has made me feel, I move away from him to the window, part the study curtains and look out. From up here, the pond looks so tranquil. Sunlight glittering on its surface.

'Funny that it's fenced in.'

'What?'

'The pond.' The wind is blowing the reeds at its edge, and I wonder what creatures lie beneath. Whether its surface skims with pond skaters. 'It's a shame. I think the railings make it look ugly.' I turn back to Owen. His head is tipped back now, his eyes closed. Has he even been listening? 'Don't you think?'

He opens his eyes but doesn't swivel his chair round to look. 'I hadn't really thought about it.'

'Well, I think it does.'

I'm about to drop the curtain when there's a movement below. A woman in her mid-forties, her hair pulled into a topknot, comes out of the house next door carrying a bagful of rubbish. She skirts the blue people carrier on the driveway, lifts the lid of the bin around the side of the building and drops the bag in. I'm transfixed by the turquoise silk kimono-style dressing gown she's wearing, birds of paradise printed on its shiny surface, and the white fluffy mules she has on her feet. Trying, and failing, to imagine myself in them. As the bin lid shuts, she looks up at our house. I raise my hand, but she can't have seen as she turns and walks back inside.

'I'll make us some breakfast,' I say, turning back to Owen, but he doesn't answer. His thoughts somewhere else.

'What were you thinking of doing today?' Owen bites down on his toast, crumbs scattering on his plate. 'After the unpacking, I mean.'

I look around us at all the boxes; it's a miracle I found the crockery at all.

'The unpacking will take longer than you think, even with two of us, but once we're done, I thought I'd maybe start looking for a job.'

I hold my breath, not sure what Owen's going to say. Watch with faltering heart as he carefully places what's left of his toast onto his plate.

'You don't need to do that,' he says. What I knew he'd say.

'I know I don't, but I want to.'

I look at my husband, hoping he'll believe me. Because, although I won't voice it, I *do* need to. The money we made on the sale of the house won't last for ever, and even though good royalties still come in for *Dead Air,* each quarter I see how the numbers go down. I can't let Owen know I'm worried, though; his confidence is at rock bottom as it is.

He blinks behind his glasses. 'Why would you want to do that when you could be in your new home?'

'Moving to a new area is difficult... unsettling. I thought getting a job might help me make friends. I'm not thinking of anything serious. Maybe a day or two. Something local.'

Owen screws the lid back onto the marmalade jar. Dabs at his beard with the back of his hand to make sure it's not sticky.

'I can't see why you need to.'

I pour myself some tea, surprised. 'Need to what? Get a job or make friends?'

'Either. Both.'

I take a sip of my tea, not bothering to explain. Owen's always said that we're more than enough for each other, but that's not true any more.

There's a sharp blast of a car horn, then a few seconds later it comes again. Longer. More urgent. Used to no sound except the birds on the feeder in the mornings, I quickly remember that we're not at our old home any more and stand to see what's happening. The blue people carrier on next door's drive has its back door open. A man in a grey suit and striped tie sits at the wheel, and as I watch, his hand raises to press the horn again. I'm relieved when, before it does, the woman I'd seen earlier, dressed now in cream blouse and smart black trousers that graze her ankles, hurries out of the house, a child of around eighteen months on her hip. She ushers two older children, a girl and a boy, both in red blazers, in front of her, slamming the door of the car closed once they've got in. The girl straightens from having fastened her seat belt, kisses her palm, then presses it to the glass. But her mother doesn't see. She's already back inside the house. The front door closed.

'What are you looking at?' Owen takes his plate to the sink. He tries each cupboard in turn until he finds the dishwasher, then slides it in, scratching his beard when he realises the dish-washer tablets are still packed in one of the many boxes that surround him.

'Our neighbours.'

I look at the clock and see it's eight thirty – time for the school run and the reason why a woman in a soft black-leather jacket, tan ankle boots and shiny hair, is hurrying along the pavement on the other side of the green. She's pushing a pram and talking to a boy of around five or six whose hand grips the metal frame as they walk. This child's uniform is different to the one worn by next door's children, the navy blazer with its school emblem swamping his small frame. When she reaches the end of the cul-de-sac, she crosses the road and disappears out of sight. To anyone else, this morning school routine would be something to be seen and forgotten, but for me it's another painful reminder of what I'll never have.

I'm about to sit down again when the woman with the silk blouse and the impatient husband reappears from her house. She's carrying her daughter on her hip as she was before and, a few moments later, the shrill ring of the doorbell echoes through our house.

'It's the woman from next door,' I hiss at Owen. 'What do you think she wants?'

Owen frowns. 'There's only one way to find out.'

Pushing back my nerves, I go into the hall and answer the door. Give my friendliest smile.

'Hi.' I hold out my hand. 'It's so nice to meet you. I'm Rachel.'

'I'm afraid you can't leave the bin there.' Ignoring my hand, the woman points to the recycling bin under our kitchen window. 'It's an eyesore.'

She lifts the child from her hip and sets her on the ground where she stares up at me with large blue eyes. Her pale hair is caught at the side with a red bow, her little shoes patent black, and I fight to rid myself of the dull ache behind my breastbone.

'I'm sorry. We had a lot to put in and it was easier to have it here. We weren't left any information about the rubbish days.'

The woman sniffs. 'We have an unwritten rule in the close

that the bins should be hidden around the side of the house unless it's a rubbish or recycling day.'

'Really?'

'It spoils the look of the place, don't you think? Lexi stop that. You're leaving marks on my trousers.' Bending down, she peels her daughter's fingers from her leg, then straightens again. 'So you'll move it?'

The last thing I feel like doing is placating this rude, unwelcoming woman, but I haven't the energy for an argument.

'Yes, I'm sorry. It's been a bit chaotic since we arrived. I'll move it when I've finished the unpacking. My next job will be to cut the grass,' I add quickly as I see her eyes slide to the unruly lawn. 'I know it's a mess.'

This seems to satisfy her. 'Thank you. I'm Phillipa and this is Lexi.'

The little girl lifts her arms to be picked up, but the woman pays her no attention. Instead, she presses the back of her slim hand to her brow. 'They're so demanding at this age, don't you think?'

I bristle but hide it well. 'I'm sure they are, but she's very cute.'

Ignoring what I've said, Phillipa waves a hand vaguely in the direction of the other houses. 'There was another reason I called round. I'm the chairperson of Pond Close Residents' Association.' She pauses, and I realise she's waiting for some response.

'Oh, you have a Residents' Association?' I try to sound impressed, though I'm surprised it's necessary when there are only five houses.

As if reading my mind, Phillipa lifts her chin. 'It was my idea. Its purpose is to represent the residents' views and concerns. Promote a community spirit. I'm sure you'll agree that's important.' She continues without waiting for my reply.

'We meet once a month. It's expected, in the name of harmony, that everyone attends.'

I try to imagine Owen at one of these meetings and fail. 'I'll see if—'

'Anyway.' Phillipa cuts me off. Looks distractedly around the close. 'At the last meeting, we decided we should do something to welcome you. We have a garden party every year on the green. It's this coming Saturday, and this one will be in your honour.'

'The green?'

Phillipa nods towards the grassed area surrounding the pond. 'It's where we hold all our events.'

My head fills with images of the Pond Close wives dancing around a maypole as the husbands look on, the children dressed as Easter chicks or pumpkins, depending on the occasion, and smile.

'And this party is for *us*?' I don't know whether to be flattered or horrified. Neither Owen nor I have ever been ones for parties. Even at Owen's numerous book events, once the main panel talk or reading was over, he'd make an excuse and slide away as early as possible, leaving me to make the apologies.

'Yes.' There's something in the way she says it that makes me guess it wasn't her idea.

'Really, you don't have to do that. We don't want to put anyone to any trouble.'

'It will be at two thirty. We don't expect you to bring anything. I've checked the weather and it looks fine, but Geoff on the other side of you has a small marquee we can put up in case that changes.'

A strange panic rises in me. I'm unused to being told what to do and she's very assertive.

'So that's all right then? You'll be there.' Phillipa's voice cuts through my thoughts and, although it's a question, the way she's said it makes an answer unnecessary. 'Lexi! What did I tell you?'

The child's plump arms are wrapped around her mother's leg again, her head pushed against the fabric of her trousers. I crouch down to her, and she turns her head. Gives me a shy smile.

'I'm sure that's okay,' I say, pressing my palms to my face, then removing them quickly to reveal the funny expression I've pulled. Lexi laughs and I do it again.

'Good. I'll let everyone know. Is there anything you don't eat? Any allergies?'

So there's going to be food as well. Owen will hate that.

'No, no.' I look up at her. Give her my best smile. 'We eat practically anything.'

Phillipa nods as though I've said the right thing. Picks up her daughter and swings her onto her hip. 'Time for her nap,' she says, although the child doesn't look remotely tired.

I smile. 'Thank you for coming over.'

'Two thirty then.'

'We'll be there.'

I go back inside and close the door, wondering how I'm going to break it to my husband... this unexpected invitation. What I do know is he's not going to like this. He's not going to like it at all. Because, from what he's told me, he'd imagined this little close to feel private.

But he's wrong. It turns out it's going to be quite the opposite.

FOUR

RACHEL

So these are our neighbours, I think as I cross the road from our house and step onto the springy grass. I watch the women fuss around a wooden picnic table covered with a checked cloth, unwrapping cling film from plates of sandwiches, vol-au-vents and slices of pizza. Dropping halved strawberries and sprigs of mint into the two large glass jugs of Pimm's.

The men stand to one side of the table, glasses of beer already in their hands, happy to let the women do all the work. The breeze carries snippets of their conversation on its breath, *Never a dull moment in politics these days. Heard the company just launched a new product line. Worst goal I've seen in a decade!* Looking back at the house, I think of Owen. Wonder how on earth he's ever going to fit in. If he's even going to try. He's still writing, has elected to come at his own pace, and I left out clothes I hope he wears.

It's hot today, the thin material of my sundress sticking to my legs and my carefully applied make-up tacky to my finger-tips. I don't know why it feels so important that I make a good impression, but it does. No one's seen me yet, and I take a moment to centre myself, taking in the women's clothes, the rise and fall of their voices, the way they seem so at ease with each other.

Children race around the grass or sit together with their phones. A couple of little ones are asleep in their buggies under the shade of a small marquee. It's like a painting or an advert for washing powder. Too perfect. Unreal.

A ball bounces off my leg, and the boy I'd seen getting into his father's car a few days ago runs over and apologises. He's around nine or ten, fresh-faced, a flop of sandy hair swept across his forehead. I'm impressed by his manners, decide that maybe Phillipa isn't such a bad parent, after all.

'You're all right.' I pick up the ball and hand it to him with a smile. 'No bones broken.'

Seeing this, a man breaks away from the group. Comes towards us. 'Not giving you any trouble, I hope.' He holds out his hand. 'I'm Carl and this is Neil.'

'No, no trouble at all.'

'That's good to hear.' Although he's dressed in casual clothes, an open-necked, light-blue shirt and beige chinos, there's still an air of the professional about him and his hand keeps rising to his throat as though surprised not to find a tie there. 'Husband not here?'

I glance back at the house. 'He'll be over in a minute.'

I feel the women's eyes on me. The food is unwrapped, and they're standing at the drinks table, glasses of Pimm's in their hands. Heads close together as though they've been talking about me.

Carl sees me looking. Gives a laugh. 'You'd better go and meet the others. They won't be happy until they've given you the third degree.' Seeing my face, he stops. 'Only joking. They're harmless.'

I force a smile. 'I'm sure everyone's lovely. It's been nice to meet you, Carl, and you too, Neil.'

They leave me and I wander over to where the women are standing. Phillipa is bent over a quiche, cutting it into portions with a clean, efficient slice of her knife. As she starts on another, I can't take my eyes off her manicured nails. Each one blood red, emphasising the curve of the cuticles. She looks up and nods, then goes back to her task. Today, she's wearing a silky turquoise jumpsuit, a narrow white belt buckled around her slim waist.

I move closer, trying not to show how awkward I'm feeling. Relieved when someone steps forward with a friendly smile.

'I'm Simone.' She's pregnant and leans back against one of the tables. 'Little blighter's been kicking me since three this morning. God help me when he eventually decides to come out.'

I smile. 'You know it's a boy then?'

'Yeah. I didn't care either way, but Kevin wanted to know so he could get the nursery done up before he went away.'

'I'm Rachel.' I hold out my hand to her. 'It's so nice to meet you.'

'Everyone, I want you to meet Rachel.' She takes my hand and pulls me towards the other women, then reaches for a glass of Pimm's, even though I haven't asked for one, and hands it to me. I'm grateful for her confidence.

'This is Chantelle.' Simone smiles at a slight girl in a short, figure-hugging dress that shows off her long legs – the one I'd seen walking her son to school. 'She's married to Steve. He was a premier footballer back in the day. Before he had his injury.'

I look at the man who's Chantelle's husband. He's older than her by a good few years – his greying hair cropped close to his head, his strident laugh carrying across the green. He's wearing shorts that show off toned muscled calves, but I can't help but notice how his loud Hawaiian shirt is stretched almost to breaking point over a stomach that has seen more pints of beer than it should.

'Pleased to meet ya.'

The girl offers me a soft hand, her long nails the same shade as the strawberry in my glass. I tuck my own bitten ones into my palm, assessing her. She's very pretty, her straight black hair drawn from her face into a high ponytail that falls down her back like a horse's mane. Her face is heavily made up, eyeliner swooped into perfect wings, and as she purses her lips to sip her drink, I see they are the same shiny red as her nails.

'Hope he ain't thinking of drinking too much.' The large gold hoops that hang from her ears swing as she moves her head to look across at the men.

Simone puts a hand on her arm. 'Don't worry. I'll keep an eye on him.'

There's a cry and we all turn to the sound. The little boy I'd seen Chantelle taking to school is lying on the ground, holding his knee.

'Bleeding hell, what now?' Chantelle hurries away and a few minutes later has the boy on her lap. She dabs at his knee with a serviette. Wipes away his tears. She looks barely older than a child herself, and I can't help thinking she should have been watching him.

'You're okay, sweetie,' she croons. 'No need to cry now.'

As though reading my mind, Simone smiles. 'Jake isn't hers, if that's what you're thinking. He's Steve's. He has a teenage boy too, Charlie, who lives with his mum but stays with them at weekends. The baby in the pushchair's hers, though. Her name's Jo Jo.'

'Is Charlie not here today then?'

'Oh, he's around somewhere. Probably hanging out with Aaron, Pam and Geoff's boy.' She leans closer to me. 'Though, between you and me, she'd prefer it if he didn't.'

'Who? Chantelle?'

'No, Pam. She thinks Charlie's a bad influence. Doesn't like the way he talks. Or Chantelle for that matter. Says they didn't shell out for Aaron's expensive private school to have him hang around with a WAG's kid. Even if he's not hers.'

I haven't been introduced to Pam and Geoff yet, but now I turn to look at them. Although older than the others, it's difficult to put an exact age on them. They're both smartly dressed, more high-end chain than designer, and Pam's hair is expensively highlighted in honey and caramel tones. Her husband, Geoff, is tall and wiry with the air of a banker or a solicitor. Whatever his profession, the silver Mercedes in the drive outside their house boasts of his success.

'I'd better say hello, or they'll think me rude.'

Leaving Simone, I walk over to them. See how close they stand together. I hold out my hand. 'Hi. I'm Rachel. I've just moved into Number 2.'

Pam blinks, something that in time I'll come to recognise as a nervous habit, and moves closer to her husband. 'I know.'

The way it's said makes me feel foolish. Of course they know. They live next door, and this party is, after all, to welcome us.

There's an awkward silence, and I look towards the road, hoping to see Owen crossing it. But he's not. A surreptitious look at my watch shows it's gone three. He'd said he'd be five minutes. Where is he?

'Have you lived here long?' It's all I can think of to say.

Pam purses her lips. Looks at her husband as though for support. 'We moved to the house in 1999.'

'So you must have known the Brookners well. I hope you're not too sad they moved away. We'll try to behave. Limit the number of wild parties we have.'

It's said as a joke, but Pam doesn't laugh, just gives a thin-lipped smile.

'We knew them as well as you know anyone in a community our size. He was a civil servant, and she was an accountant. We didn't see them much, and they left quite suddenly.'

'I see.'

The conversation stalls again.

Geoff hasn't said anything yet. He stands there next to his wife, the sun beating down on his balding head, looking like he has the entire world on his shoulders. I think of the teenage son I haven't met yet. Maybe it has something to do with him. They'd clearly had him late in life and that must take its toll.

'They kept it as it was. Just a lick of paint in the living room and a new carpet. Never did the place up... the Brookners.' Geoff's eyes are on our house. 'Like they had no intention of staying.'

'Really?'

'That's what we felt anyway. Are you planning on doing anything to the house?'

'We are... and as soon as possible. I thought I'd make a start on the kitchen. Get rid of that awful vinyl tile-effect wall covering. It weirdly reminds me of something out of Blue Peter. Sticky back plastic!'

I laugh, but Geoff remains stony-faced, and I'm relieved when I see Simone coming across the grass towards me, a paper plate of food in her hand. But before she can reach me, she's waylaid by Phillipa who's carrying a jug of Pimm's. They stop walking, exchange a few words, then Phillipa takes the plate from Simone and carries on over to me.

'I took the liberty of making up a plate for you.' She holds out the jug of Pimm's. 'And I thought you might be ready for a top up. It's your party, after all.'

I'm surprised by this sudden change in her manner – the way she's smiling at me. So different from the Phillipa who'd accused me of letting down the close with my recycling bins.

'Thank you. I won't say no.'

Geoff and Pam move away, and I get the feeling they're relieved. The conversation had been awkward. I take the plate Phillipa's holding out and wait for her to refill my glass, glancing over to where Carl and Steve are standing, fresh beers in their hands. I'd been hoping that Owen might have slipped out of the house when I was talking and joined them, but of course he hasn't, and when I look across the road to our house, I think I see him at the window.

Phillipa catches me looking. 'Your husband's not keen on parties then?'

'No, it's not that, it's...' I stop, feel the sides of my neck redden. I won't be able to lie with conviction. Not about this when the truth is so obvious.

'You're right.' I sigh heavily. 'To be honest, he'd rather have his teeth pulled than have to socialise. I'm so sorry.'

Phillipa stares at the blank window a moment, then looks back at me. 'Some people would call it a blessing. Carl exudes bonhomie, and it can be exhausting at times. It's easy to feel like the bridesmaid to his bride when he gets going.' She turns her head to look at him. Frowns when she sees him talking to Chantelle, then scans the green. 'What's he done with... oh, bloody hell!'

A little body has pushed between us. It's Phillipa's daughter, Lexi, a small hand reaching up to grab a handful of her mother's silk trousers. 'Up. Up.'

'Jesus. Why can't Carl look after her for one bloody minute.' Phillipa looks down at her daughter's curly head. 'What now? No, I'm not picking you up.'

Taking Lexi by the shoulders, she moves her away. Bends and hisses something in her ear. I hear the word *smack* and wince. Phillipa can't really have said that, can she? Lexi's a toddler, and she's done nothing wrong.

'Sorry about this. I'll be back in a minute.' Holding Lexi's hand tightly, Phillipa marches back across the green to where her husband is standing, laughing at something Chantelle has said.

Seeing me standing alone, Simone comes over. Points to one

of the deckchairs and rubs her rounded belly. 'Fancy a seat? Standing too long makes my ankles swell.'

I'm glad she's back. Phillipa's sudden friendliness has confused me, whereas Simone seems genuinely nice. 'That's a good idea. It's hard to hold a glass as well as food.'

Putting my plate on the ground, I pull a couple of the deckchairs into the shade, and we sit. I take a bite of quiche and watch Pam and Geoff wander back to the food table.

'Those two seem different to the others. Quieter. More serious.'

Simone pushes the hair back from her face, then shields her eyes with her hand against the sun. 'They're all right.' She looks as though she's going to say something else but takes a sip of her orange instead.

'And the boy... Aaron, was it?'

She nods. 'He's okay too when Charlie's not here. He's a year older, and I agree with Pam that he's a bad influence. I've cut across the green sometimes after they've been out here and the place stinks of weed.'

'Well, I wasn't expecting that.' I look around at the houses. 'Not here.'

Simone smooths her dress over her bump. Slips off her sandals and wiggles her toes. 'I probably shouldn't have said anything. You've only just moved in, and I don't want to put you off the place.'

'Don't worry about that. To be honest, it makes the close more human if anything. After my encounter with Phillipa, I was beginning to imagine I'd stepped onto the set of *Stepford Wives*.'

Simone laughs. 'Hardly. We rub along together okay, and that's probably all I should say. We have our moments. In a small road like this, things can be magnified. Mountains out of molehills, if you know what I mean. It's hard not to feel everyone knows everyone else's business.'

I think of Phillipa's visit to our house. How I'd been called out for leaving the bin in the wrong place. She's right there.

My eyes slip over to her. Watch as she hands Carl their daughter. I want to say something to Simone about what I'd heard but am not sure how to broach it. 'Have you noticed the way Phillipa talks to Lexi?'

Simone follows my gaze. Frowns. 'What do you mean?'

But now I've brought it up, it's impossible to elaborate. How can I tell her I thought I'd heard Phillipa threaten to smack her daughter when we've only just met?

'Ignore me. It's nothing.'

I say it light-heartedly, but still I'm watching Phillipa. Feeling on edge.

Simone leans forward in her chair. 'Phillipa was in her early forties when she got pregnant with Lexi. She wasn't expecting it to happen, and it's been difficult for her.' She stops. 'Are you okay, Rachel?'

'Yes, I'm fine. Sorry. A bit tired from the move, that's all.'

I stretch out my legs so they're in the sunshine. Sip my drink and listen to the men talk about the state of the golf course. How it's gone downhill and how they really should complain. I know I'll have to go over and talk to them in a minute, but something holds me back – the thought of Owen. If he looked out of his study window and saw me standing with them, he wouldn't be happy. Not that he'd say anything... I'd just know. See it in his eyes.

Wanting to think of something else, I look away towards the pond.

'It's haunting that place. So wild compared to the green. It's a shame about the fence.'

Simone looks too. 'A little girl drowned there, a toddler. It's why they fenced it off, to make it childproof. So it doesn't happen again.'

My hand shoots to my mouth. 'Drowned? Oh my God.'

Simone looks at me with sympathy. 'I know. It's terrible, isn't it?'

'But how did it happen?'

She glances over at Phillipa, then back at me. 'No one really knows. There was an inquest, but it was inconclusive. The front door had been left open, and it's believed she wandered out.'

'I don't understand. Where was her family? Which house did she live in?'

Simone doesn't say anything. Instead, she turns and looks at my house, the one Owen and I moved into yesterday, and I have my answer. The reason it was a bargain.

The little girl who died, lived at Number 2.

She lived in *our* house.

Simone changes the subject – something about her husband Kevin's flight home. Disappointed, that she hasn't said more, and more than a little rattled, I watch Chantelle lift her stepson so he can see a butterfly that's landed on one of the buddleia plants that overhangs the metal fence enclosing the pond. And, as the party moves on and the voices ebb and flow around me, I can't stop thinking how strange it is to be sitting here eating party food and drinking Pimm's next to the place where something so terrible happened.

Lexi is on her own again. She toddles on her plump legs, bends to pick a daisy, and I try to imagine someone as young as that making their way across the road. Across the green.

On their own.

She's near the pond now, keen to show Chantelle her flower. The girl with the long dark ponytail hasn't seen her yet, and I offer up thanks to the person who thought to have a fence put around the area. A gate with a secure latch to protect little fingers from opening it. Because Phillipa certainly isn't watching her child. She's too busy keeping her eye on Carl.

Anger creeps up on me, pulling me back into a past I don't

want to revisit. My husband and I sitting on hard chairs in the consultant's room as he tells us we'll never have our own biological children. The pain in my chest as my heart breaks.

Yet here is Phillipa. A woman who has a child, even though she's undeserving of her.

My thoughts are broken by a shout, and I turn my head. Chantelle has put her son down and is running towards the pond. I stand, one hand on the back of the chair, unsure of what's going on. Others are running across the green now. Carl. Steve. Beside me, Simone is looking worried.

I look around, my eyes searching for Lexi, not finding her. Then I see why. The gate to the pond stands open; she must have gone through.

My paper plate drops from my hand, and I run. Get to the fence at the same time as Carl. In front of us is the pond, its edges fringed with reeds and the tall moleskin-brown heads of bullrushes. Chantelle is crouched by the side of the water, Lexi pressed to her.

'Ya gave me a bleeding fright. You know you shouldn't be in here. You could have fallen in.'

Carl hurries over to her. Lifts the little girl out of Chantelle's arms, and anger stirs beneath my breastbone. Not because of what might have happened, but because Phillipa isn't here. Hasn't even bothered to find out what all the commotion is about.

I stand aside to let Chantelle and Carl past me and give Lexi a warm smile, hoping she wasn't too frightened. Next to the pond, the silver birch rustles its leaves, its reflection surrendered to the still water, and its then I see the faded pink ribbon that's tied to the flaking bark of its trunk. Frayed edges flapping in the breeze.

I shiver. Guessing why it's there.

Being careful to shut the gate behind me, I go back to the

garden party, noticing how more neighbours have gathered around Carl and his daughter. Not Phillipa, though, she's still at the drinks table, and it makes me all the more determined.

If I can't have my own children, then I'll have to protect this one.

FIVE

RACHEL

When I get home later, Owen's study door is shut. Usually, I'd knock, but, this time, I walk straight in.

'I can't believe you did that?'

Owen is at his desk, his pale hair lit by the sun that's streaming through the window.

'I'm sorry.' He takes off his glasses and pinches the soft space either side of his nose. 'I meant to go, you have to believe me I did, but...' He points to the screen. 'I'm really getting somewhere, and that's why we're here, that's the most important thing. You agree, don't you?'

I do. Although I wish Owen wouldn't put so much pressure on himself because, when he's in full flow, it can take a mountain to move him. He'd miss meals if I didn't bring them up to him. Miss sleep too if I didn't remind him that a tired brain equals one that will be less creative.

'I had to make excuses for you, you know. I said something had come up. That you had an important meeting with your agent. Not that I think they believed me for a minute.' I close my eyes, remembering how awkward it had been. The look that had passed between the men. They didn't need to say it; it was clear what was going through their heads – Owen thought he was better than them. Had better things to do with his time than go to a garden party that was so important to them – one that they had dedicated to welcoming us.

What made it worse was knowing they were right. That my husband *did* think himself better than them.

'You know how I hate lying, Owen.'

'Really?' He looks up at me. Without his glasses, his eyes look smaller, sadder, and I feel the burn of shame.

'You know what I mean. I wanted us to be there together... as a couple. I wanted to stand by your side and show everyone how proud I am of you and what you've achieved.'

'You're proud of me?'

'You know I am. I always have been. Right from that first day I met you.'

Owen smiles, and I'm relieved. These last few months I've been worried about him. His confidence is at an all-time low, and I haven't been able to do anything about it. If only he'd talk to me. Confide in me and let me help him. But that's never been Owen's way. He's a proud man and his problems are his own... no one else's. And, because he's like that, it makes me the same. Unable to open up. Unable to share my feelings... my worries.

Owen shuts down the computer, walks over to the window and looks out. He's still wearing his T-shirt and cords. Had not got as far as changing for the party.

'We have a good view of the green from here,' he says.

I join him. 'I know.'

I wonder what Owen saw when he looked down during the garden party. Whether he was trying to catch me out. Persuade himself he was seeing something that wasn't there – an accidental touch of a hand or a look that lingered longer than it should. I'm thankful I'd stayed in my deckchair most of the time with Simone. I can't risk him spiralling. Not again.

'I saw a couple of kids,' he says, leaning his shoulder against the glass. 'Teenagers. They were inside the fenced-off pond area by the tree. When the commotion started and everyone ran to the gate, I saw them jump the fence at the spot where the road comes into the close. They clearly didn't want anyone to know they'd been there.'

So Charlie and Aaron had been at the party all along... only no one had known.

'What were they doing?'

Owen shrugs. 'Not a lot. They rolled a joint and smoked it. Drank the beer that one of them must have nicked from the drinks table. The usual things kids get up to when they're out of their parents' radar.'

'What *you* did, you mean?' I try to imagine my husband as an irresponsible teenager and fail. He would have been the sort of boy who preferred to sit in his bedroom reading or playing solitary computer games. Polite. Well behaved.

He doesn't answer, moves back from the window. 'They think themselves so big at that age. So smart. They'll learn... probably the hard way like the rest of us.'

'Do you think I should tell Pam and Geoff... about the drink? The drugs?'

Owen stops at the swivel chair. Rests a heavy hand on it, making it turn. 'Pam and Geoff?'

His face has taken on a pinched look, and I wonder whether he's heard something about them. Has bumped into them. But that's hardly likely as he hasn't been out in the few days since the removal van left.

'They're the parents of one of the boys. They live next door.' I jerk a thumb to the right. 'That side.'

'I see.' He presses his fist against his forehead as though trying to remember something.

'What is it? Are you okay?'

'What? Yes... I'm fine. Just a headache. Too much staring at the screen.' He drops his hand. Breathes in. 'So, what were the others like?'

I think. Trying to put together everything I saw. Everything I heard.

'It's difficult to know on a first meeting. None of them are like I imagined, if I'm honest. Steve from Number 5 was a footballer in his day... a well-known one according to Simone.'

I know better than to think this will impress Owen. He doesn't follow football, or any other sport. Says the rise of the super-rich is disgusting, though I've never heard him say that in relation to the literary world.

'Can't have been that good if he lives in Pond Close. Thought half of them lived in mansions in Alderley Edge.'

I smile at the thought. 'Apparently, he used to have a house in Cheshire with an underground gym and a swimming pool. Another in Cannes. But after his injury, he had some sort of breakdown – started gambling and lost most of his money. That's why they had to move here.'

The irony of their situation mirroring our own is lost on Owen, and he only shakes his head. 'More money than sense. What about the others?'

'Phillipa, the one who invited us to this thing, was a surprise. After the issue with the bins, I wasn't expecting her to speak to me, but she was surprisingly friendly.' I don't tell Owen about what I saw her do; my concerns about her. After everything that happened before, it would only worry him. 'And Simone at Number 4. She's...' I'm about to say pregnant, then think better of it. 'She's there on her own at the moment as her husband's working away. Maybe when he's back, we could invite them round or something. Be a bit more sociable than we've been in the past.'

Owen doesn't answer. He looks distracted, and it frustrates me as I want to share this with him.

'She told me something terrible.'

That gets his attention. He looks up, worried. 'What?'

'Apparently, a little girl drowned in that pond on the green. She lived in our house. Did you know that? Did the estate agent tell you?' I rub at my arms. Look around me as though expecting to see her.

Owen pushes his glasses up his nose. Takes a moment to answer. 'Of course not, but it's no big deal, Rachel. Think about it. Our old house was over a hundred years old. The place of many a death, I imagine.'

I'm irritated that he doesn't understand. 'That's completely different. We're talking about a child. A toddler who was clearly being neglected.' I jab at the window of Owen's study. Imagining it. And I can't help but think of Lexi. 'Oh, my God. Her poor parents. How do you ever get over a thing like that?'

'Humans are designed to cope with adversity. If we didn't, the whole of society would flounder and go under.'

I hate it when Owen talks like this. It makes me want to shake him. He's always wanted me to be more pragmatic, but I can't help the emotions boiling up inside of me. It doesn't help that I can't get the image out of my head. The little girl, whose name I don't even know, toddling across the road in front of our house. Wanting to see the goldfish or the frogspawn or whatever it was that was in the pond when it happened. Crouching at the edge of the water, her chubby finger poking into the reeds. Her mother unaware the door was open. Unaware her daughter was entering the last minutes of her life.

'Which was her room, do you think?'

'What?'

'Which room?' I look around me, unsettled. 'This was the smallest of the bedrooms, maybe it was hers.'

Without realising it, my eyes are scouring the walls for marks where a cot might have been, for the evidence of small sticky fingers on the wallpaper. Finding nothing.

'Put it out of your mind.' It's Owen's turn to be irritable. 'What do you want to do? Leave before we've even unpacked?'

'Of course not. It's just—'

'Just what? We liked the house. We bought it. Even if I'd known, I wouldn't have told you about it because I'd have guessed this would be how you'd react.' He looks around. 'If anything, it makes the place a little more interesting.'

I shake my head, dumbfounded. But there's no point in arguing with him.

'Don't you think it's strange, though?'

'What?'

'A child of that age wandering off. How can they know that? What if they're wrong and someone took her from her house? She couldn't have been much older than Jade and—'

'Stop it, Rachel.'

I swallow back the words. I shouldn't have let Jade's name slip out.

Owen's right. There's no point in harping back. No point at all.

'I'm going to make a cup of tea,' I say, wanting to change the subject. 'Do you want one?'

Owen shakes his head. Sits in his chair and wakes the computer again. I leave him to it and go downstairs. Through the kitchen window, I see Carl and Steve upturning the wooden trestle table onto the grass and folding its legs. Phillipa hovering, Lexi on her hip. Making sure they're doing it right.

I'm about to turn away when, as one person, all three turn and look at the house, and although they can't see me, I take a step back. They've clearly been talking about me, about *us*, and I wonder what I might have done wrong. Whether at the party I'd said the wrong thing. Not behaved as I should.

I thought I'd been friendly. Interested. Happy to ask their advice about the close and compliment their children. But maybe that had been the problem... maybe I'd been *too* eager to please. Maybe Phillipa had noticed me with Lexi. It's only been a few days and yet, already, I feel as though I've made the wrong impression. That living in Pond Close is going to be harder than I'd imagined.

Thank goodness for Simone, I think as I fill the kettle. At least she seems to like me. The jury's still out on Phillipa. I think of how the neighbours have been with me. The way Geoff and Pam's eyes had slid over to our house as we'd been talking at the party. I'd thought that, like Owen, they were socially awkward, but now I'm wondering if it was something else entirely. That they think misfortune, death even, is catching... as infectious as a disease. Even if it's not personal, our move to Pond Close might be doomed to fail simply because, by some misfortune, we are living in a dead child's house. A little girl who managed to get herself over to the pond without anyone noticing. One who no one wants to talk about. Or is *allowed* to. Are they protecting someone?

SIX

RACHEL

'What are you doing?' Owen hovers in the entrance to the kitchen.

I climb down the stepladder and put the metal scraper on one of the steps, enjoying the satisfaction of the work. 'What does it look like? I'm stripping this bloody awful wall.' I laugh and tear at a strip, enjoying the moment when the wet paper peels away to reveal the white matte surface underneath. At the garden party, I'd told Geoff and Pam I'd do it, and it had spurred me on. 'It's quite fun, grab a scraper.'

Owen tuts. 'Don't be ridiculous, Rachel. You know I don't have time for that.' He comes into the room and studies the wall. 'What's wrong with it anyway?'

'It's hideous, that's what's wrong with it. No one has vinyl wallpaper. Whoever put this up had no taste.'

'As long as it makes you happy.' Owen goes over to the kettle. He takes it to the sink and refills it.

My arm sweeps an arc to take in all of the room. 'Once we've updated Number 2, it will feel like it properly belongs to us.' I stand with my hands on my hips, considering the strips of wallpaper, sticky with old glue, hoping I haven't bitten off more than I can chew. 'A coat of paint in a nice light colour is all it needs, then when we can afford it, we can change the cabinets.'

Owen remains silent, and I realise what I've done. What I've said. I squeeze my eyes shut, hating myself for my thoughtlessness. It's not Owen's fault money is tight at the moment. Everyone knows how up and down the publishing industry is, and it's no reflection on his ability. I want to say something to make it better, but the chances are I'll only make things worse. So, instead, I bend and take the yellow sponge out of the bucket of warm water by my feet and press it against the ragged edge of the paper. Watching it darken. Hoping that this piece will come off as easily as the last.

'I'll leave this here for you.' Owen steps over a pile of soggy wallpaper strips and puts my mug on top of the stepladder. 'I'll be upstairs if you need me.'

'Fine.' I don't mean to be short with him, but, like the emptying of the packing cases, I'd been hoping this was something we could have done together. But I need to remember that Owen has to focus on his work; I need to support him, that's my job. The two of us will make our marks on our new home separately. Christening it in our own ways.

I press the metal stripper to the wall again and loosen the paper. As I take the edge between my thumb and finger and strip it away, the birth congratulations card that had arrived through our door comes into my head again. There will be no christening for me. No first birthday to celebrate. What had that been all about?

The tea Owen made tastes bitter, but I can't complain; it's so seldom he makes it. I put the mug down again, push the wallpaper strips aside and crouch to do the lower part of the wall. The work is tedious, but I'm happy with that as it takes my mind off things.

The wallpaper is stuck more firmly here and is harder to peel off. Using two hands, I force the stripper up through the wet paper. Watching as it rucks up, intent on sticking to the surface.

I wipe my forehead with my sleeve. 'Come on. Give me a break.'

The paper, instead of coming off in strips, is now coming away in large confetti-shaped pieces. It's frustrating and I'm tempted to give up, but I don't. I won't let this wall get the better of me.

Trying another angle, I manage to tear a larger piece off, but now that more paper has been removed, I see that the paint underneath is a different colour to higher up. I jab at the vinyl with the corner of my stripper and manage to loosen another piece. I peel it away, revealing the wall beneath. It's brown in parts as though spattered with something. A different coloured paint, maybe. Blood even.

I shiver and look behind me as though someone is there. But, of course, they're not. As I loosen more paper, the dark patch grows. Takes shape. It's no longer a random pattern of brown against the white wall but something else.

With thudding heart, I lean forward and place the flat of my hand against the wall. The pad of my palm fits the largest smear and the smaller pads, below my finger joints, match the blobs above it. It's as though someone has leant against this wall with a bloodied hand.

I straighten up. Step away. Not liking the direction my mind's taking me.

'Owen.' I run to the bottom of the stairs. 'Owen, come down.'

I hear the door of his study open. 'What now?'

'I need to show you something. It's important.'

He sighs loudly, giving himself away. I know that he'll think I'm being hysterical, but I have to tell someone.

I drag him into the kitchen. Point at the stain on the wall. 'There.'

Owen's eyes squint behind his glasses. 'What are you showing me?'

'It's a handprint... see?' I press my palm against the wall like I did before. Wait for him to understand.

'How can I see anything when your hand is over it?' I lower my arm, and Owen steps closer. Presses a finger to the stain. 'It's nothing. Just old paint.'

'It's blood.' His dismissal has made me petulant. Childlike. I'm desperate for him to see what I'm seeing. Jab at the wall with my finger. 'It's right there. See?' The pattern matches the protruding parts of my hand. 'Something happened in this kitchen, Owen. I feel it.'

I don't expect Owen to laugh, but that's what he does. 'That's priceless. You should see the look on your face, Rachel. As though you've seen a ghost. That brown stain is nothing but paint.'

I'm not listening to him. 'Someone may have harmed the child. Or maybe...'

'Maybe what?' His voice has turned serious. 'Why are you doing this? Trying to turn our beautiful home into a... a...' He looks around for inspiration. 'A scene from a slasher movie? Is it any wonder you don't sleep? Is it any wonder you have night-mares? Stop it, Rachel.'

I sit back on my haunches. Hear the thump of Owen's feet as he goes back up the stairs. The slam of his door. Tears sting my eyes as I look at the stain again. Maybe he's right and it *is* paint. Would bloodstains even remain on a wall this long after it's been decorated over? I run my hand over the surface. The paint underneath is matte, porous, and it would have made it difficult to clean off. That's if they'd even bothered – after all, the vinyl paper would have kept it hidden.

Instinct makes me pick up the stripper again. Shove it against the paper. There's more to this. I feel it deep inside me.

With two hands, I drag at the paper, revealing more of the

dark stain. Letters appearing. Forming words. First one then another.

Why Phillipa?

I stare at it. Goosebumps raising the hairs on my arms. What went on in my house? What did Phillipa do?

SEVEN

OWEN

Owen crouches by the wall, his forehead creased into a frown. He places his hand over the brown stains as Rachel had, but his palm is too big, the soft pads beneath the joints of his fingers not matching the marks that are there. Pushing himself up, he stands back, studying the words written on the plaster with curiosity.

Why Phillipa?

Phillipa. The woman next door. The one who was so rude to his wife on their doorstep. The one whose garden party he'd never had any intention of attending – not that he'd told Rachel that. As far as she knew, he'd simply been tied up with his writing. Forgot the time.

He bends. Half-heartedly stuffs some torn wallpaper into a black bin liner before glancing back at the wall. This is all he needs. Something more for Rachel to latch onto... to mull over and worry about. Because he knows his wife. Knows that she won't be able to leave it alone. Those two little words on the bare wall will torment her. Will be twisted and pulled out of shape until they have a darker meaning.

He rubs his hand down his face, his stomach clenching at the possibility of what could happen. Already, the move has started to give Rachel nightmares. Last night, he'd woken to the sound of her rapid breathing. Had rolled over and seen the whites of her eyes as she'd stared at the ceiling.

Did you hear that, Owen?

But of course he hadn't. It was all in her head, and, besides, he didn't believe in spirits or ghosts from the past. Didn't have time for nonsense like that. He'd told her it was a dream. Whatever sound she'd heard, simply the house settling. But when he'd offered to go downstairs and check all was okay, she'd said no. He was right. It was nothing. She hadn't meant to worry him.

He looks at the wall again, giving a heavy sigh. This isn't going to help with her recovery, and it's times like this when he questions whether his decision to move here had been the right one. But they'd had little choice. They could no longer afford to live in their old house, and, even if they could, the awkward business with Jade had made continuing to live in the area untenable.

An image comes to him – Rachel in the days after the consultant had spoken to them about the results of their IVF. He remembers the hours she'd spend up in their bedroom, her face wet with tears he couldn't comprehend. A dark despair settled over her that made her turn to face the wall whenever he came into the room. Waving away all offers of food. All offers of company. There had been days and days of it until, one morning, he'd come downstairs to find her in the kitchen making breakfast. As though it had never happened.

The relief had been massive. And once the status quo of their marriage had been resumed, he'd been able to go back to his writing. Or tried to at least.

They'd never talked about that time, and he'd been glad, for what could he have said? They both knew that their future life would be different to the one they'd intended, and he'd presumed that, in time, his wife would come to accept it. But although her mood had improved, she was different to the old Rachel. Something in her had shifted, and she no longer seemed content to look after him while he was in the thick of his writing.

And that wasn't all. The bad news they'd been given at the hospital had affected not only her mood but her judgement. The old Rachel would never have done what she did. Would have known where the boundaries were and stayed inside them.

He goes over to the window. His wife is across the green at Simone's house, disappointed that he'd not wanted to talk more about what she'd found under the wallpaper. Should he be worried about that? After what happened at their last house, is getting chummy with the neighbours a good thing?

Owen pushes his glasses up his nose. He wishes he had the old Rachel back. The one she'd been when he'd first met her. He leans his head against the glass, remembering what it had felt like to be on that stage. The room darkened. The spotlight on him. How confident he'd felt... how alive. Of course, there had been many more such events in the years following, but none that had felt as powerful as that one. And the reason was because it was the first time he'd set eyes on Rachel. She'd been sitting in the second row, in his line of vision. Close enough for the light that bathed the stage to pick her out from the audience behind, the ones whose faces merged into the gloom.

Her eyes were fixed on him, and he knew she had been listening to his every word. His every sentence. Even then, before he'd even met her, he'd loved her for it.

He'd faltered then, struggled to find his place in the text – something he never did. But when she'd smiled, a smile that said it didn't matter, he'd found his place again and continued. Basking in her faith. Buoyed by it.

When the talk had finished and the audience had started to leave their seats, he'd left the stage and torn a strip of paper from the bottom of his notes. Scribbled some words. He'd known she'd be waiting when he got to the auditorium to sign the books the publisher had provided.

What he hadn't known was what would come next.

Come after.

A car pulls into the drive next to theirs and Phillipa gets out, her coat over her arm. She goes to the back door of the car and bends, unbuckling the straps of Lexi's harness.

His mind turns back to Jade. To the policewoman who had stood in their living room.

No good will come of fraternising with the neighbours. No good at all.

EIGHT

RACHEL

I look around Simone's living room, marvelling at how different it is to ours even though, from the outside, all five houses in the cul-de-sac are identical.

'I can't believe it's the same house.' Simone and Kevin have painted their walls sunshine yellow and above the mantelpiece hangs a modern print of a window with blue shutters looking onto the sea. A stone vase full of shocking pink hydrangeas sits in the fireplace and the armchair I'm in is covered with a cream, wool throw. A strange eclectic mix... neither one thing nor another. Yet the sum of them all is oddly pleasing.

Simone hands me my mug, then sits down opposite, her hand resting on her belly. 'You should see Chantelle and Steve's place. All faux fur and shag pile carpets. Can you believe the whole garden is artificial grass? Saves them having to mow it but rather ironic considering Steve's profession?'

I smile and nod. 'Ex-profession,' I add.

'Yes, you're right. I've no idea what he does now, keeps things very close to his chest, but I don't really want to know, to be honest.'

I laugh. 'He does seem a bit of a Jack the Lad. There's a big age difference between him and Chantelle. I wonder what attracted her to him.'

Simone rubs her thumb and first finger together. 'He was still playing football when she met him. Guess she didn't count on how things would turn out. But I'm being unfair. Chantelle comes over as a bit ditsy, but she's all right. More astute than you'd imagine from the way she looks and acts.'

I take a sip of my coffee. 'So, when are you expecting Kevin home?' I'm interested to meet him.

'Oh, didn't I tell you? He'll be home tomorrow. He wasn't supposed to be coming back until next weekend, but he managed to push it forward. You must come over and meet him. Both of you.'

I bite my lip, knowing already what Owen will say. *Why would I want to meet someone I can guarantee I'll have nothing in common with?* He's right of course, if Kevin's anything like the other husbands, but if he's finally making headway with the book, maybe he'll make the effort.

'I'll have a word with him.'

Simone looks at me over her coffee mug. 'You never told me. What does Owen write?'

'He writes crime.'

Her eyebrows raise. 'Really? Anything I'd know?'

'It depends if you're into thrillers. His most successful one was *Dead Air*. He wrote it five years ago, and it was a bestseller.'

'Are you kidding me? Of course I bloody know it! I read it after Kev. Think I may still have it somewhere.' She rubs her hands together in glee. 'Wait until I tell him!'

I smile, still finding it odd when people say they know his work. To me, he's moved on from being Owen Packard the writer to simply Owen, my husband. Though sometimes, when he's in the middle of a book, it's hard to distinguish between the two.

'Well, that's Owen, but what did *you* do, Rachel?' Simone's gaze is direct. 'Before you moved here.'

'Me? Oh, I was a pharmacy assistant. Nothing exciting.' With the spotlight so often on Owen, I'm unused to people asking about me. 'Not that I've had a job for a while unless you count the bit of childminding I did.'

An image of Jade, her little hand in mine, comes into my head and I push it away. She doesn't want to know about that.

Simone puts her head on one side. Presses her hands into the small of her back and winces. 'Oh, Why's that?'

'When Owen's career took off and we no longer needed two incomes, he suggested I give it up.' Although it hadn't bothered me at the time, I feel myself colour. 'I was happy to. The house needed a lot of work. We had a big garden...'

I know I sound defensive and clear my throat to cover my discomfort.

Simone puts down her mug. Leans forward, her baby bump resting on her thighs. 'I'm sorry. I didn't mean to make you feel awkward. As far as I'm concerned, people's life choices are not anyone else's business. I'm planning to go back to work once my maternity leave finishes... but who knows?'

I watch her hand circle her stomach – a reminder that there's one big difference between us. As if reading my thoughts, Simone's hand stills. Her cheeks flush a pale pink, and she looks away. She won't ask me, it would be rude to, but now the elephant is in the room, I know it will be easier for our friendship if I address it now.

'Owen and I would have liked to have had children, but it wasn't meant to be.'

Reaching over, Simone gives my hand a reassuring squeeze. 'There's still time, you're—'

'No.' I cut her off before she can say any more. 'It's not going to happen. We had a round of IVF, but it didn't work.'

My body feels light as if it might float away. She's the first person I've told. The only person who knows. Well, almost.

Simone places her hands on her knees. Her forehead creases. 'Oh, Rachel. I'm so sorry.'

'It's okay. It was hard at first, but I've accepted it.'

Simone winces. Rubs at the space under her ribs, the fabric of her black jersey top moving with her hand.

'Are you okay?' Without realising it, my own hand has moved to the same place as I imagine what it must feel like to have a living thing growing inside me. When I realise what I'm doing, I drop my hand back into my lap, colour rising to my cheeks. Hoping Simone hasn't noticed.

'Yeah, I'm fine. Doctor says he's breech, and it feels as though his head's stuck right under here.' She massages the hard dome below her ribs, then looks at me. 'But you don't want to hear my boring pregnancy stuff.'

I give a tight embarrassed smile. Having told her about my failed IVF, the last thing I want is for her to feel bad about it. Think she can't mention her own pregnancy. For, even though it's hard for me to hear, it wouldn't be fair on her. And it is, after all, just the hand Owen and I have been dealt.

'I don't mind, honestly. Bringing a child into the world is a wonderful thing and, regardless of what happened to me, you should celebrate it.' My smile is genuine now. 'Please, I really do mean it.'

Simone is clearly relieved. She looks down at her swollen belly. Softens her voice. 'I'm not surprised you're causing trouble already, little man. Just like your father. Anyway, we were talking about you, not me. How are you now? How's Owen?'

Through the living room window, on the other side of the green, I can see our house... Owen's study. But the window reflects back the clouds, and I'm too far away to make him out.

'He says he's happy it being the two of us. That having children was my dream not his.'

Simone digests my words, her hand straying back to her stomach. 'And you believe him?'

I turn back to her. 'To be honest, I don't really know. It's hard to tell with Owen. He's never been good at opening up, admitting his true feelings – neither of us have. I wonder, sometimes, if he only says that to make me feel better.'

'I think that's sweet.'

I nod. 'Yes, it is. And, true or not, it helps. Our future isn't going to be how we thought it would be, but we have each other, and we know we're luckier than some. We'll have the freedom to do things we wouldn't have been able to do with children in tow. Once Owen's finished his next book, we'll embrace that freedom. Maybe travel.'

Knowing how worried Owen is about money, it's another thing we haven't actually talked about, but I'm hoping I can persuade him. It's a long time since we've been anywhere together, something that hasn't involved a book tour or a literary festival, and some time away would do us good. Owen especially. Spending so much of his week in front of a screen isn't good for him.

'And in the meantime?'

I smile. 'Actually, I've been thinking about getting myself a part-time job. Just a couple of days a week. Owen's not keen, doesn't see why I'd want to, but, if I'm honest, this move has made me unsettled. A job might be a way of getting some stability back into my life.'

'If that's what you want, then I think it's a great idea.' Simone puts her head on one side. 'I've had a thought. It might not be what you had in mind, but I know Phillipa's looking for someone to help her out.'

'Really?'

'Yeah. A bit of housework, babysitting the kids, some ironing... stuff like that. You said you'd done some childminding. I could have a word with her if you like.'

I sit straighter, knowing Owen wouldn't like that.

'It's kind of you to suggest it, but I was thinking more along the lines of something in town. In an office.'

Simone laughs. 'I get what you're saying, and it was only an idea... probably not my greatest. Phillipa and I are friends, don't get me wrong, but sometimes...' She hesitates. 'Let's just say time with her is something you only need in small doses. Like camping.'

She gives a snort of laughter, holds her hand to her mouth, and I can't help but join in. The coffee is warming my insides, but it's not just that. I feel that, in Simone, I've made a friend. Something I hadn't imagined happening straight away.

'There's something I wanted to ask you, Simone.'

She looks at me quizzically. 'Yeah? If it's the name of the capital of Kazakhstan, then I'm not your person.'

'No, nothing like that. I wanted to ask you about the people we bought the house from.'

'The Brookners?' Simone pushes a plate of biscuits towards me. 'Ask away.'

'I was wondering how old their daughter was.'

Simone's brows pinch. 'They didn't have a daughter.'

Now it's my turn to be confused. 'They didn't?'

'No, it's why they...' Simone looks down at her hands. 'Anyway. No, they didn't have any children.'

There's something Simone's not telling me, and I can't let it go. 'What were you going to say? Why they what?'

Simone's eyes raise to meet mine. She knows I'm not going to let it go. 'Why they left. I think living in the house where the little girl had lived, the one who died, had been playing on Lisa's mind. I didn't know her well, but, from what I heard, she wasn't happy living there once she found out.'

I feel a tightening in my stomach. 'Really?'

'Apparently, she'd started to hear things. It was her imagination, of course, but it clearly unsettled her.'

'She never said anything to us. The agent never mentioned it either.'

Simone shakes her head. 'Why would they? Saying you think the house is haunted is hardly going to help with the sale, is it? Look, I shouldn't have said anything either. It's a beautiful house, and I know you'll be happy there. I, for one, am over the moon to have you living in Pond Close. It's nice to have someone I can really talk to.'

But I'm only half listening, my mind wandering back to my phone call with Lisa Brookner. Remembering how animated and happy she'd sounded as we'd discussed the cooker she was including in the sale, the curtains she'd decided not to leave, after all. I'd thought her to be someone with a generally cheerful disposition, but now I wonder if her upbeat tone had simply been relief at having left the house behind her.

The child who died hadn't been hers at all, but the daughter of someone who'd lived in the house before her. Had Lisa Brookner believed her spirit still lingered in the house? I think about the bloodstain, Phillipa's name scrawled on the wall, and try to ignore the cold lick of apprehension that has crept up on me. I'd woken too, that first night, thinking I'd heard a sound in the house.

I lock eyes with Simone. 'What exactly was it Lisa thought she heard?'

'Don't quote me on it, but I think it was a child's cry.' She looks down, no longer smiling. 'Look, Rachel. Don't take this the wrong way, but it's been decided that we're not to talk about it.'

I'm confused. 'Decided by whom?'

'By the Residents' Association. What happened was awful, but it's been agreed that having a tragedy like that forever hanging over the close is no good for anyone. We want Pond Close to be a positive place. A happy place.'

As she speaks, I hear Phillipa's voice. Can guess whose idea it was. The thing that I'm finding strange is that Simone is happy to go along with it. I hadn't taken her for someone so compliant, but, then again, I've never lived in a small community such as this one. Perhaps conformity is the way to promote harmony.

Simone stands, gives me a warm smile, and the atmosphere returns to what it was before I'd mentioned anything.

'It's been really lovely to chat, Rachel, but the house is a tip, and with Kevin coming home tomorrow, I really should get the place sorted. Make it look like I haven't been having wild parties every night.' She snorts back a laugh, rubs her belly. 'As if that's likely.'

I smile back at her. Stand too. 'You never know. Thank you for the coffee and I'm sorry about—'

'Forget it. Rules, eh! Look, I'll pop over tomorrow sometime when Kevin's back. Introduce the old man. That way it won't be so formal, and it won't give Owen the chance to make an excuse.'

I laugh. 'I won't mention it to him. I'll let it be a surprise.'

'Good plan.'

I pick up my bag, feeling grateful for having met someone who understands my situation. Who doesn't question it.

Leaving Simone to her tidying, I let myself out of the front door and cross the green. As I near my house, I see Phillipa's car in the drive next to ours. A light is on in her kitchen, the shutters open, and I'm tempted to look in but force myself not to. For some reason I don't want to see Phillipa playing with Lexi or giving her a snack in her highchair, her hair brushing the little girl's cheek as she bends to kiss her head. Not that my imagined scene is likely, considering what I'd witnessed at the garden party: Phillipa's fingers gripping the little girl's shoulders. Her hissed threat of a smack.

As I get my front door key out of my bag, I realise I never

told Simone about what I'd found on our kitchen wall – the bloodied handprint, Phillipa's name beside it. Still, she'll see it when she comes over with Kevin, and maybe they'll be able to shed some light on it.

I step onto my porch and, unable to resist any longer, turn curious eyes to Phillipa's window. When I see the kitchen is empty, I'm left feeling strangely deflated – as though I've stepped into an auditorium during the interval and found the stage deserted.

Perhaps I should consider taking that job at Phillipa's, after all. At least that way I'll be able to keep an eye on the two of them.

That night, I have the nightmare again; it's one I've had, on and off, since the day we found out the IVF hadn't worked out as we'd hoped.

I sit up and reach for my dressing gown, the child's cry still in my head, unsure if I'm asleep or awake. All I know is I have to save her.

Pushing back the covers, I stumble out of bed and feel along the wall for the light switch, panic rising when it's not where I think it should be. For a moment, I can't think where I am – in my old house or my new.

'Owen,' I call out. 'Owen!'

He doesn't answer, and I press my back against the wall, the room so dark I can't see anything. Where is my husband? Where *is* he? With my arms outstretched in front of me, I find the door and open it. Step out onto the silent landing.

As I walk down the stairs, I see the moonlight that shines through the glass panels of the front door. Instinct makes me go to it. Stand in the white rectangle of ghostly light to check it's closed. It is and I move away, the only thought in my head that I must find the child from my dream. Let her know she's safe.

'It's all right. I'm here,' I whisper into the darkness.

The kitchen is empty, the outline of the counters indistinct. The only light coming from the digits on the cooker that glow yellow in the gloom.

I know it's my house, yet it feels different as though it belongs to someone else. As though I'm trespassing on someone else's life.

I can see Jade. Can make out her pale skin and the pink bows on her little sandals. My head is filled with her cry. The wail of a police siren.

A light flicks on. Fingers grip my shoulders. Shaking me.

'Rachel, wake up. It's me, Owen.'

The kitchen melts away. The child's face too, replaced by my husband's. His hair is mussed. His cheeks lined from the pillow. I'm no longer in the kitchen but in my bedroom. In my bed.

'I heard her cry,' I say. 'I had to find her. Stop her.'

But even as I say it, the dream is moving away from me. Too far for me to grasp properly.

'Please, Rachel. Not this again.' Owen switches off the bedside light, turns over so his back is to me. 'Go back to sleep. It will all seem different in the morning.'

I lie back, my heart still thudding. I want to believe him, but I can't.

NINE

RACHEL

The next day, while Owen is up in his study, I scout the job websites on my computer. There are no pharmacy jobs locally and the only interesting vacancies seem to be full-time – something I know Owen wouldn't be happy with.

I jot down a couple of things that might do in the short term and make a mental note to apply later. Neither position fills me with enthusiasm, but I tell myself that once I've secured something, I can always move on in a few months if a more compelling job comes along.

Closing the computer, I go into the kitchen and start to prepare lunch. As I dice the cucumber and cherry tomatoes for our salad, take the stone out of an avocado and slice it, I see Phillipa walking down her front path. The older two children will be at school, but Lexi toddles in front of her, her plump legs encased in white lacy tights. The black patent shoes and red velvet dress she's wearing making her look as though she's going to a party or a Sunday church service.

As I watch, Phillipa hurries after her as best she can in the high shoes she's wearing, her arm outstretched. When she reaches Lexi, she takes her hand, but the little girl twists and pulls away. Runs out onto the pavement, looking as though she's heading for the road.

I run to the window, gasp in horror as a blue sports car appears out of nowhere. It's going to hit her, I know it is. I cry out and close my eyes. Waiting for the impact. The sound of Phillipa's scream or Lexi's.

When neither come, I open my eyes again and let out a long breath of relief. Phillipa is crouched on the pavement in front of her daughter, her hands either side of her shoulders, her mouth wide. She's shouting at her, and as I watch, Lexi's face crumples in shock.

Beside them on the road, the sports car has wound down its window. Charlene's husband, Steve, leans out, his elbow on the window frame. I can't hear what he's saying, but, from the look on his face, it's clearly not complimentary. I want to shake them both, tell them how irresponsible they've been, but it's not my place. No one was hurt, and Lexi's not my child. As Owen would say, it's none of my business.

I go back to the salad, hook my finger under the ring pull of a tin of tuna and strip off the lid. Fork out the contents and add it to the cucumber, avocado and tomatoes. But I can't stop thinking about what happened and my heart thuds with anger. With fear. Another second and Lexi might have been dead. Crushed under the wheels of Steve's car. And even if no car had been coming, in another few minutes she could have crossed that road. Been heading across the green towards the pond.

I picture her little body, white tights turned brown by the water, hair tangled with the reeds, and feel her mother's heartache as if it were my own. But would Phillipa really be heartbroken? It's hard to believe when her name is slashed across my wall... an accusation clear for all to see in that simple question. *Why Phillipa?*

One thing is certain, I need to find out the link between my neighbour and the little girl who lived in our house. Why her name is on the kitchen wall. I also need to make sure Lexi is safe in her care.

'What's going on?' Owen appears at the top of the stairs. 'What was all the shouting?'

I point to the window. 'Phillipa let her child run down the path unattended. She could have got run over. Nearly did.'

'Who, Phillipa?'

'What? No, her little girl, Lexi. You should have seen the ridiculous heels the woman was wearing. No wonder she couldn't run after her.'

'You shouldn't make judgements, Rachel. For all you know, Phillipa may have been going out to work or a meeting. She could have been taking the child to a childminder or something.'

It's true, I suppose, and Owen's right I shouldn't judge. But after what happened, it's hard not to. If I had a child, I'd look after them better than that. Wear sensible shoes when I took them out and change them later if I needed to. Above all else, I'd know where they were at all times.

I swallow. Worried that my face is giving me away and that Owen might somehow read my thoughts. Because all of these things are hypothetical. Have been since the moment the consultant at the hospital told us our chances of another round of IVF being successful was slim.

I force a smile. 'Anyway, from the way Steve was yelling at her, he must have felt the same way.'

Owen leans on the banister. 'Which one is Steve again?'

'Ex-footballer. Young wife. One of the kids you saw drinking by the pond is his son from a previous marriage.' I close my eyes. 'Jesus. I really did think his car was going to hit Lexi. He was driving way too fast for a residential street.'

'Sounds an idiot to me.'

Owen turns to go, but I call after him.

'You might as well stay down now. It's almost lunchtime.'

He shakes his head. 'No, I need to get on. You can call me when it's ready.'

He disappears up the stairs and a few moments later I hear the study door shut.

I sigh and turn back to the salad. We've only been here a couple of days, I know, but I feel as though it's someone else's house I'm standing in. Preparing food in. As though I'm a visitor or a holidaymaker in an Airbnb. The kitchen, the house, the big, grassed area front and back, doesn't feel like mine at all, and I wonder when it will start to. My eyes drift to the peeling wall-paper and my scattered tools.

I reach up to one of the cupboards and get out two plates. When the unpacking is finished, it will be different, I tell myself. Of course it will.

I'm taking the plates to the table, coming back for the salad, when I see Simone crossing the green, her arm linked with that of a tall man with broad shoulders. They're heading towards the house, and I glance up at the ceiling, wondering whether Owen will have seen. Should I have warned him that they'd be coming today?

Not wanting to alert him to their visit until after they're safely inside, I hurry into the hall. Perhaps this is my chance to find out a little more about Phillipa, Lexi... the child. I open the door.

'Hi.' I give them a welcoming smile.

'Blimey, you opened that door quick. I didn't even ring the bell. Rachel, I presume.' Kevin offers his hand and I take it, liking the firmness of his grip.

'You presume right. It's nice to meet you, Kevin. You must be happy to be back.'

He smiles, showing white teeth in a classically good-looking face. 'Nice to be back home to the wife but...' He nods his head towards the close. 'Can't say I missed this place much. Dubai's fucking amazing. Ever been?'

'No, never.'

'Shame.'

I kiss Simone's cheek, then turn and wave my hand at the boxes. 'I'm sorry the place is in such a state. We haven't got around to unpacking everything yet. To be honest, the whole move has felt a bit like a dream, and I keep expecting to wake up back in my old place. Please, come in and make yourselves at home. There are still loads of boxes in the living room so we might be better in the kitchen, if you're okay with that?'

'Of course.' Simone links arms with me. 'We don't care where we sit, do we, Kev?'

''Course not.'

At the kitchen door, Simone stops. She's seen the salad. The plates on the table. 'Oh, I'm sorry. Have we disturbed your lunch?' She looks at her watch. 'I didn't think.'

'Please don't worry. We haven't started yet, and there's nothing to get cold. What can I get you? Tea? Coffee? Or there's white wine in the fridge, if you'd prefer.'

'No wine for me, thanks.' Simone looks down at her bump. 'But Kev might. I'll stick with tea, if that's okay.'

Kevin pulls out one of the kitchen chairs. Sits down and links his fingers behind his head, elbows wide. 'Yeah. I'll have a glass of wine. Why not?'

I go to the fridge. Pull out the bottle of white Owen opened last night, then reach up to the cupboard for glasses. Wondering if the cheap Sancerre we bought in the local supermarket will be good enough for Kevin – how much of a connoisseur he is.

'Where's the old man then? Keeping a low profile?' Kevin looks amused, eyes flicking up to the ceiling, and I guess Simone must have told him about Owen's no show at the welcome party.

'Nothing like that. He's working, that's all. I'll call him down.'

I switch on the kettle for Simone's tea and hand Kevin his wine. I take mine to the bottom of the stairs. Call up.

'Owen, can you come down? We have company.'

When there's no answer, I place my glass on the newel post and run up. Knock on the study door. 'Owen, can I come in?'

'Of course.'

I step inside, shutting the door behind me. Owen is at his desk as I expected him to be, but the computer is switched off. The monitor blank.

'Is lunch ready?' He takes off his glasses. Cleans them on a corner of his shirt.

'No, but I need you to come down. We have visitors.'

He holds his glasses up to the light, then puts them on. 'Visitors? Who?'

'Simone and Kevin from Number 4.'

'Couldn't you have told them it was lunchtime? That it wasn't convenient?'

I feel my mouth tighten. Lean my back against the door, arms folded. 'No, I couldn't. These are our neighbours, Owen. I know it doesn't bother you being rude, but it does me.'

'And you don't think turning up at lunchtime is rude?'

I look at him, exasperated. 'No, I don't. They weren't to know what time we have lunch, and it won't hurt us to eat later for a change. We have wine, and I'll find some nibbles.'

Owen places the flats of his hands on the desk and stares at the blank screen of his computer. It looks as if the universe is on his shoulders, and my irritation slips away.

'Please, Owen. Come down. If not for you, then for me. A few minutes, that's all... to say hello.'

I hold my breath, waiting for his reply.

He swivels his chair round so he's facing me again. Looks down at the gold band on his finger and back up at me.

'All right. If it will make you happy.'

'It will. You'll like them. I know you will.'

He shakes his head. 'I doubt that.'

As we go downstairs, Simone's voice comes to us from the kitchen, followed by Kevin's loud laugh.

Please, Owen. Make an effort. Let them see how nice you can be.

It's what I'm thinking as we join them. What I'm hoping for as Kevin looks up from his drink, his brows pulling together in confusion, and the colour leaches from Owen's face.

TEN

RACHEL

'Don't I know you?' Kevin taps the tips of his first two fingers to his forehead as he tries to remember. 'Hold on. It will come to me.'

Owen hasn't moved. His eyes behind his glasses give nothing away.

Simone and I look at one another, and her shrug tells me she's none the wiser. She puts her hand on her husband's arm. 'Well, whether you do or you don't, let's all have a drink and get to know one another. It's lovely to meet you, Owen. I'm Simone and this is Kev. I was going to say we live across the road, but it would be more accurate to say we live across the green.'

'Owen?' I give my husband a nudge.

While Simone's been talking, he's been staring out of the window, miles away, but now his eyes focus. He looks at Simone and smiles.

'I'm very pleased to meet you. You too, Kevin.'

He steps forward. Holds out his hand. Kevin takes it and the two men shake, but I can see Kevin is still thinking. His eyes roving across Owen's face.

'Could you take your glasses off?'

'Kevin!' Simone slaps her husband's arm. 'Stop being an idiot.'

'No really, mate. If you take your glasses off, it might help me remember.'

Simone shakes her head at her husband, her frown deepening. 'I'm sorry, Owen. Don't you do any such thing. When Kev gets a bee in his bonnet about something, he's insufferable. Sit down and tell us about yourself. We're not used to having celebrities living in the close.'

The colour has returned to Owen's face. He pulls out a chair and sits, happy to be able to talk about something with which he's comfortable.

'I'd hardly call myself that. I get ideas, I write them, and my publisher pays me for the pleasure. Rachel told me you've read *Dead Air*.'

Kevin nods. 'Fucking good read, mate. Hats off to you... I never saw that end coming.'

'Not many do.' Owen gives a rueful smile.

Simone grins. 'Maybe you could sign it sometime?'

'With pleasure.'

I watch Owen and feel my shoulders relax, not realising how tense I'd been. When Owen talks about his work, he's like another person. Warmer. It takes me back to the day I met him. To the day I fell in love with him.

Kevin leans forward, elbows on the table. 'It's your voice. I'm sure I know it.'

Owen had been smiling, but now his smile slips. 'Maybe you've heard me—'

'Wait a minute. Wait a minute.' Kevin sits back again. Places both palms either side of his head and squeezes. 'It's coming to me.' He looks up and points, triumph written across his face. 'Manchester Uni. Were you there?'

'As it happens, I was.'

'Then that's where I know you from. I just can't recall why and how.'

'I think you're mistaken.' While he'd been talking about his work, Owen had poured himself a glass of wine, filling it almost to the brim. Now he picks it up and takes a couple of large mouthfuls. 'As far as I know we've never met.'

But like a dog with a ball, Kevin won't leave it. 'What course were you on? English, I presume.' He leans back in his chair, remembering. 'I knew a few people from the English department. They were always banging on about the uni rag. Wanting me and the other guys in the rugby club to contribute something to it.' He laughs. 'As though we were ever sober enough to remember our matches!'

'I wasn't in the English department. The course was over-subscribed, so I studied psychology.'

Kevin gives a shrug. 'English. Psychology. All the same to me. I knew it, though, the minute I set foot in here. Knew it.'

Owen closes his eyes as though it pains him to be having this conversation.

'It's a well-known fact I was at Manchester. It says it on the cover of my books, in every interview I've given. The point I was making, Kevin, was I don't remember you, and I think I would know if I did. Now why don't you have another drink?' He picks up the bottle and pours more wine into Kevin's glass. Turns to Simone. 'How rude of us to hog the conversation. When is your little one due? It's been a good pregnancy, I hope.'

I sit and listen to the conversation. Pleased at the effort Owen's putting in even though I know he's not interested in either of them. Not really.

Yet as he talks, asks questions about the close and the other neighbours, I see how Kevin's eyes haven't left Owen. See how his face has frozen into a frown. Something feels wrong, but I've no idea what it is.

The conversation Owen and Simone have been having has

fizzled out, and Kevin, remembering his manners, drags his eyes away from my husband.

'So, Rachel. How have you settled in? Simone's been telling me you're on the hunt for a job.' He stretches out his legs and crosses his arms. Quite at home in our kitchen.

I see Owen's face tighten and know what he'll be thinking. That it isn't anybody's business but our own. That I shouldn't have been discussing it with a neighbour I've only just met.

'It's only an idea,' I say quickly. 'Not one I've thought through properly. There's no hurry and it's not as if there isn't plenty to do here.'

Kevin's eyes have caught the half-stripped wall, and I take my chance.

'I found writing over there, underneath the old paper.' I point and Simone and Owen look over too. 'Odd, isn't it?'

Kevin gets up, looks at the writing. '*Why Phillipa?*' He gives a forced laugh. 'I've wanted to ask her this question a few times myself. *Why* she's such a pain in the arse? *Why* she rules the roost here?'

'But what's it doing here? Don't you think that looks like blood?'

He looks closer. 'Nah... that would be old paint.'

'Exactly what I told her, Kevin.'

I glare at Owen. Hating that he's taken Kevin's side. They're wrong. It's blood, I know it is.

'Anyway,' he continues. 'I told her there's nothing wrong with the kitchen.' Owen looks around him. 'I've never understood people who want to make changes for change's sake. It looks fine to me.'

'It *is* pretty old, mate.' Kevin sits back down. 'These kitchen units are the original from when the houses were built. Early nineties when unpainted wood was still popular. Ours had exactly the same ones. We stripped them out a few years ago.'

Owen sucks in his cheeks, won't meet my eye. We both

know we don't have enough savings left for things like new kitchens, but he's too proud to say.

'I was thinking more along the lines of painting the doors,' I say, placing my hand on his. No one else seems to think it odd to have writing hidden beneath the paper on a kitchen wall, so maybe I'm overreacting. 'It would be nice to have a project.'

'I think that's a great idea.' Simone pulls her eyes from the faded writing. It's the first time she's spoken since I pointed out what I'd found under the old wallpaper, and I'm grateful to her for rescuing me. Although I hadn't been so indiscreet as to tell her the exact reason we moved here from our large country home, I'm sure she must have had her suspicions.

Beside me, Owen's eyes lift to the clock on the wall. Now that the conversation has moved on from his writing, his attention is starting to drift. He pushes back his chair, the suddenness of his action making us all look at him.

'I hope you don't mind, but if you'll excuse me, I have things to do.'

I feel myself colour. Embarrassed that Owen's show of hospitality has come so abruptly to an end.

'Please, Owen—'

'It's all right, honestly.' Simone gives me an understanding smile. 'We need to be going anyway. I would have rung before coming over, but we never got around to swapping numbers. We should do that now, Rachel.'

She gives me her number and I ring it. 'There we are.'

'Great.' Simone stands. Rubs her belly. 'Drink up, Kev. This little one's getting restless. It's been nice to meet you, Owen. I hope you'll both be very happy in Pond Close.'

'That's very kind of you. I'm sure we will.'

'I'll see you out.' I get up and accept Simone's kiss on my cheek. Refuse to look at Owen as I'm so mad at him.

Kevin stands. Offers his hand to Owen. 'Let's fix up a round of golf, mate. Next weekend, maybe?'

Owen forces a smile, and I know he's already thinking of an excuse not to take up Kevin's offer. 'I'll check my diary and let you know later on in the week. Thank you both so very much for coming over. It was very thoughtful.'

Feeling flustered, I follow Simone to the front door and open it for her.

'I'm sorry. Owen doesn't mean to be rude. It's just his way.'

Simone puts a hand on my arm. 'You don't need to apologise. Your husband's a busy man, and we stayed longer than we'd intended anyway. Thank you for the drinks. It'll be our turn next.' She looks over my shoulder. 'Come on, Kevin. What are you doing?'

I turn. Kevin is staring intently into our dining room, but from where I'm standing, it's impossible to see what he's looking at.

'You don't mind if I take a look, do you?' Without waiting for an answer, Kevin disappears into the room.

'Kevin!' Simone looks at me and sighs. 'Now it's *my* turn to apologise. Husbands, eh?'

Wondering what's caught Kevin's attention, I leave Simone at the door and follow him in. He's leaning against the shiny surface of the sideboard, one ankle crossed over the other, a framed photograph in his hand. It's the one of Owen on his graduation day. He's wearing a dark gown and mortar board and has his degree certificate clutched in his hand. The earnest way in which he's staring into the camera, adds seriousness to the capture. Makes him look as though he can't quite believe his luck.

'Owen Two-Pack Packard living in the same close as me.' Kevin shakes his head in disbelief. 'Who'd have bloody thought it.'

He holds the photograph out to me, and I take it. Try to see what he's seeing. Behind the polished glass, Owen looks a lot younger than his twenty-one years. His fine hair is cut short at the back, falling into a side curtain across his forehead and without the glasses he wears now, his clean-shaven face looks naked.

Kevin's looking at me strangely, the intensity of his stare disconcerting, and I'm relieved when Simone's voice comes to us from the hall.

'Kevin. Come *on*. Are we going or not?'

'Right with you,' he calls back.

With a last look at the photograph, Kevin goes out into the hall. 'Sorry, love,' he says to his wife. 'Had a date with the past. Goodbye, Rachel. It's been...' – he looks past me to the kitchen door – 'enlightening.'

I wave them off and watch them as they cross the green. When they're out of sight, I shut the front door and lean my back against it, not ready to go back in. A question on my mind.

Why hadn't Owen recognised Kevin?

Unless he had, I think, my eyes moving to the kitchen door. *And didn't want me to know.*

ELEVEN

OWEN

Owen sits at the kitchen table, his head in his hands. He'd known it was Kevin Wellbeck the minute he'd clapped eyes on him as, in the years since they'd last seen each other, the smarmy bastard hadn't changed a bit. Same physique, except for the beginnings of a paunch that he'd be able to hide if he sucked his stomach in. Same smirk. Same confidence.

He thinks of the way Kevin had sat at their table. Legs stretched out in front of him, feet crossed at the ankles. His fingers linked behind his head, elbows wide, in that way he remembered. As though it was *his* bloody house, not theirs.

Owning the place.

Owning the air they breathed.

And him having to pour the bastard his wine. Having to ask after his wife's pregnancy, when all he wanted to do was punch his smug face.

Time heals all wounds, but memories last a lifetime... That's what they say, isn't it? And it's true. For the last twenty-five years, he'd striven not to think back to those university days, but he'd never managed to completely forget them. How could he, when his graduation photograph was there on display, eyes following him whenever he walked past to eat his supper. He'd hoped that, with the move, Rachel might forget to put it back up, but it was one of the first things she'd done. Setting it along-side the one of him signing his books and their wedding photo.

He hadn't wanted it framed at all, but Rachel had found it in a cupboard after she'd first moved in with him. Had insisted. And, like a fool, he'd allowed her to persuade him. Flattered by what she'd said. Her words massaging his fragile ego. Words he can only partly remember now – something to do with being proud of him. That he was the only person she knew with a first-class degree.

He could have told her that the photograph is a painful reminder of his mistakes back then. Secrets he needs to keep from Rachel.

He twists his wedding ring around his finger. Listens to Kevin's voice shouting goodbye. Too loud. Too bloody cocksure. He'd noticed how his pregnant wife Simone's eyes had stayed on her husband the whole time he'd been sitting at their table as though he was some bloody superhero or something – not the boor he knows him to be. The question he'd not dared ask himself was whether Simone's eyes had been the only ones on him. It's a question he asks himself now. Might Rachel have been taken in by him too? Had she also been unable to see beneath Kevin's shiny veneer?

He presses his fist to his forehead. What were the chances of Kevin living here? What were the bloody chances?

There's a click as the front door shuts. Knowing he only has a moment to compose himself before his wife comes back in, Owen knocks back the last of his wine. Sits up straighter in his chair. And by the time Rachel enters the kitchen, he's arranged his features so the tension which had tightened both his eyes and his lips is hidden behind his smile.

Rachel sits down. Pours herself some more wine. She looks lovely. The sunlight, streaming in through the kitchen window, picking out the golden highlights in her hair. His wife is his rock. His anchor. He chews at his cheek... there must be a better metaphor. Ah, yes. She's the knot that keeps him from unravelling. Always was. Always will be.

He must protect her.

He remembers how he'd stood on the doorstep and listened to the reasons Jade's mother, Julie, gave as to why she would be terminating the arrangement. Yes, of course she understood that things had been difficult for his wife, she'd said, but recently Rachel had been getting too needy. Ringing her to ask if she could keep Jade another hour. Turning up at her house to see if she wanted her to have Jade another day. The final straw had been the late winter afternoon when she'd come to their house to collect her daughter and found the place in darkness. Rung the police.

They'd discovered Rachel and Jade at the bottom of the garden, staring at the moon reflected on the surface of the pond, even though darkness had fallen and it wasn't safe for a child to be out there. Too close to the edge. Much, much too close. Rachel's hands on the little girl's shoulders.

He shudders at the memory.

But they were different people then, he reminds himself, shifting his eyes from her hair to her hand where her diamond engagement ring glints beside her wedding band. Very different people. Weren't they?

TWELVE

RACHEL

I wipe the sweat from my forehead, then press the starter button, grip the lever on the lawnmower's handle and carry on mowing. Forcing the blades through the unruly grass of our front lawn. Stopping again as the engine strains and whines before I do some damage to it.

I unplug the mower from the circuit breaker and am kneeling to pull out the clogged grass from the blades when I see one of the teenage boys, Aaron I think Simone said his name was, come around the corner of the close. In his dark-red blazer and school trousers, he looks different to how I'd imagined. Younger. He has a rucksack on his back, and as he reaches his driveway, he looks up. Catches my eye.

I start to say hello, but before I can, his head is down again and he's swinging his bag off his back. Searching in it for his key. A key he has no need of as the door has already opened. I squat by the mower, clumps of wet grass clutched in my gardening gloved hand, as Pam steps out. She looks from right to left, then ushers Aaron in without a word to either him or me.

It's odd behaviour, but as I stand and start the mower again, I reason that maybe she hadn't seen me, though the sound of the mower's engine would have been hard not to hear from her house.

A car passes by. Phillipa is back now too, her car slipping into the space on her drive next to where her husband parks his when he's home from work. I watch as the passenger door opens. One of the back doors too. The two older children scramble out and run around the side of the house, squabbling over something. I wait and watch, expecting to see Phillipa get out, but she doesn't. Instead, she remains in the driver's seat, staring at the white double garage doors in front of her. In her car seat in the back, I can make out Lexi's little face, eyes screwed up, mouth wide. Her cries audible through the open door on the other side of the car.

I release the lever on the mower and the engine stops. Why isn't Phillipa doing anything? Why is she sitting there rather than picking her daughter up? Comforting her? I wait and watch, expecting the driver's door to open and for Phillipa to get out, go around to the back and release Lexi from her straps. But she doesn't. Instead, she folds her arms on the steering wheel and rests her forehead on them.

The other two children have disappeared, and I step out from behind the mower. Lexi's cries are becoming louder, and I'm not sure whether I should do something.

I look behind me, wondering if Pam would have heard the child's cries from her house, but there's no sign of her at the window. Owen's not looking out either. Is it only me who cares? Not able to stand the sound of Lexi crying any more, I take off my gardening gloves and drop them onto the half-mown grass. I cut across the lawn to Phillipa's drive, go to the driver's window and knock on it.

Phillipa jumps. Looks at me as though she's seen a ghost.

She winds down the window. 'What is it?'

I point to the back seat. 'Your daughter... Lexi. She's crying. I... I wondered if something was wrong.'

Her face hardens. 'Nothing's wrong. She's overtired, that's all.'

Lexi's face is red. She rocks forward and back in her chair, the straps pressing into her coat.

'Do you want me to get her out of her seat?'

Phillipa sighs. 'Do what you want. It's only attention seeking. Jesus Christ. If I'd known it would be so easy to get pregnant at my age, I'd have bloody well slept in the spare room.'

I stare at her, shocked, then open the back door and unbuckle Lexi's straps. I lift her out and onto my hip, rocking from foot to foot in the hope that the rhythm will comfort her. The little girl's face is wet with tears, strands of fine hair stuck to her cheeks. I wipe them away.

'There, there. You're all right now.'

'I'll take her.' Phillipa lifts her daughter from my arms. I thought I'd been doing her a favour, but her face has tightened. She waves me away dismissively. 'I'm sure you have things to do.'

I stand on her drive, my arms feeling oddly empty. 'Yes, of course.' I force a laugh. 'The lawn won't mow itself.'

'No.' She puts Lexi down, and as she straightens the little girl's skirt, I think I see a red mark on the side of her plump leg. Has Phillipa smacked her? Is that why she was crying?

I want to say something, but I don't want this woman to hate me. I need her to trust me. Is now the time to try to ask Phillipa what she knows about my house? But by the time I finish my thought, she's gone.

I cross back across the lawn. Picking up the mower's wire, I hook it over my shoulder and take up where I left off. I've almost finished when I see someone jogging across the green in navy tracksuit bottoms and a white T-shirt. He's heading towards our house, and I stop mowing. Take off my gloves again.

Kevin stops in front of me. 'Hi. Wanted to have a word with your other half. See if he wants to join me and Carl for that game of golf next weekend. We can sign him in as our guest, then if he's up for it, he can join too.' He folds his arms. 'Is this a good time?'

I look up at the study window. No time is a good time when Owen's working, but I don't want him to think us rude.

'Do you want me to go in and see?'

'You're busy.' Kevin points at the half-open front door. 'Why don't I pop in? Call him down.'

Surprised by his suggestion, I don't answer straight away and, taking this as a yes, Kevin grins, then jogs up to the front door. Before I can act, he's disappeared inside.

I know I should stop him, that Owen won't be happy, but a part of me is rebelling. Telling me that this might, in fact, be a good idea. He wouldn't tell me why he'd been acting so strangely with Kevin, and if I'd gone up and told Owen that Kevin was here, he'd have made up some excuse or other. But if Kevin calls him... well, then he'll have to come down. Have to make an effort. It's only now I realise how much I want this. To make friends in this new place. Not just me but Owen too.

I finish the rest of the grass, unplug the mower and wind the cord around the handle. Kevin hasn't come out yet. The front door is open, but, from where I'm standing, there's no sign of him in the hall.

Placing my gloves on top of the lawnmower, I remove my grass covered shoes and go inside, surprised when Kevin is nowhere to be seen. I frown. Look up at the stairwell. There's no way Owen's going to be happy about this. Unsure of what I'm going to find when I get there, I climb to the turn of the stairs. Stop when I hear voices. Kevin is in Owen's study, and the door is shut.

Even though it feels wrong to eavesdrop, I move across the landing and press my ear to the study door. Owen is talking. He sounds agitated, his naturally quiet voice coming in fits and starts.

I wait, for what I'm not sure, the flat of my hand against the shiny wood. It's Kevin who's speaking now, and his voice, louder than my husband's, is clearer to hear. But now that he's spoken, I wish I'd never gone up. Never put my ear to that door.

'Don't worry, Owen.' Kevin's voice is a mixture of contempt and amusement, and I feel gooseflesh rise on my arms at what he says next. 'Your secret's safe with me.'

THIRTEEN

RACHEL

The study door opens, and Kevin comes out. I step back into the shadows, and he doesn't see me, takes the stairs two at a time, a smile on his face. I wait until I hear the front door shut, then go in to Owen. He's at the window, watching Kevin jog down the street. His face is pale. One hand gripping the other behind his back, the flesh whitening beneath the press of his fingers.

'Owen?'

He turns. 'What is it?'

I think about making something up, but I have to know what Kevin wanted. The real reason he came here and the meaning of what he'd said. One thing I'm sure of is that if we're to make a go of things, we can't have secrets from one another. Not so soon into our move.

'I heard what Kevin said.'

I think Owen's going to be angry, accuse me of listening in to his private conversation, but that's not the case. Instead, he moves from the window and lowers himself heavily into his chair.

'Oh.' The single syllable conveys his despair.

'What did he mean *your secret's safe with me*? What secret,

Owen? What was he talking about?'

Owen snaps out of his despondent mood. His voice is brittle. 'It was something and nothing. Don't worry yourself about it.'

'It didn't sound like nothing.' I go up to him. Crouch next to him, my hand on his knee, wishing we were able to talk like other couples. 'Please, Owen, don't keep things from me.'

His expression is closed. Defensive. 'I said it was nothing, Rachel. The man's an idiot.' He shakes his head. Tries to lighten the mood. 'Why would he ever think I'd want to play golf with him and his idiot friend?'

'Carl, you mean? You haven't even met him yet. How can you be so quick to judge?'

Owen gives a mirthless laugh. 'It's not hard considering the company he keeps. Kevin's a jerk. He was one when we were at university, and he hasn't changed.'

I stand. Try to work out from his expression what he's thinking, but it's impossible. If only I didn't find it so hard to read him. 'I think you should give him a chance. And anyway, I told you before, I like Simone.'

He doesn't answer but gets up and paces the room, his head bent. The place where he writes is the one place guaranteed to help him relax, give him peace when the world around him gets too noisy, but today, he's like a caged animal. Something's wrong, but he's not going to tell me what.

'Why don't we go out somewhere? Just you and me. A walk, maybe, or that new shopping centre we drove by the other day.'

Owen looks at me as though I'm mad, and I realise how foolish I'm being. Wonder why I even said it. Owen's never liked shopping and walking is something he prefers to do alone. An activity done not for fresh air or health, but in order to gather his thoughts... untwist his tangled plotlines. I'm desperate, though, knowing that if things are going to work out, something must change.

And that's the problem. Nothing can change between us if Owen's unwilling to try. As I stand in his study, surrounded by his books and folders, I can't help wondering if the loneliness I'm feeling now isn't because I miss him, but because I miss the *idea* of him. The man I thought he was the night I met him. The man I wanted him to be. Not that I don't love him. I do.

It's just...

Unable to stop it, James's face has come into my head, as it does from time to time. Usually, I manage to push it away, file it under the label of *no regrets,* but today it's harder and I know why. Sometimes, I wonder if Owen even knows I'm in the room, but James... well, he had that way of looking at me. A look that said he really saw me, really knew me, and what he knew made him want to know more.

Want *me* more.

'I'm rather tired.' Owen takes off his glasses and cleans them. 'I might have a lie-down.'

I break away from my thoughts, feel a rush of tenderness for my husband. A sadness. Today, Owen seems older – the tendons in his neck strained, his shoulders more hunched. Kevin's visit has bothered him, and it makes me want to reach for him, comfort him, but I don't. I can see from the angle of his body that he wants to be alone.

I often wonder if Owen believes it was his fame that first attracted me to him, but it wasn't. It was the hint of vulnerability he'd shown when he'd struggled to find his place in the text at his reading. A sensitivity that had drawn me in and which still, to this day, makes me stay. The urge to look after had started after my dad died – a time when I'd been eaten up with guilt for not having been able to do anything to stop the cancer that had eventually taken him. Not that a child could have done anything.

I take in the four walls of Owen's study. The view from the window that still doesn't feel like ours. Sometimes, I wonder if my need to nurture is simply a coping mechanism to stop myself from going under.

'A nap's a good idea. You look tired.' I brighten my tone, not wanting him to know that I, too, feel unsettled by what I overheard. 'The move has taken it out of the both of us, and I'm sure you'll feel a whole lot better after. If you don't mind, I'm going to pop round to Simone's and then we can have supper.'

I'd thought that Owen might protest, considering Simone is Kevin's wife, but he only nods. He follows me out of the room and goes into our bedroom, shutting the door behind him. It makes me wonder if I'm right in leaving him alone when he's in this sombre mood. His melancholy evident in every movement. Every expression. Not that he's ever given me reason to believe he'd be desperate enough to try anything.

Not when he has his writing.

His books are his saviour – he's told me that many times. His characters a distraction for him when things are tough. When Owen's at his lowest, he can lose himself in whatever world he's created. Real life, and the worries it brings with it, all but forgotten in the press of a computer key. It makes me envy him sometimes. If only it was that easy for everyone. For me.

I let myself out of the house, admiring the newly cut lawn as I walk down the front path. Across the street, on the other side of the green, Phillipa's husband, Carl, is walking quickly, head down. When he reaches Steve and Chantelle's place, he ducks into their drive where Chantelle's little pink Fiat is parked. He doesn't go to the front door but stops, glances towards his own house on the opposite side of the close, then disappears around the back of the house.

I wait, intrigued, and a few minutes later, my patience is rewarded. Someone has appeared at one of the upstairs windows – a shadowy form before the curtains close, but I'm pretty certain it's Carl. If the two of them are up to what I think they're up to, he's sailing very close to the wind. I look across to

Phillipa's house, wondering what she's doing and whether she might suspect. Yes, very close indeed.

Don't shit on your own doorstep. It's a term my mother used to use. I've never liked the expression, but as I look back at Chantelle's house, I decide it's one that Carl should heed. He might like the thrill of nipping into their house when Steve is out with the baby, but although Steve lacks height, he looks strong. I wouldn't want to mess with him. Also, behind his affable cocksure manner at the welcoming party, I'd thought I'd seen something else. Suspicion mixed with something darker.

I carry on walking, my steps taking me across the green. Carl's playing a dangerous game. I stop and look back at the window of our house. The reason I know this is because I recognise that look.

I've seen the same in the eyes of my own husband.

When I reach Simone's house, I see Kevin's car has gone from the drive. Glad that she'll be on her own, I ring the bell. It opens straight away. 'Well, this is a nice surprise. What can I do for you? Would you like to come in?'

'Thank you, but this won't take long. There's something I want to ask you.'

'That sounds intriguing. Fire away.'

I take a deep, nervous breath, hoping I'm doing the right thing. 'Did you know Kevin came over to our house earlier?'

She looks surprised. 'No, I didn't. What did he want?'

I hesitate. 'He said he wanted to invite Owen to play golf with him and Carl.'

I think of Carl up in Chantelle's bedroom, what they might be doing, and blush.

Simone looks at me, head on one side. 'You don't sound sure it was the real reason for his visit.'

I look away, trying to decide if I want to tell her or not. I feel uncomfortable talking about Owen behind his back, but what

Simone's husband said to him... well, it's too important to ignore. Too worrying.

'That's because I don't think it was. I believe golf was simply an excuse and he wanted to talk to Owen about something else.' I lower my voice, even though the road is empty. 'Has Kevin said anything to you about the time he was at university?'

She frowns. 'Not really. I get the impression he had a bit of a raucous time there, him and his mates. I expect there's a lot I wouldn't want to hear... wouldn't want to know. I get the impression he was a bit of a womaniser back in the day.'

'And Owen? Was he one of this *raucous* group?' I draw imaginary quote marks around the word, finding it hard to imagine.

Simone shakes her head. 'I don't think so. To be honest, Kevin's never mentioned Owen. The first I knew they were both at Manchester was when we came over to your house the other day. I don't think they could have been friends or I'm sure I would have heard something. Why do you ask?'

I look down. My attention taken by the diamond ring that sits above my gold wedding band. A ring that had once belonged to Owen's mother. One I'd felt it would be rude to refuse.

'It was something I overheard.' I look up again. Meet Simone's eye. 'Something odd that I didn't understand.'

'Yeah? Doesn't sound like Kevin. He's pretty straightforward. Says things as they are. What was it?'

My eyes scan the cul-de-sac. This isn't anything I want anyone else to hear.

'I heard Kevin say to Owen that he needn't worry as his secret was safe with him. What secret, Simone? What does Kevin know that I don't?'

Simone frowns. 'I've no idea. Considering they haven't seen each other in over twenty years, it's presumably something that happened at university. He was probably teasing him. Kevin loves a good wind-up.'

'It didn't sound like that. He sounded serious.'

'Then I've no idea. Have you asked Owen?'

'Yes, but he brushed it off. Didn't really tell me anything. I don't get the impression he liked Kevin very much back then. Said he was an idiot.' I stop, give an embarrassed laugh. 'I'm sorry, Simone. That came out badly. I didn't mean to be rude.'

To my relief, she laughs. 'Believe me, I've heard him called worse. My husband is like Marmite. People either love him or hate him, and it seems your husband falls into the latter category.'

I move closer to her. 'Would you ask him for me? What it was about... this secret? Find out if it's something I should be worried about.'

'Of course. Though I can't guarantee he'll tell me. And remember, whatever it is, it will be Kevin's take on it that we're hearing. There are two sides to every story.'

'True. But I'd like to know all the same.'

Simone looks at me for a long while, and when she eventually speaks, I know why.

'I know I haven't known you long, Rachel, and you honestly don't have to answer this, but...' She pauses, bites at her lip. 'Are you and Owen okay? From some of the things you've said, well, it's made me wonder. Also, you look so sad it makes me want to wrap you in a big hug.'

I smile at this, but she's right, I'm not happy. Not really. I can't get Phillipa and Lexi out of my mind – the way she treats her, her lack of care. It wouldn't be so bad if I could share my concerns with Owen, but he's always shut away in his study, and when I've tried, I'm not sure he's really been listening.

One thing I do know is this move isn't turning out as I'd hoped. Because, in this close full of children, with Owen so distant, I'm as lonely as I've ever been.

FOURTEEN

RACHEL

It's strange to be sitting in Phillipa's living room, watching her pour tea into cups from a pure white teapot, but I give my best smile as I accept the offered cup from her. Using the opportunity to look around the room, taking in the minimalist furniture, the white walls and the large modern canvases that take up most of the space – blank squares with geometric shapes in different colours. An odd choice for a family home.

Not that you'd know any children lived here from the tidiness of the place.

'Thank you. It's lovely of you to invite me over.'

The invitation to come to her house for tea had been a surprise, a simple note through the door, and even though it's nice that she's made the effort, I can't help wishing it was Simone's living room I was sitting in instead of Phillipa's.

'You have a beautiful home.'

'Yes, it's very different now to how it used to be when I lived here with my parents. We've remodelled it throughout.'

The house is so quiet. The older children will be at school, but there's no sign of her little daughter. The playpen in the corner empty. 'Where's Lexi?'

'She's in her cot. It's her nap time.'

'That's a shame, but I'll be seeing a lot more of her soon.'

Because now I have a job. Before I'd even got through the door, Phillipa had told me Simone had mentioned I'd been searching for one. Said she was looking for someone to help out with housework and childcare and that I'd be welcome to it. The offer had come so quickly, so unexpectedly, that I'd accepted without thinking.

Now Phillipa takes her own cup from the table and sits back, crossing long legs.

'So how are you settling in?'

I take a sip of my tea, wondering what I should say to her. I want to know her connection to my house, so I'm hoping if I get her to like me, feel for me living somewhere *haunted*, she might reveal more about what happened there. She was obviously involved somehow.

'If I'm honest, it's all been a bit strange. Since I moved into Number 2, I've been having these awful nightmares. Then, when I wake up, I believe I can hear a child crying.' I shake my head, give a nervous laugh. 'Stupid, isn't it?'

Phillipa's face sets. Her eyes flick to the door. 'It doesn't surprise me in the least. Everything is new for you at the moment, not just the place but the people, and it's simply your mind playing tricks on you.'

'I don't know. After what Simone told me—'

Phillipa's eyebrows raise a fraction and I stop.

'What *did* she tell you?' she asks.

'It was nothing.'

'I don't think so. Please, I'd like to know.'

I sigh. 'It was the reason Lisa Brookner moved away from the close.'

Her eyes don't leave my face. 'I see. And that was because...?'

'Because she thought she heard crying as well. Thought the house was haunted.'

'Ridiculous.' She tips back her head and gives a laugh that's tainted with something I can't read. 'Lisa Brookner always did have an overactive imagination.' She stops laughing, her face serious again. 'Please don't tell me you believe such nonsense?'

'I... no, I suppose not.' I lean forward. 'It's just that what with the little girl drowning...' I trail off.

'She was my best friend, you know.' Phillipa jerks a thumb towards our house. 'Like sisters. I never wanted her to leave the close. After she had her baby, though, things were different. She didn't have time for me any more.'

A bitterness has crept into her voice. Are those tears in her eyes? Didn't Simone tell me Lisa hadn't had any children?

I want to ask her about it, but before I can, she has a question of her own.

'What about Owen? How has he coped with the move? It must have been a wrench.'

I look at her, surprised, before remembering that since Owen became well known after the publication of *Dead Air*, he's become everyone's property. She'll have read about our big house in the country. Wondered why we moved here.

'He's getting used to it,' I lie. 'Hopes the change of environment will give him inspiration.'

Phillipa doesn't answer, a habit she has, and I carry on, hoping to befriend her further. Maybe she'll tell me more.

'I just wish Owen and I talked more. We had a bit of a rough patch a few years back, but we got over it. Now I'm worried things are slipping back to how they were then. It's as though, since the move, all the ground we'd made up is slowly being eroded.'

I feel Phillipa's eyes on me and wish I hadn't said so much.

Phillipa sips her tea. 'I'm sorry to hear that. You probably don't want to talk about it, but if ever you do, I'm here if you feel the need of a friendly ear. Carl's not interested in gossip so whatever you say will go no further than these four walls, I promise.'

That silence again.

I twist my engagement ring around my finger. This has been bottled up inside me for so long that I'm desperate to tell someone. Even Phillipa.

'It would be good to talk.'

She leans forward. Pats my hand. 'I'm glad. I don't like to see you unhappy. Tell me about that husband of yours.'

I draw in a breath, remembering. 'When I first met Owen, I thought he was the most charismatic, the most thoughtful and attentive man I'd ever met. He dazzled me, Phillipa. Really dazzled me with his intellect. His depth of character.' I remember the conversations we used to have in the early days. About poetry, music, politics. Never about feelings, I realised later. Never that.

Through the wide patio doors, Phillipa and Carl's back garden stretches away like ours does. There's a bird feeder hanging from one of the trees and two blue tits are squabbling for the seeds. Watching them makes it easier to talk.

'When he asked me to marry him, I thought I'd burst with happiness, but we'd never lived together, and it was only after the wedding that I realised being a couple with Owen wasn't how I thought it would be.'

'In what way?'

I think about it. 'I suppose I hadn't realised how much his writing meant to him and how much time his books would take up. There would be weeks when I would hardly see him. He'd shut himself away with his computer, and when, eventually, he did come down, I'd be lucky if I got more than a handful of words from him. You know, Phillipa, it was as though the rest of the sentence had been used up in his work. He'd be tired. Stressed. Expect me to look after him. Sometimes, when things got really bad, he'd end up sleeping in the spare room.' I feel tears welling. 'He didn't realise I had needs too. Not just physical but emotional.'

Phillipa looks at me with sympathy. 'Oh, Rachel. You poor thing.'

I cover my face with my hands. The memories coming back. The bleak nights. The weekends that seemed to stretch forever once I'd given up my job. 'I'd thought it would be different once we started a family, but that never happened.'

I think of the nights I'd cried myself to sleep. Owen's side of the bed cold. The tap tap of his fingers on the keyboard coming from his study. When the time had come to accept it wasn't meant to be, the heartache of knowing I'd never have a child was borne alone.

'But you said things got better. What changed? What did Owen do?'

Tears slide down my cheek and I wipe them away.

'He didn't do anything. It was me.'

I let the words hang in the air. Knowing what I'm about to say might change the way she sees me. I also know that once said, it can never be unsaid.

'You.'

'Yes.' I close my eyes. Remember how it had started and how it had changed me. 'I did something I never thought I'd do. I had an affair.'

I want to say that I regret it, but I don't. Never have.

Not really.

Because there are two sides to me, the one Owen sees, prefers, and the one I'd been before... the one James allowed me to become again.

No. I could never regret James.

FIFTEEN

RACHEL

I look at Phillipa. Try to gauge from her expression what she's thinking. Is she shocked at what I've told her? Does she think any less of me? Instantly, I regret what I've said. I want her to like me, but this may have had the opposite effect.

'I was desperate.' I bite at my lip. 'James saved me.'

'You know, Rachel. Sometimes, we need to do things that others might not understand.' She stares into the distance as though remembering something. 'For our own mental health. For our own sanity. It's not for me to judge you... I'm sure you wouldn't have done it unless pushed to it.'

She smiles, and I wish I could be more honest, more open about it, but I can't. It wouldn't be fair on Owen. I think of him in our house next door and wonder what he's doing. Whether he's recovered from Kevin's unexpected visit.

'Please don't tell Owen I said anything.'

Can I trust her, this woman whose name is written on our kitchen wall?

'You have my word I won't mention it to a soul. Not Owen or Carl or anyone.' She thinks for a minute, frowns slightly. 'James is our little secret.'

My thoughts move from Owen to James. The affair had only lasted a few weeks, and although wonderful while it lasted, it had felt wrong. I'd met him in a café of all places. I was walking to my table with a coffee when he bumped into me, leaving half my coffee on the tray. The sort of thing that only happens in cheesy films. My lips curve into a smile at the memory of it, the shock of it, remembering how I'd accepted his apology and his offer of a fresh cup. Some strange part of me knowing, even then, that this chance meeting was going to change everything.

He'd told me his name was James. Had taken the tray from me and carried it back to the counter while I'd found a table. And as he'd ordered me a new coffee, I'd taken in the faded jeans. The khaki parka. The trainers. Clothes Owen would never wear. Never approve of. And I wonder now, as I had then, whether that difference had been the reason for me liking them. Liking *him*. That he could have worn an undertaker's suit and I'd have felt the same.

We talked a bit. I drank my coffee and then I left. I was confused. Excited. Full of guilt even though nothing had happened. It had been twenty minutes at the most but enough to know I wanted more. And for the next week, when I was making the bed or Owen's lunch, when I was doing the weekly shop or digging the garden, the encounter would come back to me. The way James's finger had touched mine as he'd lifted the tray from my hands. The way he'd looked at me, if only for a moment, as though he really saw me. Really *knew* me.

Because, sometimes, to Owen, I was invisible. Like a minor character in one of his books when what I should have been was the lead. The protagonist. Was that too much to ask as his wife?

The next week James was there again. We hadn't arranged it, but I'd hoped. My heart gives a lurch as I remember how he'd asked if he could sit with me and I'd said he could. He had, after all, bought me that coffee the previous week. I needed someone to talk to, really talk to, and here was this man who listened in a way Owen never had.

'You don't think having an affair was a little risky?' Phillipa purses her lips as she sips her drink, and I wonder if she's thinking about her own husband. The risk he's taking.

'Not really. In a weird way, I saw James as a means of saving our marriage.'

Owen and I couldn't have gone on as we were – keeping our true feelings from each other, not saying things in case it hurt or offended. If it hadn't been James, it would have been someone else and the outcome might have been worse. I didn't fall in love with him, but I *needed* him. Falling in love would have been much more destructive.

I'd been close, though. Very close.

'I started meeting James regularly and, even though he never talked much about himself, he became my sounding block. I know it sounds odd, but I felt safe with him as though I knew nothing I told him would go any further.'

The truth was he made me feel I was worth something. Valued. He had this way of coaxing, of encouraging me to cut the bullshit. To be honest and speak from the heart.

Phillipa regards me with interest, breaking my thoughts. It's as if she knows I'll only admit so much and needs to be careful with her questions. 'Was it you who broke it off or him?'

'It was me. It always had an end date.'

Phillipa nods, and I realise I might have reassured her that her own husband's affair won't last.

'Owen knew, but once it stopped, we carried on as though it had never happened. We kept our feelings to ourselves more than ever.'

What I haven't told her is something much worse. It wasn't just our feelings. We started keeping secrets from one another.

SIXTEEN

OWEN

Owen turns off his computer and pushes back his chair. He's in no mood to write. Not since Kevin Wellbeck muscled his way into his space. Pushed his way back into his life.

Just a terrible coincidence, he knows. A quirk of fate. But still it's there, the knowledge that the guy he once detested lives across the street from him. Washing his flashy car. Flaunting his pregnant wife.

And there's nothing he can do about it. Not a damn thing.

He'd tried to put that time at university out of his mind. Even getting in hadn't been the celebration he'd expected. His mother had said she was disappointed in him. That she'd presumed, as an only child, he'd want to do the right thing by her. Had he forgotten about her heart condition? Had he considered who would take her to the hospital appointments she more than likely would need?

Owen hadn't been fooled by that. Had never been susceptible to emotional blackmail. It was all an act; his mother was as strong as an ox. But his certainty had been called into question the day he'd received the call from her neighbour.

His mother had been found unconscious in her hall.

She'd died of heart failure before she could reach the hospital.

Owen moves his keyboard so it's level with the edge of his desk. Dusts a crumb from the return key as the guilt comes back. There are things now he wishes he'd told her before she'd died. Like how he'd started his course with a broken heart – the outer layers peeled away like the skin of an onion.

Owen scoots his office chair over to the other end of the desk. Picks up the wedding photograph he'd put there after he'd unpacked it. Rachel in a plain white wedding dress, the only adornment to it a sprinkling of seed pearls at the neckline. He in a charcoal-grey suit. In the photo it's he who is signing the register, Rachel by his side. Her bouquet of white roses on the desk in front of them.

When was the last time she'd looked at him like that? Owen wracks his brains but can't remember. Was it before or after their crisis, as he likes to call it?

He remembers how he'd accused her of having an affair. How he'd been right. Owen wipes a smudge from the glass of the photograph with his sleeve, then puts it back on the desk.

He won't let that happen again.

SEVENTEEN

RACHEL

The atmosphere in the room has changed, and it's hard to believe that only a few minutes ago Phillipa was seeking my friendship. Encouraging me to talk about my personal life. About James. Now, from the way she's sitting, her back straighter, her face set, it's clear she's reappraised our relationship.

She's brought Lexi down, and the child is in a playpen in the corner of the room. Staring at us through the mesh side.

'You've done ironing before, I take it?'

'Yes, of course.' I'm surprised at the question. Who hasn't done ironing? 'But only for my family. Not that I mind doing yours,' I add quickly.

The constant effort to smile is making my cheeks ache, and I'm acutely aware of how I'm sitting. Knees and ankles pressed together, my hands clasped in my lap – as though I'm Mary Poppins discussing the nanny's position. So different to earlier. But, weird though this feels, I need this job. For however much Owen wants to bury his head in the sand and deny it, our savings, and the money we made from the sale of our large country house, won't last forever. And it's not just that. I'm scared that with Owen so distant, if I don't do something with my time, I'm in danger of going mad.

'That's good because with three kids there tends to be rather a lot.' She closes her eyes briefly. 'Sometimes, it's quite overwhelming.'

I don't reply, for what can I say? I have no experience of a large family. Or any family at all apart from Owen. I push thoughts of Jade away. She hadn't been part of my family and I need to remember that.

I look at Phillipa expectantly. She's already run me through a list of the chores she'll expect me to do: the washing, the hoovering, tidying the children's bedrooms and, when she's out, looking after Lexi. When I'd asked if she needed me to pick the older children up from school, she'd said there was no need. She would do that herself. After all, she wouldn't want the other mothers to think she didn't have time for her children.

I hadn't commented on that either. I could hardly tell her that I'd already made that assumption myself.

'There's one other thing.' Phillipa adjusts the neck of her blouse. Smooths down her skirt.

'Yes?'

'Do you have any experience with young children... not having any yourself, I mean?'

It's said pointedly as though it's a fault, a disability, and I feel myself bristle. I want to tell her that being childless is not my fault, that I have more maternal instinct in my little finger than she has in her entire body, but I don't. I've decided I want this job – if only to be sure that Phillipa is treating her small daughter properly.

'I've had many friends with children Lexi's age.'

Jade to be precise. Her mother, Julie, hadn't been my friend and now never will be, but Phillipa doesn't need to know that.

'If you're happy with the arrangement and the salary,

maybe we can agree on a starting date. As soon as possible if that works for you.'

'I can start tomorrow if you like.'

'That's good.' Phillipa gets up, offers me her hand across the coffee table. A gesture that seems too formal, considering we're neighbours. Considering it was only fifteen minutes ago I was telling her about James. 'I was beginning to think I'd never find anyone.' She goes over to a pot on the sideboard and picks out a key with a yellow fob. 'Take this. It's the spare.'

I stand too, take the key from her outstretched hand. So that's why she'd made an effort to be cordial. Not because she wanted my friendship, but because no one else had applied – or maybe they had and had been put off by Phillipa's attitude once they got here.

I look over at Lexi in her playpen. 'Shall I say hello to Lexi? She needs to get used to me.'

'That won't be necessary. It's her quiet time, she knows that. I don't want to break the routine.'

'No, of course not.'

I hate seeing her in there. Apart from the doll she's holding, there are only a couple of toys in the playpen with her, and she's taking no interest in either of them. I want to talk to her, make her smile, but I know that's not what Phillipa wants so, instead, I follow her to the living room door, feeling the child's eyes on me even though I can't see them. I look back. Wave my hand and call goodbye to the little girl. But she only stares at me with her big blue eyes, and it makes me sad for the both of us.

Phillipa is waiting in the hall, her expression making it clear that the interview is over. Pulling my eyes away from Lexi's, I walk quickly to the front door.

'I'll see you tomorrow then. What time would you like me?'

'Seven thirty, if it's not too early. The children will need their breakfast.'

'Okay.'

Phillipa hadn't mentioned anything about giving them breakfast. Owen's not going to be happy about this early start, but I agree nonetheless and slip off home. At least it gives me more time in Phillipa's house. More time with her. What did she mean about being friends with the woman who used to live in my house? Is that why her name is on my wall?

I let myself into the house and step into the hall. The air feels too cold, and I rub at my cheeks, not just to warm them up, but because I've been smiling so hard this last hour my face hurts. Thinking I'll start supper, I go into the kitchen, my eyes sliding to the half-stripped wall – the dark stain. It's as though the ghosts of the people who once lived here can't let go of the place and, even though I didn't know them, and no one will talk about what happened, the thought sends shivers through me. What is Phillipa's connection? Why is her name here?

Hating the sight of it, I bend to the cupboard below the sink. Look for something with which to clean off the writing. There's a bottle of white spirit in there somewhere, and I shove aside the dusters, the double packs of kitchen roll and a dustpan and brush in my search for it. It's as I'm lifting the bottle out that something catches my eye. It's stuck to the back wall of the cupboard, and as I reach my arm in and run a finger over it, I realise it's some sort of sticker, the edges fraying away from the melamine. Pulling my phone from my pocket, I turn on the torch and shine it at the smooth surface. A closer look shows it's a *Hello Kitty* sticker, the red bow on the cat's head now faded with age – like the ribbon that's tied to the birch tree. Across the bottom of it are the words *Good Girl*.

A chill grips me. The only way the sticker could have got there is if the child who'd lived in our house had climbed into the cupboard and pressed it to the wall. The sight of it is unsettling, and I snap off the torch, not wanting to see. Not wanting to be reminded of her and what happened. Her little life cut short in such a tragic way.

Without thinking, my gaze moves to the window, where, obscured from view behind the metal fence, a faded pink ribbon ripples in the breeze.

Perhaps it's *me* who can't forget.

And, even if I wanted to, I have this feeling that the house won't let me. That it's telling me I need to do something before it happens again. Before another life is lost.

EIGHTEEN

RACHEL

Owen doesn't answer when I knock on the door of his study. I'd wanted to tell him about the sticker, ask him what he makes of it, but I'm not sure he's there.

'Owen, are you in there?'

When I still hear nothing, I turn the handle, push open the door and look in, only to find the room empty. There's a noise above my head, and I look up, wondering what it is. An attic runs the length of the house and, as I listen, I hear the creak of a joist. Muffled footfall. Owen must be up there. Stepping away from the computer, I go out onto the landing and cross to the spare bedroom opposite. It's where the loft hatch is, and as I step into the room, I see the gaping hole in the ceiling. The metal ladder that extends down to the floor.

I walk over to it. Call up into the dark space. 'What are you doing, Owen?'

'Moving stuff around. Making space.' His voice is faint, and I can only just hear him. He must be at the far end of the attic.

'Space for what?'

'I haven't thought that far, but there's bound to be something. You know how much junk we accumulated in the old house. I thought we could put some of it up here, the empty packing cases too.' His feet appear at the edge of the hatch, his knees coming into focus as he crouches down.

'I thought you were working.'

'I've finished for the day.'

His hands grip the sides of the ladder as he climbs down. There are cobwebs on his jumper. Dust on the knees of his old cords.

How long has he been up there? Not working? I worry that this continued drought could really be the end of Owen's career. That he's reached that stage every writer dreads – when the block that has temporarily stifled creativity becomes permanent. When they know there's nothing more they can do and it's time to give up.

Something my husband would find hard to accept.

Although I'm only guessing, as Owen certainly hasn't said any of this to me, I know it's this worry that makes it hard for him to get to sleep at night. What makes him wake in the early hours in a sweat. It's why I need to be certain that this neighbourhood is safe for us; to find out what happened here.

'What is it? Why are you looking at me like that?' Owen runs a hand across his chin, and I see how much greyer his beard has got recently. At forty-two, Owen's still a relatively young man, but the last couple of years have taken their toll.

I reach out, take his hand, and he looks down at it in surprise. Hand holding and other signs of affection are not things that have ever come naturally to us. Some strange, misplaced formality holding us back. Or rather, holding Owen back as, before I met him, I was very different.

There's a small double bed in the spare room, and I lead Owen over to it and make him sit. I sit next to him. 'I want to talk to you about something.'

Owen pulls his hand away from mine. Crosses his arms. 'If

it's about Phillipa, I need you to stop it. Don't think I didn't see you going in there today.'

I frown, imagining him at the window. Forehead pressed against the glass. He's been watching me. Checking up on me.

'As it happens, I was talking to her about a job. I'm going to be doing a few hours for her. A bit of cleaning. A bit of child-care. It won't affect you.'

'Of course it will.' Owen's gaze hardens. 'We're married. Everything you do affects me. *Everything*.'

I look away, knowing what he's talking about. Sometimes, James seems so long ago it's hard to believe he ever really existed. If only Owen could feel the same way. Move on from it and be content with what we have. But it's harder for him. So much harder.

'I'll make sure it doesn't.' The words feel inadequate, but I have nothing else. Not when he's blindsided me.

And even as I'm saying it, I realise that Owen hasn't brought this up because he cares what I do with my time. What he's doing is little more than deflection – his aim to move the conversation on. Away from him and his book and his inability to write – so far away that it will be difficult to draw it back again. But I have to try.

'I'm sorry is hasn't worked out the way you planned with your project. That things haven't got any better. Is it the move? Is it the house? You said that moving back to Gloucestershire, being near to your childhood home, would be all that was needed to get you going again.'

Beside me, Owen puffs out his cheeks. Sighs out a stream of air. 'I know.'

'Then you need to give it time.' I take his hand in mine again, and it feels easier this time. 'But I need to know you're all right, Owen. Since we've been here, you've been so...' – I search for the word – 'so withdrawn... not just from me but from everything. I'm scared that if we go on like this, things will go back to how they were.' I look down at my hands. 'In the bad times.'

It's a relief to have opened up to him, and I feel less anxious now. Talking like this is good for us. Cathartic. Maybe this is the turning point in our relationship I've been hoping for.

But I should know better because Owen stands. Rubs at the dust on his knees.

'You don't need to worry about me. You're my wife not my mother. I'm fine.'

I feel the ache of disappointment. How stupid to have allowed myself to believe things had changed.

'I'm glad,' I say, but my heart's not in it.

Owen walks over to the ladder. Rests his hand on one of the metal rungs. 'You might think I've been doing nothing with my time, Rachel, but there's something you don't know. It's all in here.' He points a finger to his temple. 'I'm getting on with things, I'm fine.'

I look at him in surprise, want to ask more, but his expression tells me he's said all he wants to say. That the conversation is at an end and there's no point in asking him any more questions.

NINETEEN

OWEN

Owen stands at the window and watches his wife as she waits on the doorstep of their neighbours' house. Sees how nervous she is as she lifts her finger to the doorbell and presses it. He waits too, until Phillipa comes out. Mouth pinched like a cat's arse until she remembers herself and forces a smile.

Rachel smiles back. That sweet smile she gave to him when he caught her eye at his book reading all those years ago after he'd lost his place in the text. The one that said, *It's okay. You've got this.*

He presses himself back into the curtain, not wanting to be seen. He's worried about her. Worried the same thing will happen as before. Will she be able to draw the line this time? See what side of it she should be on? Perhaps he should have been firmer. Put his foot down and told her she wasn't to look after Lexi. That her mental health might not take it.

There's only one car in the drive this morning. Phillipa's husband, Carl, has left already. Taken the older kids to their posh school. He'll return later, eat his dinner and tell his wife about his godawful day in the office. How the coffee machine didn't work – gave him flat white instead of cappuccino – and how he'd cc'd the wrong manager into his email. He'll compliment her on the haircut she's had while his own wife, Rachel, has been looking after their kid. Then later, when Steve on the other side of the green has left for the pub, he'll sneak over and screw his wife. He would feel sorry for Phillipa, but only a fool wouldn't see what's going on right under their nose.

Only a fool.

Rachel's voice is in his head, *I want to talk to you about something.* Had she not realised how her words had turned him cold? Been aware of how it drove a stake through his heart to hear them.

Because she'd used those words before. In that time they both try to forget.

You have to believe me, Owen, it's over. Truly over. I know now it's not someone like James I need, it's you.

He knows he should have felt relief – like an athlete on the podium with his gold medal. Taken comfort from the fact that she'd chosen *him* over the sort of person he'd been sure would have crossed the winning line before him. But what he'd actually felt was nothing. A big fat emptiness that neither he nor Rachel had known what to do with. Known how to fill.

He looks across the green to the pond. Thinks about the child who'd drowned there. Rachel's still having her nightmares, but if he tries to comfort her in bed, she always moves her hand away from his. It had been the same after the failed IVF. If only he could find it within himself to be that person. The one Rachel needs. Deserves. Someone like James.

But he can't. Never will be.

Turning away from the window, he throws himself into his office chair. Pounds his forehead with the heel of his hand as he remembers Kevin's visit to their house. The things he'd said.

With Kevin living in the close, his secret will never be safe.

TWENTY

RACHEL

'What would you like me to do?'

I stand in Phillipa's hall clutching my bag. Last time I was here, I was already on an unequal footing with her. Something that would be obvious to an observer in the way we spoke to each other, the language we used, the way we sat. Phillipa straight-backed, thin-lipped, a little remote. And me? Well, I might as well have had a sign around my neck. *Employee.*

I give Phillipa a bright smile, one designed to please, and see that today is no different. Our roles are set, and I can't imagine them changing in the near future.

I look around me, taking in the large, white-framed mirror on the wall above the glass console table, the pale carpet that looks so clean and fresh it could have been laid only yesterday. And when I follow Phillipa into the living room, the show house impression continues through, deliberate I'm sure, with the same cream carpet, the same off-white walls. *Linen* or *orchid white* I imagine the paint's called. Anything to keep the purchaser from believing they're buying magnolia. God forbid.

Phillipa takes a seat on the pale settee as she did before and indicates for me to do the same. As I sit, I notice that, apart from the playpen I'd seen on my previous visit, there is no evidence that children live in the house. No toys. No books. And I don't just mean things that would belong to the little one, Lexi, but to the older children as well. For the place is so tidy: no evidence of family life. I'd expected to see games consoles abandoned beside the TV, white AirPods left on the arm of a chair. And, as I'd walked through the hall, there had been no trainers kicked off at the front door. No hoody slung over the banister at the bottom of the stairs. The image I'd had of how a family home should be. How *mine* would be if things had turned out differently.

But it isn't my house, it's Phillipa's, and she's telling me something about Lexi.

'So if she makes a fuss and doesn't eat it, take it away. She has to learn.'

I blink. Try to focus on what she's saying.

'Lexi's lunch?'

'Her breakfast.' Phillipa frowns, points a finger at the page of typed notes she's made for me, the word breakfast highlighted in yellow, followed by a list of things I should and shouldn't do. I blush. Hate that I've been caught out for not listening.

I read the list upside down.

- *No sugary cereal.*
- *Don't allow her to hold the spoon as she'll make a mess.*
- *Don't let her get down until she's finished all her milk.*

'And if Lexi cries when you put her down for her afternoon nap, ignore her. She's just trying it on.'

'The child I looked after, Jade, stopped having naps when she was fourteen months old. Lexi's older than that. Maybe she's grown out of them.' I say it without thinking. Stop, when I see Phillipa's expression. 'Not that I know your daughter,' I continue quickly. 'All children are different, of course.'

The corners of Phillipa's mouth tighten. 'No. You *don't* know my daughter and, yes, you're right, all children are different. As Lexi's mother, I know what's best for her.' She picks up the pages of notes and shuffles them. 'I'd be grateful if you don't make judgements when you haven't children of your own. It's very undermining.' Phillipa picks an invisible thread from her bright-red culottes. 'Anyway, the evidence is clear in the research. Daytime naps provide the child with a host of benefits. Improved attention, reduced irritability, higher performance.'

She gives me a look that says she's not sure about me. That maybe I wasn't the right choice of person to look after her child and that perhaps she should have held off and interviewed someone else. I want to tell her that her answer is flawed. That the benefits only apply to a child who is asleep, not one who is awake and crying to be taken out of their cot, but I don't. I want this job. If only to see for myself that the little girl is being cared for properly.

'Yes, I'm sorry. I'm sure you're right.' I look around me. 'Where *is* Lexi?'

'I don't bring her down until I've got myself ready.' She looks at her watch. 'The ironing basket is in the utility room. If you get the chance...'

'Will you be here? In the house, I mean.' I have no idea what Phillipa does with her time.

'Here?' She looks at me as though I've gone mad. 'I'll be at Chantelle's. She has a personal trainer and has suggested I join her for a workout. Then I expect we'll go into town for lunch and some shopping.'

I cover my surprise. I'd presumed Phillipa knew her husband was having sex with the pretty young woman across the green with the shiny hair and expensive tan, but clearly not.

You have to give full marks to Chantelle for brazening it out... after all, it's a dangerous game she's playing. One with unforeseeable consequences. I should know.

Phillipa scrutinises her face in a hand mirror, widening her eyes to check for mascara smudges. 'When it's time to get Lexi up, you'll find her highchair in the kitchen. All the information you'll need is in the notes I left, and I don't expect you to ring me unless it's an emergency.' She adjusts the neck of her exercise vest. 'Oh, and if you could try not to make too much mess...'

I try not to show what I'm feeling. 'Of course. Have a nice morning. What time can I expect you back?'

Phillipa pulls a lime-green running top from the back of the chair and slides an arm into it. 'Five at the latest.'

'Five?' I hadn't imagined she'd ask me to stay that late. Had presumed she'd want to get back to see the older children once they'd got home from school.

Phillipa zips up the top. 'That's all right, isn't it?'

'It's a bit later than I was expecting, but I suppose so.'

Owen likes to eat at six. He comes down for a meal and then goes back up to his study for another couple of hours of writing. It's how he's always worked. Now I'll have to change those plans.

'That's good. It's not as though you have children to get back for.'

Her words hit me hard. I'm not sure whether it's deliberate or whether she really doesn't see what she's doing. How thoughtless she's being. Whichever it is, Phillipa taps at the screen of her smartwatch and smiles.

'Need to go. See you later.'

I think of the little girl up in her bedroom. 'Don't you want to say goodbye to Lexi? Won't she wonder where you are?'

'It's not good for a child to be mollycoddled.' She looks at me, head on one side. 'You're not worried you won't be able to cope, are you?'

'No, of course not.'

But how do I know that for sure? I'd thought I could once before.

Phillipa seems satisfied. 'Then I'll be off. I probably won't have my phone on while I'm exercising. That's all right, isn't it? I can't think why you'd need to call me anyway. Unless you think—'

'No. It's fine.' I give a shiny smile. 'It's all here in your notes.'

She picks up her bag and leaves, and I go to the living room window. Watch as she jogs across the green. Knowing there's no point in starting the ironing, I go into the hall, listen for a few minutes to hear if Lexi is calling and when she isn't, wander back into the living room. I sit on the settee and place my hand on the cushion next to me, wondering whether Lisa Brookner, her supposed best friend, had sat on this very same settee sharing secrets with her neighbour as I had the last time I was here.

Or maybe Phillipa had shared secrets with *her*.

My mind turns to the bloodstained wall. The writing there. *Why Phillipa?* What had made Lisa move from Number 2 Pond Close? Leave so suddenly and sell the house for such a low price? Was it simply because the little girl had lived there, or had she known something about her neighbour that she'd not wanted to divulge to the estate agent? Was that it?

I stand again, no longer able to sit still. I'm not usually one to snoop, but I can't get it out of my head that Phillipa is hiding something from me. Something to do with my house... with the little girl's death. There's a large, modern sideboard on the other side of the room with wide doors and brass handles. I go over to it and pull open one of the doors, see that it's full of fine china – the sort you might use for a dinner party.

I close the door again, kneel and slide open the long, deep drawer beneath it. It's full of photo albums and my heart quickens. I lift the top one out and open it to a large photograph of a younger Phillipa. She's sitting in the room I'm in now, smiling widely, a baby in her arms, and at first, I think the baby's Lexi, but then I see that instead of shutters at the windows, there are curtains. Also, instead of the pale paint Phillipa has chosen for her living room, the walls are covered with a patterned wallpaper. It must be her elder daughter, Talia, she's holding, not the child who's asleep upstairs.

Laying the album on the floor, I take out the next one and open it. In this photograph, the living room wallpaper is the same, but the baby is different – unmistakeably a boy. Neil is sitting in a highchair, his hands covered in chocolate, and behind him is Phillipa. It surprises me to see her face screwed up with laughter and it makes me wonder what happened to change her from this happy woman to the one I've had to endure these last few days.

I close the book and put it away. Choose more. I want to find photographs of Lexi when she was first born... see if Phillipa had that same look of love for her youngest child. I pull out album after album until it dawns on me how stupid I'm being. Lexi is ten years younger than Talia. Most likely, any photos of her will have been captured on Phillipa's phone, not printed out.

I'm putting the albums back in the drawer when I see a smaller one with a padded vinyl cover, just big enough to take one photograph per page. I take it out and open it, seeing that the photos inside are of Phillipa as a teenager. Plumper certainly, her hair longer, but still recognisable. In one of them she's listening to music, headphones pressed to her ears. In another she's sitting cross-legged, a poodle on her lap. I turn the page. In the next photo, Phillipa's arm is looped around the neck of a girl of around the same age whose straight fair hair is partially covered by the baseball cap she's wearing.

I'm turning the page when my hand stills and I look up at the ceiling. Someone's calling. *Mumma. Mumma.* My face breaks into a smile, and I close the album. There's no time to look at any more. Lexi wants me.

I push myself to my feet and am about to put the album back in the drawer when I change my mind. Instead, I take it over to my bag and slip it inside. Telling myself that Phillipa won't notice. That I've done nothing wrong.

TWENTY-ONE

RACHEL

'I'm not happy with the amount of time you're spending at the Wellbecks'.'

I put my coat on the back of the kitchen chair and stare at my husband. It's the weekend and I hadn't expected to see him until lunchtime as, for Owen, every day is a writing day. Even now there's a pad and pen in front of him.

His statement has annoyed me. The reason I'd gone over to Simone's is because when I'd returned from Phillipa's the day before, Owen hadn't enquired about my first day at work. And when I'd tried to tell him about it, he'd stopped me, saying he was busy. I'd been desperate to talk to someone about the odd childcare rules and strict nap times, and with Owen's lack of interest, Simone's invitation to come over this morning had arrived at the right time.

'It was a coffee, Owen. That's all. I wanted to offload about my first day at work. It wasn't what I'd been expecting.'

Owen reaches for his mug and takes a mouthful of coffee, his Adam's apple bobbing as he swallows. His hair is touching the collar of his shirt, and I note that it needs a trim, his beard too.

'I told you, you don't need to be doing this.' He puts the mug down. 'We don't need the money.'

He's wrong. We *do* need the money, but I don't say it. It will only make things worse if I do. Owen is a proud man. Always has been.

'I know, but it's not just that. I'm doing it for me. I didn't mind not having a job when we were in our old place. There was the garden. Things that always needed doing. Here though—'

I look around helplessly, my eyes alighting as they always do on the half-stripped wall I haven't the energy to finish. Making me wonder, as I have countless times, what the mother of the little girl who died was doing when the child wandered out. Feeling her presence, I rub at my arms, my jumper wrinkling beneath my fingers.

Owen is studying me. 'What's the matter?'

'It's nothing. Just a bit cold.'

'You're thinking about that child again, aren't you?'

It's as if he knows. Can read my thoughts.

'No, of course not.' I feel foolish, knowing that Owen doesn't feel her presence like I do. 'Don't you think it strange that no one talks about it, though?'

Owen writes something on his pad, then leans back in his chair. Gives it some thought. His feet are crossed at the ankles, fingers linked behind his head in a mirror of Kevin when he and Simone came to visit.

'Not really. It's human nature. A fear of contagion and a desire to protect yourself from ill luck. If you don't talk about it, it can't happen to you.'

I pull out a chair and sit down. 'You really think that's the reason?'

'Can you think of a better one?'

I shake my head. 'Not really. It doesn't bother you, though, knowing what happened? Knowing that a mother will have sat in this very kitchen grieving the loss of her child.'

He looks at me with interest, head on one side. 'Don't you think you're being rather melodramatic? It's a house with four walls and a roof. No different to any other.'

'No, it's more than that.'

'Really?' Owen raises his eyebrows, and I know I have to be careful. Next, I'll be telling him about finding the sticker in the cupboard and that amused expression will turn to something else. The look he'll give me saying it all – that he's concerned about me. Like he was before.

I don't need to worry about that, though, as this morning Owen has more important things on his mind.

'So, getting back to the Wellbecks. It's not what you want to hear, I know, but I really would appreciate it if you didn't spend so much of your time there.' He rubs at the back of his neck, his fingers leaving a red mark on his pale skin. 'In fact, I'd really rather you didn't see them at all.'

I stare at him wordlessly, hardly believing what he's said. In those few words he's vetoed my one and only proper friendship in the close.

'Why on earth would I want to do that?'

Owen pushes his mug away from him. 'Believe me, I don't say it without good reason.'

'Which is...?'

I wait. If I'm to go along with his wishes, this had better be good.

'It's not Simone I have an issue with, it's Kevin.' He curls his fingers into fists. Presses them against the shiny surface of the table. 'Look, I didn't want to have to tell you this before, but unless he's changed, he'll do everything he can to make my life hell.'

I look up, shocked. He'd told me he didn't like him, but this is different.

'Why ever would he want to do that?'

'Because that's his *thing*. At university, he was a manipulator and a bully. He loved nothing more than to play on people's weaknesses.' Owen closes his eyes, pain etched into the crease between his brows. 'So arrogant. Never the victim. Always the victor.'

I wonder why he's never told me this before. Why, until I'd met Simone at the welcome party, I'd never even heard of Kevin. 'What did he do, Owen? Please, you have to tell me.'

I think he's going to, but then his face closes down. He looks at his hands as though seeing someone else's. Uncurls his fingers and studies the palms where his nails have left their mark.

'It doesn't matter. It was a long time ago. But I want you to trust me, Rachel, when I tell you that man is bad news.' He pushes back his chair, goes over to the window and looks out. 'I don't expect you to understand, but if you have any feelings for me, you won't go over there again unless you really have to.'

I bite my lip. 'But what about Simone? She'll think me so rude?'

'I'm sure she'll get over it.' He turns to me, his eyes pleading. 'Will you do this one thing for me? It's bad enough him living across the green, but...'

He tails off, and I feel his helplessness. I hadn't known about this part of my husband's life, and I suspect there's more he's not telling me. Whatever Kevin did, it was bad enough to cause this reaction, and I don't want Owen's mental health to suffer more than it already has. Hard as it is, I'll do as he asks. What other option do I have?

'All right. I've no idea what I'm going to say to her, but I'll think of something. Make up some excuse next time she invites me over. If I see them about on the close, I'll have to talk to them, though. We're neighbours, after all.' I sigh, hating what I'm doing. 'We were going to go for a walk tomorrow, but I'll cancel it.'

Owen gives me a rare smile. 'Thank you, Rachel. That means a lot and I appreciate it.'

I don't answer, I'm too sad for that, but continue sitting at the table while my husband gets up, puts his mug in the dishwasher, then heads out of the room. When he reaches the stairs, he looks back at me through the open kitchen door.

'You know I couldn't have done this without you.' His voice has taken on a serious tone. 'Honestly, Rachel, I couldn't.'

I look at him questioningly, a tightness in my chest. 'Done what?'

He sweeps a hand around the room. Palm flat. 'Any of this. My work... this house... my very existence.'

'Don't be silly.' I feel awkward. It's not like Owen to talk this way, not like him at all, and although I'm always saying I wish he'd do it more, I find it unsettling.

His smile is grim. 'Oh, believe me. I need you more than you could ever know.'

He disappears up the stairs, leaving me with a head full of emotions fighting for supremacy. Relief that I still mean something to him. Resignation that for the sake of Owen's mental health I will, once again, have to sacrifice my own needs. But most of all, I feel regret that he hadn't told me this sooner. Years sooner.

Before I had the need to turn to someone else. To James.

Feeling at a loose end, I go to the cupboard under the sink, the one where I'd found the *Hello Kitty* sticker, and feel inside for the small photograph album I'd taken from Phillipa's. I take it out then, knowing Owen wouldn't understand why I had it, go and close the kitchen door.

I sift through, finding more photographs of Phillipa with her friend. In all of them they look happy, goofing at the camera, and in one they're lying top to toe on a single bed in what is clearly a teenager's bedroom if the posters of the Spice Girls are anything to go by. There are more photographs of this other girl throughout the album and then they suddenly stop, their place taken by pictures of the poodle... other teenagers.

But what's this?

I've come to the last page of the album and there, under the plastic film, is a lock of pale hair, tied with a piece of red cotton. Next to it is a photograph which I guess has been taken on a hospital's maternity ward, the transparent-sided cot positioned beside an empty bed.

I stare at the picture trying to make sense of what I'm seeing. Not because the baby is beautiful or anything like that, but because of what's been done. For where the baby's face should be, there's nothing to see but the thick marker pen that obliterates it.

TWENTY-TWO

RACHEL

It's Monday, my second day at Phillipa's, and as I open the front door, I'm not sure how I feel about it. It's seven forty-five and I'm not used to these early starts, my back still aching from a weekend spent emptying the last of the packing cases, pulling out weeds that seem to have pushed up from nowhere through the gravel of the drive overnight, and dragging the mower across the ankle-length lawn at the back of our house.

Phillipa meets me in the hall. 'What are you doing?'

I look back at the door. 'I'm sorry. I thought...'

'I gave you the key to use for when I'm out, Rachel. I didn't expect you to let yourself in willy-nilly.'

I put my hand to my neck. Feel the flush of red. 'No, of course not. I wasn't thinking.'

Because all I can think of is the photograph of the baby in the hospital cot, scrawled over with marker pen.

She turns away. Walks back down the hall, heading for the kitchen. She carries on talking, presuming I'll follow. 'Anyway, you're here now. That's good. I wanted to have a word with you about yesterday.'

'Yesterday?'

'Yes, mowing the lawn when I had guests round. It was rather thoughtless, don't you think?'

I remember the barbeque smoke that had drifted over my garden to my aerial washing line – how I'd had to wash everything again, knowing that Owen and I had been left out of a get-together.

'What would you like me to do?' I cock my head, listening for a sound from the little girl upstairs. 'Is Lexi awake?'

'I've no idea.'

Phillipa climbs onto one of the stools by the breakfast bar and picks up a cup of coffee. She flips through a magazine, stopping at a page full of shoes, their eye-watering prices printed next to them inside gold stars. I haven't been offered a drink and stand there awkwardly. If only there was a baby monitor, then I could see for myself.

'Shall I start on the living room carpet? See if I can get it done before Lexi wakes.'

Phillipa looks up as though she'd forgotten I was there. 'That would be good. I'll be going out soon.'

'Somewhere nice?'

I kick myself as soon as I've said it. Phillipa has made it obvious where the boundary lines are: I'm not here as a neighbour to chat but to clean her house and look after her child, our friendly talk the first day a distant memory.

She yawns but answers. 'Not really. Talia is playing the flute in assembly along with some other kids and the parents have been invited to watch. As if we don't have better things to do.'

I balk at what she's said. Hearing my child play an instrument would be a privilege not a chore. How could she speak like that about her own daughter?

'Maybe I could go instead if you have something else you should be doing. I could take Lexi. I'm sure she would enjoy it.'

Phillipa looks up from her magazine. Laughs. 'I don't think so, do you?'

And I know what that laugh means. Why would the home help be at the school, sitting amongst the other parents?

'Carl then?' I know I've gone too far, that she'll take it as a criticism, but I no longer care. Why be a parent if you have no interest in your children?

'Carl's at work.' Her face tightens and I say no more. Last night, through the open window, I'd heard them fighting. Not the actual words they were throwing at each other, but the rise and fall of their voices. One cutting through the other. Sparring like fencers waiting for the final lunge that would win them the argument.

What had the children thought, lying in their beds? Had Lexi been scared? Had the older two? Or were they used to it?

'Anyway.' Phillipa looks down at me from her stool. 'I have a job for you. These are some of Lexi's baby clothes.' Placing one foot on the ground, she bends and lifts the large supermarket carrier bag at her feet. 'God forbid we have any more. I want to get rid of them all, then Carl will know I mean it.' She holds the bag out to me. 'If you could sort through them, decide what's good enough for the charity shop and what can be chucked, I'd be obliged.'

I stare at the bag a moment, then take it from her. On the top is a little stretch suit with pandas on. So tiny it looks like it would fit a doll.

As if reading my mind, Phillipa smiles. 'Diddy, isn't it? Hard to believe Lexi's grown into such a lumpen child. I guess that's Carl's genes coming through. She's going to have to watch it when she's older.'

I bite my lip. Lexi's not even two yet. How can she talk about her like that?

Scared I might say something I'll later regret, I put the bag down and am relieved when Phillipa looks at her watch, then slips down from the stool.

'Well, I suppose I'd better get this over with. No rest for the wicked.'

She goes into the hall, and I follow, hearing Lexi's cry when I reach the bottom of the stairs. My instinct is to get her out of her cot, but Phillipa is looking at me in that way she has. She picks up her leather jacket from the newel post and puts it on. Checks her hair in the white-framed hall mirror, then digs into her bag for her lipstick. Our eyes meet in the glass.

'There's no need to get her up yet. You understand that, don't you?'

I nod my affirmation. Watch as she slings her bag over her shoulder and opens the door. If Friday was anything to go by, she's unlikely to be back until much later. As I hear her car reverse out of the drive, I go back into the kitchen.

The bag of baby clothes is on the floor by the breakfast bar. I pick it up and carry it into the living room. Empty the contents onto the settee. As I pick up a tiny vest, my heart contracts. Seeing this small item of clothing brings it all back. The endless trips to the hospital, the invasive procedures, then worse than that, the waiting, followed by the crushing disappointment.

I set the vest aside, it's in good condition and someone will be grateful for it, then look through the rest, dividing them into two piles, one for the charity shop and one for the clothes bank. Small dresses. White tights. Towelling stretch suits in a variety of pastel colours and some bibs.

I pick up one of the bibs and look at it, a frown on my face. Whereas the others are plain, this one has a fancy lace edge and, embroidered on the white fabric in purple silk thread, is the letter M. I think for a moment. Phillipa and Carl's older children are called Talia and Neil. Who is this child whose name begins with M? Knowing it's unlikely I'll find out, I move the piles of clothes onto the coffee table. Taking them to the charity shop and the charity bin in the car park in town will be a long-overdue trip out.

Lexi's still crying, and my heart quickens. She's the sweetest child and it's not right. The previous time I'd been here, she'd followed me around on her chubby legs, tugging at my trousers when she wanted to show me something. Laughing when I sang to her or read a story from one of the few books in her bedroom. Phillipa said I shouldn't get her up until the stated time, but she's not here and I am. Anyway, what mother would leave her child crying in their cot? It's cruel. Heartless. While Phillipa is out, I'm in loco parentis and I need to do what I think is right.

Sod Phillipa's ridiculous rules.

I climb up the stairs and go into Lexi's bedroom. Her cot is on the far side, but the curtains are still drawn, the blackout material making it hard to see. Walking over to the window, I draw back the curtains and see that Lexi isn't lying in her cot but is standing at the end of it. Her thumb in her mouth. Snail trails of tears drying on her pink cheeks. I go over to her, and she holds out her arms to me, and as I lift her up, the damp curls at the side of her face stick to my cheek.

'It's all right, darling. I'm here.'

As I carry Lexi downstairs to give her some breakfast, I know that however rude Phillipa is to me, however insensitive, I won't leave this job. I can't. Because someone has to show this little girl love. Someone has to care.

And if it's not Phillipa or Carl, then it has to be me.

There's no one else.

TWENTY-THREE

RACHEL

The street is ordinary. A terrace of houses built sometime in the seventies, their flat blank fronts facing onto a row of identical ones on the other side of the road. A band of grey tiles, with scalloped edges, separating the uniform windows of the upper floor from those of the ground in an attempt to make them appear more pleasing to the eye. An attempt that fails miserably.

A *For Sale* sign is attached to the fence in front of the house we're looking at. Through the downstairs window, I can see the front room is empty of furniture.

'So this is it? This is where you grew up?'

Owen nods. 'Yes, this was home.'

The way he says it stops me. The underlying note of sadness unexpected.

I'm glad he's brought me here. After all, it's only ten minutes away from where we're living now, and being nearer to his birthplace had been one of the reasons he'd given for wanting to move back this way. Bringing him closer to his past, he'd said. His roots.

Owen's never really talked much about his childhood, just

bits and pieces, and when I've asked him more, he's clammed up. Dismissing my questions with a shrug. Saying it was a childhood like everyone else's. Now he stands with his hands on his hips surveying the property.

'I told you it wasn't much to look at.'

'It's interesting.' I look at the small front lawn outside Number 29, the house where Owen lived from the time of his birth until he left for university. Trying to imagine a bicycle on the lawn. A football. A face at the kitchen window, maybe – his mother's face, as she watched her only son play. 'When you see the place where someone you're close to grew up, it helps you form a complete picture of them. It's difficult to explain, but when you tell me things about your childhood, I like to picture you somewhere. Does that make sense?'

Not that he's told me much.

Owen folds his arms. 'Not really. People change, you know. I'm sure *you* must have.'

I think about it. Trying to decide. 'To be honest, I don't think I'm very different to how I was growing up. I was always pretty quiet.' I give a short laugh. 'Not much has changed.'

Except that I was too eager to please back then. Didn't want to upset anyone. The IVF, the loss, changed that. I've learnt to put myself first.

'Anyway.' Owen looks at me. 'It's not as if I've seen where *you* grew up.'

'That's because there's nothing worth seeing. Unless you think a house on a military base worth viewing. We moved so often when I was young, the word *home* started to lose its meaning.'

I think back to those days: the houses that had different numbers but invariably looked the same. The teachers whose names I kept forgetting because I'd been taught by so many, the friendships made in the knowledge that soon they would be lost again.

I look around me. There's not a lot to compliment here either, but I try anyway. 'It must have had a nice community feel with the front gardens open like this. Kids playing outside. Mums chatting over a coffee. It's south facing. Maybe they brought chairs outside.'

Owen looks at me as though I'm mad. 'It wasn't exactly Pond Close.'

There's a face at the window of the house next door. A woman. Middle-aged. Clearly wondering what we're doing loitering outside her house. I smile at her, and the face disappears. Seems like nothing's changed.

'Didn't she have any friends then... your mum? With your dad gone, it must have been lonely for her.'

'She wasn't on her own. She had *me*.'

'Yes, I know, but it must have been hard when you were little. Bringing up a child on her own couldn't have been easy with no one to help. No one to sound off to.' I see the set of his shoulders. Something's off, and I realise he's never really talked about his mother before.

'Did something happen?' I ask tentatively.

Owen doesn't answer. His face is closed and the tightness around his mouth tells me he doesn't want to talk about it. And then he smiles. 'I suppose I want what I never had,' he says.

And I know then that my quest to have a family, to make this life in Pond Close work is more important than ever. I didn't see it before. I thought he wanted the house for me, but maybe he needs it too.

We get in the car and drive, Owen's reassuring hand on my leg a surprise. The close is as you'd expect on a sunny weekend afternoon as we return. On the drive next to ours, Pam snips faded-pink rose heads into a pail by her feet. She nods to us as Owen locks the car door. And then I see Geoff. He must have been hosing dirty suds off his car because his shirt is dark with water splashes, but now his face is turned to our house. His expression closed.

'Geoff.' Pam's voice comes across the front garden. Acid sharp.

Geoff starts then collects himself. He drags his eyes from the house and, lifting the hose once more, carries on rinsing the wheel arch of his car.

What had he been thinking as his eyes had moved from my front door to me? Should I be concerned?

Before I can think more about it, their son, Aaron, pushes out of the door. He's wearing ripped jeans and a beanie hat despite the sun that's come out again. What a difference a school uniform can make, I think, as he skirts the bucket of dirty water Geoff has been using to wash his car, and steps onto the pavement. His mother calls out to him, asks him where he's going, but he ignores her. Crosses the road and breaks into a run. When he reaches the green, he checks his phone, then legs it across the grass.

Pam, no longer interested in what her husband is doing, stands beside the plastic pail of dead flower heads and watches her son as he opens the gate in the iron fence and lets himself in. She stands like that until he's out of sight, hand tenting her pale eyes against the sun's glare. Eyes that, if I'm not mistaken, are filled with tears.

Without realising it, my new neighbours are giving me glimpses inside their lives. Lives that, when I first moved in, had seemed to be content but which now appear to be as troubled as mine.

I unlock the door and Owen walks through it in front of me. I follow him in, turn to shut it, and that's when I see the police car. It's just entered the close and I step out again and watch it as it drives past our house then Phillipa's. Stopping when it gets to Simone's.

My heart falters. Imagining why they might be there and

what they could be saying. Remembering how it had felt to have the police visit *my* house that time.

I wait until Simone has opened the door, and the three of them have disappeared inside, then step back into the hall and close my own door. Surprised when I turn to see Owen at the top of the stairs. Looking at me with an expression I can't read.

TWENTY-FOUR

OWEN

Owen stands watching his wife a moment before going into his study. Across the green, he can see the police car that had passed by their open door. Looks at it thoughtfully.

Reaching a hand behind his back, he presses at the knot of tension between his shoulder blades. He wishes he could decipher what had been written on Rachel's face. Wish he could see what's going on inside that head of hers.

He waits with his hand on the curtain, but no one comes out of the house on the other side of the green – the place where, only two weeks ago, the neighbours had planned their ridiculous welcome party. No movement at any of the windows to give a clue as to what's going on inside that house.

He drums his fingertips on the glass and thinks about Rachel's calm demeanour when they'd visited his old house. Her questions, her actions, had given away nothing of what had happened the previous day. No hint of the argument she'd had with Kevin outside their house. The one she doesn't think he knows about.

He'd seen it from his window, as he sees everything. Had been shocked at the way she'd pointed a finger at Kevin's chest, her mouth moving with the words he couldn't hear through the cold pane. Something had stopped him from going downstairs to find out what was happening, and he knows what it was – the fear that Kevin might blurt out his secret. But now, as he looks at the blue and yellow squares on the side of the police car, he wonders if maybe he should have intervened? Not many things unnerve him, but uncertainty is one of them.

Like the uncertainty over James whose presence is always there between them. An unanswered question.

Leaving the window, Owen walks to his desk, swivels his office chair round and sits. The visit to his mother's old house has unsettled him, left him feeling insecure. Why else would he be thinking of the man who still haunts him?

He'd believed that by showing Rachel where he'd lived as a child, it might help to make her feel more settled. More comfortable living in the area. It was a request she'd made several times since they'd moved and he'd finally given in, even though he knew it would only serve to bring back unwanted memories. If he hadn't, he wouldn't be sitting here now with this bloody dark cloud over him.

Linking his fingers together, Owen presses down on the top of his head to ease the pain that's started there. But the relief is only momentary, and when he relaxes his hands again, the pain comes in a stronger wave.

He screws up his eyes. Massages his temples with his fingertips and thinks of Rachel prattling on about cups of tea on the front lawn. Cosy chats over a non-existent fence. Her words painting a picture of a childhood idyll he didn't recognise.

He's back there again, standing in the silent living room with its flocked wallpaper, the blank face of the TV mocking him. A TV that wouldn't be turned on until he'd gone up to his room. No pets to give him comfort. No siblings.

With his dad shacked up with his fancy woman, his mother had been Owen's only company after he got home from school, and during the long school holidays, because friendships had never been encouraged. Not that school had been any better. He'd been a serious boy. A serious teenager. Misunderstood by his peers. Smothered by his mother. His adolescent years spent up in his room.

His mother called him a bookworm, but it hadn't been his reading that had kept him there, well, not only that. He'd stayed up there because he couldn't stand being with her. Couldn't stand her fussing and her questions. Her neediness. Even the times when she ignored him totally, took herself to her bed with a bottle of Chardonnay and left him to get his own supper, had been better than that. Well, almost.

He swallows hard. No wonder his dad had left. Got himself someone else.

Who could blame him? Who could bloody blame him?

The need for comfort comes unexpectedly. He'd hoped Rachel might come up, but she hasn't. Is it because she's worried about that police car? His mind sifts through the various emotions he assigns to the characters in his novels. Checking them against what he'd seen in his wife's expression. Anxiety? Doubt? He taps fingers to his temple... ah, he's got it.

Walking over to the bookcase, he slides the faded *Oxford English Dictionary* from its place next to his university copy of *Roget's Thesaurus*. He's never believed in online word finders and checkers. Paper was good enough for Dickens and it's good enough for him.

He flips through the pages until he reaches the word he's looking for. Sucks on his bottom lip as he reads. *Despair. To be without hope.* Is that it? Is that what his wife is feeling? Has he driven her to it or is it something else that haunts her? The thing that makes her lie awake in bed at night. Makes her imagine things.

Owen puts the dictionary back on the shelf and goes to the door. Unlocks it. He shouldn't need to lock the door, he knows, but recently the idea of his wife coming into his study when he's not expecting it has been preying on his mind. It's what his mother had done. Pointing out the mistakes in his homework. Telling him he was useless. Anything to make him think he couldn't achieve anything. Hoping to keep him there with her.

But Rachel isn't his mother, she's his wife. It's what he has to remind himself every day. He loves her and, until recently, he'd thought she loved him. Yes, *him*. Owen. The quiet, serious one. The one she'd married.

Not fucking James.

Has seeing his old house again and the memories it's unearthed brought this mistrust on? He can't say for sure, but what he does know is he hates the man. The name. Even the idea of him makes his stomach churn as it did back then. Imagining his fingers grazing the soft flesh of his wife's arm and the smile on Rachel's face. The sort of smile she hasn't given *him* in years. He thumps his forehead with his fist. Despite Rachel's assurances, thoughts of the man still stop him sleeping at night. Taunting him. Terrifying him.

Worse than Kevin. Much, much worse.

But he doesn't want to think of that now. Time is moving on and he has Phillipa's book group to prepare for. What he needs is a strong coffee.

He closes the door of his study. Looks at his hand as he locks the door behind him. A hand that can't reach out to his wife. The hand of a man who's unable to love her like she wants. Give her the child she longs for.

What did she ever see in him?

Rachel's at the living room window. She jumps when she hears him, shakes the curtain back into place.

'I wasn't expecting you down so soon.'

'I needed coffee.'

She still has that look in her eyes and when he moves closer, he realises how wrong he'd been. It's not despair he sees in the dark pupils, but something else entirely. He closes his eyes as he tries to capture the essence of it. Opens them again when he knows what it is.

It's fear he sees in Rachel's eyes. Yes, fear.

Owen wants to go back upstairs. Get his notebook and make some notes but he doesn't. Instead, he puts a tentative arm around her. He feels her stiffen and it makes him wonder what she's done.

It's something that's always concerned him. Intrigued him. What she's capable of when she's trying to protect him. The family she feels is her right. Their lives.

TWENTY-FIVE

RACHEL

Simone stands at my door. The white T-shirt she's wearing is covered by faded navy dungarees, one strap slipping over her shoulder, the material stretched over her growing belly. Today her thick hair is loose, and she pushes it back irritably from her face.

'I'm sorry to bother you.'

The way she says it, the formality, saddens me. I know Simone doesn't understand why I've been avoiding her, and it's not as though I can tell her. It would be disloyal to Owen. Although Simone isn't Kevin, I have to accept that, to my husband, they are inextricably linked. The way Kevin treated Owen at university is inexcusable, and I have to respect that the idea of me hanging out with Simone, having coffee at their house, would be rubbing his nose in it. Giving him the message that I don't care. But I've missed her. Wish she was the one I'd talked to about James rather than Phillipa, as already I'm beginning to regret having told the woman next door so much about my life. Am scared she'll use it against me in some way.

'Simone. It's good to see you.' I glance behind me, step forward onto the porch and close the door. The police car that had been parked outside her house is disappearing around the bend in our road and I follow it with my eyes. 'Has something happened? Is everything okay?'

Simone's face is white and pinched. 'Not really. Kevin didn't come home last night. He went out to meet a client, and that's the last I saw of him.'

'He didn't come home?' I repeat.

'No, and I'm so bloody worried.' She takes a shuddering breath. 'He's not answering his phone and... and... Oh Christ, where is he, Rachel?'

I glance behind me. Know that I should invite Simone in but can't. Owen wouldn't like it. I did what he asked, distanced myself from the two of them, but now as I look at Simone's tear-stained face, all I feel is guilt.

'What did the police say? Were they concerned?'

Simone pulls a handkerchief from her sleeve. Blows her nose. 'They've taken details, but he's not considered vulnerable. They said he'll most probably turn up with a good excuse. I feel so stupid. I didn't even ask Kevin what the client's name was or where they were meeting. Why didn't I do that?'

'You can't blame yourself and, anyway, the police are probably right. If it was a child who was missing, it would be another matter.' I push the thought of Jade away. 'There could be any number of reasons why Kevin didn't come home. Maybe he had too much to drink and decided not to drive back.' I stop, knowing it sounds lame. 'Please try not to worry.'

Simone pulls at her sleeves. Looks down at the step. There's something bothering her; I can see it.

'What is it, Simone?'

She looks up at me. Bites at some loose skin on her top lip. 'Where was Owen last night?'

'What do you mean?'

'Where was he? Please just answer me.'

I feel wrong-footed. 'He was at home with me. Writing in

his study.' Anger stirs. Why am I having to vouch for him? 'What are you asking me for? You can't be thinking—'

There's something in my expression that makes Simone take a step back. She shakes her head, then presses the heels of her hands to her eyes. 'Oh God, I'm sorry. It's just that...'

'Yes?' Whatever she's about to say had better be good.

'It's just that you asked me to find out from Kevin what the secret was you'd heard him mention.' Simone's eyes lift to the window above my head, and I wonder whether Owen's standing at the glass, watching us. I hope not.

'And did he tell you?'

'Yes, he did.'

Simone's discomfort is catching. It feels awkward standing at my front door discussing my husband. I know she's worried about Kevin, but that doesn't excuse her rudeness in questioning me about him. I give an embarrassed laugh. The sound coming out wrong.

'All good I hope.' It's meant as a joke, something to lighten the atmosphere, but the words fall flat. Simone's not laughing. She picks at a scab on her arm.

'I don't think we should talk about it on your doorstep.' She pauses. 'Do you?'

I frown. 'Anything you want to say can be said here.'

It comes out more forceful than it should, and Simone gives a wry smile. Understanding at last. 'It was Owen, wasn't it? He was the one who told you not to talk to me? To break our friendship.'

My throat tightens. 'I didn't break it. I—'

She gives a small shake of her head. 'Oh, give over, Rachel. I've seen how you duck back indoors whenever you see me coming out of my house. How you pretend not to hear when I call out hello. It's this thing between our husbands, I know it is.' Her eyes flick up to Owen's window again, and I wonder if she's worried he might see her. 'Look, we don't have to talk at either of our houses. We could go for a walk or sit on the bench by the pond if you want.'

I look beyond her to where the iron railings rise from the close-cropped grass. A glimpse of pink ribbon visible between the bars.

'No, not there.'

There's a movement at Phillipa's window and we both turn. I think it's Lexi, but I can't be sure.

Simone looks back at me. 'You know I thought it was Phillipa who had turned you against me.'

'Why would you think that?' Despite everything, I'm interested to hear the answer.

'Because she can be possessive. Doesn't like to share. Once she thinks of you as best friend material, there's no going back... that's what I've heard anyway.'

I give an ironic laugh. 'She's made it quite clear I'm not that. Anyway, Lisa Brookner was her best friend. She told me that the other day.'

'Hardly. Lisa Brookner couldn't stand her. It was one of the reasons she left.'

'Really? But she said...' I look back at my house, trying to make sense of things.

'No,' Simone continues. 'It wasn't Lisa. She must have been talking about the girl who used to live here. The one whose child died.' She stops, places a hand on her bump, fingers spread wide. 'Anyway, it's not what I came here to talk about. This thing with Owen and Kevin...'

Colour rises through me. I don't like what she's implying. That their past has something to do with Kevin's disappearance. However much I want to know about that secret, Owen deserves my loyalty.

So instead of walking with her, finding out more, I paste on a smile. Fold my arms across my body.

'I'm sorry, Simone. I know you're worried about Kevin, but

he's a grown man and I'm sure he knows what he's doing. Besides it's only been one night.' I stand taller. 'I think it's best if you go now.'

Simone shoves her hands into the pockets of her dungarees. 'If that's what you want.' She makes to go, then turns back. 'Just one thing. It might be better if you didn't tell Owen I came here... What I said.'

'Keep secrets from him, you mean?' I stiffen. 'I don't see why.'

She holds my gaze a moment too long and I look away. Even though she hasn't voiced it, I know what that look means. What she's trying to say to me.

Of the two of us, it's not me who is keeping secrets.

I go back inside, guilt eating away at me. Simone had been worried sick, and I'd pushed her away. What friend would do that? But then I remember what she'd said about Owen. How she'd laid the blame for Kevin not coming home on our doorstep.

In the kitchen, I pull out a bottle of white wine from the fridge and pour myself a glass. I think of Phillipa sitting in her own kitchen next door and something niggles at me. Simone had said it wasn't Lisa Brookner that Phillipa had been best friends with but the dead girl's mother. I'd presumed the friendship to have been a recent one, but Geoff had said the Brookners had never redecorated. That the old vinyl wallpaper that hid Phillipa's name had been there when they'd moved in. Covered up by someone else.

Confused, I get up and find my laptop. I open it and click on the search engine, desperate to find out more. Into the search box I put in anything I can think of that might help: the name of our road, the words *pond* and *drowning*.

I search the results, almost immediately seeing what I've been looking for. It's a headline from a local newspaper. GIRL, EIGHTEEN MONTHS, DROWNS IN POND. And there she is, the child I'd only ever imagined. Dressed in dungarees, her fair hair in a topknot on top of her head. She's smiling out at the camera. Her eyes innocent. Trusting.

I stare at the date the article was written, my eyes widening. I'd presumed the child's death to be fairly recent, from the time just before the Brookners had moved into the house, but now I see how wrong I'd been. The news report is from 1998, the year before Pam and Geoff moved to the close.

I try to get my head around it. The tragedy in our cul-de-sac happened over twenty-five years ago.

My eyes race across the words, devouring them. A part of me wondering why I'd never thought to check the information out before this. But I hadn't and that's why, as I read to the end, my breath is held tightly in my chest. I stop, let the breath out slowly. I'd hoped the article might have given a reason for what had happened, an insight into how a young life had been lost, but I'm none the wiser. As Simone had told me, the inquest had been inconclusive and no one had been charged or arrested. No neighbours implicated. According to the report, the front door had been left open and Maddie had wandered out. She'd been found in the pond, an hour later, by her grandfather.

It all seems innocent enough. Yet, if it is, why do I have such a horrible feeling about this? Such a horrible, horrible feeling.

The photograph looks as though it's been taken in our kitchen, but the wallpaper behind the child is plain, not a sign of the vinyl tiles. I turn and look at our kitchen wall. Who had stripped away that earlier paper? Re-papered it with the one that still clings to it in places, waiting for me to have the energy to finish the job?

I take another mouthful of wine. Move closer to the screen. The child's name had been Maddie Leary and her mother, Kayla, had been only eighteen when she'd had her. There's no mention of a father. It might have been twenty-five years ago, but time hasn't reduced its ability to move me. That poor desperate mother. Destined by fate to live in our house with no baby to love.

Tears slip down my cheeks, and I press my hands to my sternum to fight the deep pain that's settled there. That little girl, Maddie, with the blonde topknot and dungarees, had climbed into the cupboard in our kitchen. Had pressed a *Hello Kitty* sticker to the wall. *Good Girl.*

Why had she done that? Why had she been in there?

Realising I've finished my wine, I pour myself some more, my mind turning to Phillipa whose name is staring at me from the bare plaster. She must be in her mid-forties which would mean that, at the time of Maddie's death, she would have only been a teenager. I remember her telling me she had lived in the close with her parents back then, but why was her name hidden beneath the wallpaper in her best friend's kitchen? *My* kitchen.

I think of the photograph album I'd found in Phillipa's house. Those two teenage girls had been Phillipa and Kayla, but it doesn't make things any clearer. I get up and walk to the wall, read the question out loud as I have many times since I discovered it written there. '*Why Phillipa?*'

I pinch the soft space between my eyes. As the only neighbour who had lived in Pond Close at the time of the drowning, and the person who had initiated the silence around it, it's a question I would like to ask her myself.

TWENTY-SIX

RACHEL

'Are you hungry? Would you like a snack?'

Phillipa's daughter, Talia, looks up at me. 'No, thank you.'

She's sitting at the kitchen table doing her homework and Neil is upstairs busy with something or other. Every now and again, I hear the creak of a floorboard, a burst of music that's muted quickly as though he's afraid his mother might come home earlier than she'd said and catch him. It's unusual for me to still be here when the older ones are home. Usually, Phillipa is back by now but, today, she'd asked if I'd stay longer – a feeble excuse of a hairdresser's appointment that couldn't be changed. Of course, she knew it would mean she'd miss the kids coming home from school, but her usual slot hadn't been available. What else could she do?

What else? For a start, she could have swapped it for the long coffee morning she'd planned for the following day, or the book club talk she's arranged with my husband. Apparently, everyone is keen to meet an author, and Owen was more than happy to oblige. I bite my lip and remind myself that it's good my husband is assimilating himself into the close – even if it's only with the wives.

The fact is my anger with this woman, this 'mother' and her secrets, is building. At least I'm here today, protecting the kids from her... because they need protecting.

My hand reaches to my back pocket, relieved that the letter is still there. I'd discovered it at the back of the sideboard in a box of what looked like memorabilia, when I'd been returning the photograph album I'd taken that first day. It had been written in cheap Biro, and all I'd managed to read before Talia had come home was, *Dear Phillipa. I don't want to be your friend any more...* The rest I'll have to read when I get home.

The kitchen is filling with the comforting aroma of warm toast. I smile at Talia.

'Sure I can't tempt you? It's been a long time since your school lunch break.'

Talia looks up at me. Her hair is tied back in a plain band and there isn't a scrap of make-up on her face. No hint of the teenager I imagine Phillipa to have been when she was that age. When I'd asked her why she hadn't changed out of her school uniform, she'd simply shrugged and pulled the sleeves of her jumper over her hands. *What was the point?* she'd said.

'I'm sure. Mum doesn't like me snacking. She says it will bring me out in spots and make me fat.'

I look at her pale moon-round face. So like Lexi's. Glance down at the child who's playing happily at my feet, sorting the Tupperware from Phillipa's cupboard according to size. Stacking one box inside the other. Something I used to do when I was little. I look back at Talia. I want to tell her the truth about her mother, but I don't.

'I'm sure one slice of wholemeal toast won't hurt. I'll have one too. Ironing is hungry work!'

'I won't, thank you.' Talia looks back at her books. When her mother is here, she does her homework in her room, but, today, it's as though she senses I won't mind. That I might even enjoy her company. She's right.

Lexi bangs two Tupperware boxes together, laughing at the sound. I laugh too. This is what I'd always imagined for myself. A house full of children. More than two mouths to prepare food for. Even a full washing basket.

Across the green, I see Simone at her window. Watching the close. Hoping for the first sight of her husband as he walks into the cul-de-sac. I look away, feeling guilty for not having been to see her. For not being the friend I should have been.

The toast pops up and Lexi points to it then at her mouth. 'Me.'

I laugh. Reach down and pick her up. 'You want some too, baby?'

She points again at the toaster, laughs, and I nuzzle her soft neck.

'I'll have to put you down again to butter it, Lexi. See if you can make me a big tower of your boxes while you wait. As big as can be, then we'll knock it down together. Good idea?'

I set her back down on the floor and lift the toast from the metal jaws. Pop the slices onto the waiting plates and butter them.

Phillipa's A4 page of household rules is on the worktop beside me, and I push it aside. It's not as if I don't already know what it says. Lexi must not be given a snack between meals. If ever I'm here at her teatime, it mustn't be given before five o'clock but no later than six. One pouch of the twelve months plus toddler food from the box in the cupboard. If she asks for more, I must say no. Too many calories aren't good for a child of Lexi's age.

I remember, when I was little, my own mother handing me fingers of warm buttered toast to tide me over until later. I wasn't as young as Lexi but what harm could it do? Finger foods are good for children, everyone knows.

'It's not too late to change your mind.'

Talia has the end of her pencil in her mouth. She looks up

from her books, and I wink at her, walk over and slide the plate of hot buttered toast she'd said she didn't want over to her. She takes a piece and bites into it, eyes closing in pleasure, a glisten of butter on her bottom lip, and I smile to myself.

'Me.' Lexi kicks the boxes away from her with her feet. 'Me, me.'

'All right, Little Miss Impatient.' I smile at her indulgently. Pleased that it's me who has brought some normality into this house of rules and lists. Just one piece of toast – minor rule-breaking and hardly an arrestable offence, but one that sends a thrill of illicit pleasure down my spine, regardless. 'Here you are, honey.'

I bend and hand Lexi the finger of toast. She smiles at me and holds it in her fist, puts the end of it in her mouth and sucks, even though she has a full set of teeth.

'Good?'

She nods her head vigorously. Pushes herself up with her free hand, then walks over to her sister, leaving a trail of crumbs and buttery handprints in her wake.

'You should sit down with that.' Talia removes her sister's sticky fingers from her arm, then returns to her homework. 'Mum won't be happy with the mess. Better eat it quickly, Lex.'

'Yes, let's sit you in the highchair. We don't want any accidents, do we?'

I lift her up and settle her into the chair, being careful to secure the straps around her. I know how easy it is for a child to choke if they're walking around. I close my eyes at the awful memory. Jade had been fine once I'd realised what was happening, but I can't make that mistake with Lexi. And I won't. This time I know more. Am more confident. More experienced.

Talia gets up and takes her plate to the sink, washes and dries it, then puts it away in the cupboard. Her brow is pinched, and I feel bad that I've caused this worry for her.

'Your mum needn't know. It can be our secret,' I say, and she turns and smiles.

A smile that tells me she's beginning to trust me.

TWENTY-SEVEN

OWEN

'Rachel?'

Owen reaches out a tentative hand. Puts it on his wife's shoulder. He'd come downstairs for paracetamol in the hope of catching the headache that lurks somewhere deep between his brows before it could get any worse. He hadn't known she was home. Hadn't heard the front door.

Rachel jumps, then pulls away a little as though his touch has stung her. Shoves whatever it is she's been reading into the bag by her feet. She wipes the tears with the heel of her hand before reaching into her pocket for a tissue to blow her nose.

'What was that you were reading?'

'That? Oh, nothing interesting.' Rachel reforms her mouth into the semblance of a smile. 'Have you finished writing? Are you happy with how it's going?'

There's a pain behind his breastbone that he can't recognise. Brought on by the sight of his wife's unhappiness. It cancels out his headache. Renders it insignificant. What had his wife been reading that had made her cheeks wet with tears? What had she tried to hide from him?

But he doesn't ask her again; it's not in his nature. Instead, he turns his mind to his work, an area where he feels safe. Secure.

'You know. Slow.' Grateful for the turn in conversation, he moves away from her and leans his back against the worktop. He taps his temple. 'It's *there,* though. Ready to come out.'

'That's good.' Rachel screws the soggy tissue up in her hand. Clears her throat. 'It will be great. I know it.'

But will it? Still something is holding the words back, like a river dammed. He has the bare bones of the idea, but the flesh he tries to build fails to cling to it. He can't afford for the next book to pan the way the last one did. Owen thinks of Kevin. His smirk. His smugness. *Your secret's safe with me.* Waiting for him to fall. Waiting for him to fail as he's always done. He sucks in his cheeks, fighting the cold dread that has him in its grip.

Owen the failure. Owen the joke.

But he has to remember this isn't about him, it's about Rachel and how he can lift her from the embers of her despair. He remembers the many times he found his wife like this at the old house. How it had escalated.

He can't let it happen again.

'I'm looking forward to doing the talk at their book club tonight.' He angles his head towards Phillipa's house. 'They want to know how *Dead Air* came to be a *Sunday Times* best-seller. How it changed my life.' He puffs out his chest a little. It had been good to be asked. Especially as it's been a long time since he's done a talk. It makes him feel he hasn't been totally forgotten. And maybe it will help Rachel.

'That's nice.' Rachel looks down at the tissue in her hand.

'I wish you'd come.'

Rachel looks at him, then away. 'No, I don't think so.'

He's disappointed. Likes having her in the room when he talks – a reminder of that first time when she'd looked up at him from the audience and he'd known, really known, that this time, someone liked him. Properly liked him.

'I'm sure you could—'

'I told you before. I haven't been asked.'

'Pity.'

She gets up. Walks over to the bin and drops in the tissue. 'I'm going for a walk.' Rachel lifts her denim jacket from the back of the chair and puts it on. 'I'll be back in time to make supper.'

Owen nods. 'Enjoy.'

He leaves her in the kitchen and climbs the stairs to his study. Outside the window, he hears voices. He goes over and looks out, sees that it's the husbands of the close that are doing the talking. Thighs clad in stretchy black Lycra, bikes propped up on the kerb or lying on the green, pedals pointing at the sky. Most of them are there: Carl a head taller than the rest, Steve whose lime-green top barely stretches over his paunch and Geoff, older than the others but still fit, the muscles of his calves taut and toned from regular exercise.

Owen watches him with interest as he swings his leg over the crossbar. He's only met him once as he'd gone to put out the rubbish and there's no reason why Geoff should know him, unless he's read one of his books. Yet there had been something in his expression as their eyes had locked. As though he was trying to place him. As though he'd seen Owen somewhere before but couldn't think where.

It doesn't worry him. He's done nothing to be ashamed of.

Rachel has come out now. The men nod to her, and she gives a small smile in return before hurrying down the road. It's her brave smile; one he's seen many times. The one that says, *I'm okay, don't ask.* Even when she's not okay. Even when he knows he *should* be asking.

If only he could make her happy the way James did.

James. Just the thought of him makes his palms clammy. When, against his better judgement, he'd asked Rachel about him the other day, he'd seen how, despite her shock, there had been something in her eyes. Like they'd been lit from within. It had made him realise that, despite the reassurances, the promises, he was still there in her head. Even if he was out of her life, the memory of him, the idea of him, still clung like ivy around an oak.

He looks across to the pond. Like a pink ribbon around a birch tree.

They'd agreed not to discuss it, or think of it again, but how can he keep his side of the bargain when her eyes tell him she can't keep hers.

TWENTY-EIGHT

RACHEL

I've no idea where I'm going. All I know is I have to get away from the close. As I get to the end of the road and turn left, I can still feel the husbands' eyes on me. Wonder what they'll be telling their wives later.

If only I could talk to Owen about what I'd read, but I'd seen how his face had closed down when he'd found me crying at the kitchen table. His hand pulling away from me as quickly as it had sought my shoulder – scared of the emotion he'd seen on my face. Unable to read me any better than he had that time at the hospital when the doctor had given us the news that it was unlikely that we'd ever be parents. That another round of IVF was doomed to failure.

Then, as now, Owen hadn't wanted to talk about my unhappiness, so I'd kept my feelings to myself. And, in time, the words I'd been unable to express had started to fester, turn rotten inside me. If only I had Owen's ability to detach. Be more like him.

But I haven't.

There's a bench at the side of the road, its metal legs overgrown with weeds. From the back pocket of my jeans, I take out the letter that had upset me so much and sit and read it again. It's from Maddie's mother, Kayla, to Phillipa her one-time best friend, telling her she never wants her in the house again. That she knows she's jealous of her little girl, has been ever since she was born, and doesn't want her anywhere near her. Their friendship is over.

I stare at the page that's littered with expletives and crossings out. It's clearly been penned in the heat of the moment, after an argument probably, the text filled with teenage angst.

The words swim because reading it has brought tears to my eyes again. Not because I feel sorry for Phillipa for receiving it or for Kayla for having felt the need to write it, but for what I'm reading between the lines – Kayla considered Phillipa a danger to Maddie. That little girl would soon be dead, and if Phillipa was a danger to *her*, then I'm in no doubt her own children need protecting from her too.

It's heartbreaking.

I put the letter away, begin to plan. I'm already at Phillipa's house plenty, but how can I get more time with her children? Get them to feel safe with me like Jade did? How can I give them the love they so clearly need? Also, if my suspicions are to be taken seriously, I need to find the missing piece of the puzzle... the reason for the writing on the wall of my house. Maybe I could ask Pam. She's lived here a long time or, better still, I can ask Owen to find out more when he's at the book group. Do a bit of digging.

There are voices coming from further along the street. Men's voices. A bike stops at the junction, is joined by two more, and I look away, hoping they won't be turning left. Breathing out a sigh of relief when they don't.

I lean forward. Rest my elbows on my knees and steeple my fingers against my chin. If only I had someone to talk to about all this. Someone who would really listen. Really understand.

My phone pings, taking me by surprise. Unzipping my bag,

I take it out and read the name on the screen, disappointed when it's a number I don't recognise. A cold caller most likely – a scam message from someone pretending to be from the phone company or the bank. I sit with the phone in my hands, fingers pressing into the rigid cover.

When the phone pings again, my finger clicks on it before I can think. I look down, read the message that's written there and my heart stops. For it's one I never thought I'd see again... or want.

It's James, the message reads. *It's been too long. I miss you.*

TWENTY-NINE

RACHEL

I stare at my phone. Try to regulate my breathing. What does he want? Why now when I made him promise he'd never contact me again? Made him swear on his life.

I won't answer him. Will delete the message, then put my phone away and not think of it again.

I press the cool screen to my burning face. Yet this number is a new one. If I delete it, then I'll never be able to contact him again. Ever. Guilt kicks in and I pull air into my lungs. Why am I even thinking like this? I shouldn't want to be in touch. It's not as though we've spoken to each other since the day I put an end to it.

But I know why I'm loath to make that final cut. It's because I have nobody else. A mother I'm estranged from, a couple of cousins, one in Scotland the other somewhere in America, but no one who matters.

Not someone who will talk to me.

Listen to me.

Properly understand me.

Because, for me, the thing with James was never about sex –

it was about the connection we had. The interest he showed in my thoughts. My emotions. My problems.

The phone pings again and I look down, dragging myself from the memory.

Rachel? Please reply.

He can't know how badly I want to.

My finger hovers over the comment box, but the fear of clicking on it, typing out even one word, is a physical weight on my chest. If I answer his message, what will it do to Owen? Could I go back to living like we had before? The secret I shared with James present in every thought, every word, every action – even ones as simple as emptying the dishwasher or making the bed.

The sun is starting to lower. The bright orb disappearing behind a farm building on the other side of the road. Blinding me. My skull feels like the shell of an egg about to crack, and I close my eyes, hoping it will help fight the memories that come pushing through. But it doesn't. The film still plays on against the orange inside my lids.

I open my eyes again searching for something to take my attention. To drive away the images. Finding nothing, I stare into space. All those things I'd told James; it shames me now to think about it. Things about me. About what was lacking in my life and how finding I couldn't get pregnant had been the greatest disappointment of all. I'd shared how, without children, I was afraid I might not be enough for Owen. I even told James that sometimes I wished my husband was more like him. Because Owen could so often be closed to me. I couldn't talk about any of these important things with him but, with James, it was different. He made it easy. So very easy.

What had been the most disloyal, the intimacy or the sharing? I wonder, sometimes, what Owen's answer would be. Not that he'd ever tell me. His inability to articulate his feelings stalling him and stopping the sentences from flowing. Each word pushed back inside and tamped down before it can be uttered.

I stand. Push the phone back into my bag. I should have deleted the number, but I haven't and even that little act is a betrayal.

I don't go straight home. Instead, I cross the green and let myself in through the gate in the iron fence. It closes behind me, and I'm surprised to see Chantelle standing at the pond's edge, Jo Jo's pushchair parked next to her. She's wearing tiny denim shorts with frayed edges that skim her thighs and an overlarge bat-wing white top that falls from one shoulder to reveal a black bra strap. She turns when she hears me, and I raise my hand. Back away.

'Sorry. I didn't think anyone would be in here.'

'No, you're all right. I was going anyway.'

'If you're sure?'

'Yeah, I am. Just getting meself a breather. He can be a dick sometimes.'

I frown, surprised she's wanting to share this with me. 'Steve?'

'Yeah. Who else?'

It's only now I see the small posy of flowers in her hands. Pink rosebuds and burnt orange crocosmia. Sky-blue cornflowers. Picked from her front garden. She places them at the base of the birch tree. Stands back.

'You knew her? The little girl?' I can't help but ask.

'What? No.' She blinks. ''Course not. Ain't gonna lie, though. Makes me sad thinking about her.'

'You too?' At last. Someone who feels the same. Who can, maybe, shed some light on what happened that day. 'I hope you don't mind me asking, Chantelle, but do you know what—'

But already her face has shut down. Her expression, under the thick make-up settling into a mask.

'I don't know anything. And we don't like people nosying. It ain't nice for the close.'

She looks in the direction of Phillipa's house, then away again. I get the impression it's not only Phillipa's children who are scared of her. Chantelle is too. Maybe they *all* are.

'I need to know what happened to her. For my own good. Was Phillipa involved in some way?' I hadn't meant to say this. It came from nowhere – a desperate attempt to keep the conversation going. But, instead of loosening Chantelle's tongue, her expression hardens.

'She was taken in for questioning, but they didn't find nothing, okay? Stop digging, is my advice.' She sweeps her dark, shiny hair over her bare shoulder. 'And I'd take it if I was you.'

What she's said has shocked me, but I know I mustn't let it show. Knowing she'll say no more about Phillipa, I turn the conversation away.

'I just can't help thinking about the little girl's poor mother. Having to live with that all her life. I can't even imagine it.'

Chantelle gives a dismissive lift of her shoulders. 'Won't hurt her now. She's dead. Blamed herself and took her own life.'

I stare at her. Shocked. 'Oh, my God!'

'It weren't her fault, though. That Phillipa's the one who should be searching her conscience.'

My skin prickles. 'Why?'

'I ain't saying no more. I've said too much already.' She wipes her palms down the sides of her denim shorts, then walks to the gate. When she gets there, she turns. 'Oh, and I know about Charlie's little habit if you were thinking of telling me. They're kids, him and Aaron. Having a bit of fun.' She looks down at the pushchair. 'Stop doing that, Jo Jo... it's not funny.'

Chantelle bends and picks up the blanket her baby's thrown onto the ground. Tucks it around her again before she lets herself out of the pond area. Leaving me standing, puzzled. For embroidered on the corner of the blanket had been the same letter M I'd seen on the bib in Phillipa's house.

But my thoughts don't linger on it for long because I can't stop thinking about the woman who took her own life. The tragedy that happened here made all the worse for knowing it. And that comment Chantelle made about Phillipa...

She knows more than she's saying, and I need to find out what the neighbours are keeping from me. If I'm to keep Lexi safe.

THIRTY

OWEN

The air is cold against Owen's skin. The ground hard. He forces his eyes to open against the bright glare, realising it's the security light above the sliding patio doors that's blinding him.

'Oh, my God, Owen. What happened? Are you all right?'

Rachel is bending over him, the wind flattening her dressing gown to her body. Without his glasses, he can't see the fear in her eyes, but he can hear it.

There's a sharp pain in his side. Something sticky at the side of his face. He reaches up a hand to touch it, wincing as his fingertips make contact with the split skin. He's bleeding.

Taking a handkerchief from her dressing-gown pocket, Rachel attempts to wipe it, but he pushes her hand away.

'I'm all right.'

But he isn't. With one hand clutching his side, he rolls over, a groan escaping his lips. He takes the handkerchief from her and wipes the trail of blood that's run down his cheek and mingled with his beard. Accepts the glasses Rachel is holding out to him.

'Did someone do this to you?' In the bright light, her pupils have shrunk to pinpricks. 'Should we call the police?'

Owen looks around him, his eyes sweeping the long stretch of lawn the estate agent had earmarked for a trampoline before realising it would only be the two of them living there. Sees nothing. The garden is still, the only sound the wind in the Leylandii.

'You haven't answered me, Owen. Did someone do this to you?' She looks behind her as though expecting someone to jump out at her, and he knows he must reassure her.

'Of course not. I tripped, that's all. Hit my face on the patio step. Something woke me, and I wasn't sure what it was, but the garden shed had blown open, was banging against the bin. That's what I'd heard.'

He struggles to his feet, trying not to wince. He's not going to tell her that the person had come at him with full force, his fist meeting with his kidneys. The blow knocking him off his feet. He hadn't seen who it was – hadn't had the chance to. It had all happened so quickly. Like that time at university. He screws up his eyes remembering how he'd been jumped on during Freshers' Week. A sack placed over his head, his body pushed up against the wall of the student accommodation. No fists or punches that time. The blows coming from his assailants' words. *Creep. Fucking weirdo.*

He couldn't say for sure it had been Kevin and his newly formed clique, but he'd be happy to lay a bet on it. They hadn't known Owen then, not properly, but it was as though they'd seen something in him. Something he didn't see in himself when he looked in the mirror. Something that set him apart from the others.

Anna had been the one who'd found him, sitting pale and shaken on the pavement, as she'd walked home from a fancy-dress night at the Student Union Bar. She'd been dressed in a *Where's Wally?* outfit she'd thrown together. The red and white T-shirt and matching bobble hat, borrowed from someone on her corridor. Dark-rimmed glasses framing her pretty eyes.

She'd helped him up, taken him back with her to her halls of residence and given him neat vodka to drink, straight from the bottle, to help with the shock. Told him she didn't know what her boyfriend would do if he found Owen in her room – but there'd been a twinkle in her eye when she'd said it.

Anna had been the first person to show him kindness in the week since he'd arrived, and he'd appreciated it. He'd known she was a good sort and that someone like her would make a decent friend and ally. It helped that she was on his course, and for the next week, he'd set his alarm so that he could get to the lecture theatre early enough to bag a seat next to her. He remembers how her eyebrows had raised a fraction as he'd asked if the seat beside her was taken. But she'd moved her rucksack off and put it by her feet. Given him a smile as the lecturer had come onto the stage and made a whispered joke about him behind her hand – something linked to the man's shoes. He hadn't understood the joke but had laughed at it anyway.

After that, there had been no more sacks over the head... no more taunts. Not for a while anyway. Not while he was Anna's friend.

Owen draws in a sharp breath as Rachel helps him down the patio steps and back around the side of the house. When they reach the front door, he pauses. Looks across at the Wellbecks' house. The attack had the hallmark of Kevin stamped all over it, but he was no longer here. No longer a problem for him. The knowledge disturbs him. Who else could it be?

Rachel shuts the door behind them. 'I'll help you up to bed, then get you some painkillers.'

'Thank you.'

When they get to the bedroom, Owen sits on the side of the bed. He waits until his wife has gone downstairs to get some water to wash the painkillers down, then lifts his bloodstained T-shirt over his head. Drops it onto the floor.

Lifting up his arm, he twists to inspect the damage. The

skin is purple, darker in the places where the knuckles made contact.

With his arm across his body, flat of his hand cradling the bruise on his side, he walks to the chest of drawers and pulls out a clean T-shirt. As he's putting it on, he sees Rachel's phone charging. He's never been one to snoop, but these are not normal times. There's something in the air; he can sense it. With a quick look at the door to make sure Rachel isn't coming back up, he bends and picks the phone up. He presses the button on the side and the phone lights up to show a photograph of him and Rachel on their wedding day. She all smiles and happiness. *His* face mirroring his incredulity that he'd actually done it. Proved everyone wrong.

A little voice niggles in his head as it has always done, *it was only your fame that attracted her, idiot.* Kevin's voice. His mother's. But he pushes it away. She's stayed with him, hasn't she? Even now that his name no longer appears in the *Sunday Times* Bestseller List. Even though he's not first choice for panel talks and festivals. She's proved it's *him* she loves. Despite his fame having guttered like a candle and his inability to give her the child she'd told him she wanted.

There's nothing else on the screen. Nothing to hint at what she'd been doing when they'd first gone to bed. When she'd thought he was asleep. The light from her phone brightening the room a fraction. Her fingers tapping at the screen.

He clicks onto her messages. Sees it straight away, the blood draining from his face. *I need to talk to you, James. I miss you too.*

But Rachel is on the stairs. She'll be here soon. He drops her phone onto the chest of drawers, steps away.

'I thought you'd be in bed.'

'I was changing my top.' He plucks at the soft material. Can she hear the shake in his voice?

He walks to the bed, turns back the cover and gets in.

Rachel slides in next to him and turns out the bedside light. After a minute, she speaks.

'I meant to say. I'm thinking of going out tomorrow evening. You don't mind, do you?'

His breath catches in his throat. 'Of course not. Anywhere nice?'

Her voice is too careful. The words clearly rehearsed. 'Just meeting an old friend. We have a lot to catch up on.'

Owen lies there, not daring to speak. She's meeting a friend. A *friend*.

He presses his other hand to his chest in a vain attempt to try to still his racing heart. Hears her voice from the past. *You have to believe me, Owen, it's over*. He'd thought she'd meant it? *Really* meant it.

Rachel's breath grows heavy, but, for him, sleep won't come. Eventually, he gets up again, slides his arm into the sleeve of his dressing gown. It's a struggle to put his other arm in without making the pain in his side worse, but he manages it. Goes out onto the landing and into his study, closing the door behind him.

He switches on his computer and clicks into the file containing his novel. He stares at what he's written, at the chapters that are slowly, oh so slowly, growing. It's not good enough yet, he knows that, maybe never will be, but he has to carry on. What other option does he have?

He rests his fingers on the keyboard. Pictures Rachel's guilty face.

Last time she'd had an affair, it had been the beginning of the end... the thing that showed him she wasn't his sweet, innocent wife any more. It's happening again, and he needs to stop it once and for all.

THIRTY-ONE

RACHEL

'I didn't think you'd come.'

'I didn't think I would either.' I look at James, my heart beating so fast I'm scared he might hear it. 'You look well.'

He smiles and the smile doesn't end at the corners of his mouth as Owen's does but follows the planes and muscles of his face. Reaching his eyes. Delivering a fan of lines at their corners. I've missed it. Missed *him*. So much it hurts.

'You too... look well, I mean.'

'Thank you.'

I slide into the seat opposite him. The restaurant is one I haven't been to before, and I like it immediately. It's open and modern. The plain white walls covered in paintings by local artists, their names and prices printed on little stickers at the bottom corner of each frame. More importantly, each table is far enough apart from its neighbours that conversations cannot be overheard. Through the window, I can see my car parked outside in the car park.

'I came by taxi,' James says, pointing to his glass of wine. 'So I can have a drink.'

I look at his fingers on the stem of his glass. Remember the feel of them on my skin and shiver. The fact he's drinking is a surprise. He never used to drink, and I wonder why he's decided to now. Is it because he's nervous, like me?

'Did you catch much traffic?' he asks. 'It should have only taken me forty-five minutes, but there was an accident. Nothing major but enough to cause a bit of a hold-up.'

'No, it was a straight run. Quicker than I thought.'

I wonder when we'll break out of this small talk. Address the real reason why we are here. It's as though neither of us wants to be the one to do it. There are so many things I want to say to James. To ask him. *Did we make a mistake? Did you hate me for calling a halt to it? When you lie awake at night, unable to sleep, do you let yourself think about it... about us? How we were then.*

But I don't ask him any of these things. Instead, I open the menu. Try to focus on the dishes rather than on the man who is sitting only a few feet away from me. The man I said I never wanted to see again.

'Rachel.' He reaches out a hand. Lowers the menu I'm holding so he can see me better. 'Why did you come? Why did you answer my message? The truth, please. Only the truth.'

I lay the menu down.

'I was lonely.'

He rests his elbows on the table. Leans forward, a frown etched into his brow and takes my hand. 'Lonely?'

'Yes.'

'Why is that do you think? You used to be so happy. So care-free. When you were with me anyway.'

I want to tell him it's because it's all happening again... but I don't.

'We moved house. Downsized. It's nice enough, but the cul-de-sac where the house is, is so...' I search for the word. 'So cold. I had this vision of us becoming part of the community. Making friends. Having a different life to the one we had in our old place where the nearest neighbours were half a mile away. It would be the silver lining.'

'To what?'

'To the move... to having to leave the home I loved.'

I look at him. Like how he's dressed – faded jeans and a short-sleeved black shirt. A million miles away from the cords and jumpers my husband favours.

'So you thought of me.' He smiles. 'I like that.'

I feel a sting of irritation. 'It was *you* who contacted *me*, James. Not the other way round.' I pull my hand away, hating that he's making fun of me. 'Why did you contact me again? When we promised each other we wouldn't?'

He looks thoughtful. 'Why is the sky blue? Why do rivers flow from their source? What is the meaning of life?'

'Be serious.'

'I'm sorry.' He looks sheepish. 'I guess it was because I thought we had unfinished business. Correct me if I'm wrong, but I think you do too.'

Can he read me that well? The thought unnerves me. 'We said everything there was to say, James.'

'Yet you're here, sitting opposite me.' Reaching across the table, he takes my hand again, and this time I leave it there. The warmth of his palm against mine an exquisite torture. 'Have I ever told you you're beautiful?'

'Yes.' I smile because he has, many times. The few short years, after I called it off, made barren with their absence. Each day that passed caught in that no man's land of time between twilight and moon rise when the colour is leeched out of everything.

'I say it because you are.' He returns my smile. 'Now just as much as before. More beautiful, if anything.' His eyes stay on mine, not letting them go. 'I want to know everything I've missed, Rachel. Every thought. Every feeling. I've been shut out of your life, and it's something I'll always regret. Will you help me fill in those empty spaces? Can you do that for me? Three years is a long time.'

'I know.' It is. Too long.

The waitress is hovering, keen to take our order. Seeing her, James releases my hand and picks up the menu again. 'It will have to wait until we've decided what to eat. The seafood risotto sounds good. What about you?'

'I'm not sure.' Seeing James, being here with him again after all this time, has taken away my ability to think. To make rational decisions. 'I think I'll have the same.'

'Good choice.'

He nods to the waitress, and she moves closer so we can give her our order. When James smiles at her, I see how she lingers a little longer than is necessary as though some invisible force is keeping her there. It's how it's always been with him, and I can hardly criticise. After all, it's not as though I'm immune to it. Whenever we'd meet, it would be so hard to break away... go home to Owen. It feels wrong to think it, but it's true and it will be the same tonight, I know.

'So, where shall we begin?' he asks, when the waitress finally leaves.

'You tell *me*.'

'Okay.' He picks up the glass jug and pours some water into each of our two glasses. Takes a sip. 'Why don't you start where we left off? From the night you told me it was over. What do you think?'

I look around me at the other diners. It seems too public, too ordinary a place for what I have to tell him. Yet, I'm not sure where would be a better place.

'It could take a while.'

James looks at his watch. 'We have all the time in the world. We've only just ordered, and if we run out of time, then we'll have to make a second date of it, won't we?'

There's a mirror on the wall behind James, and when I look

at my reflection, I see how excitement and nerves have changed my face. Brought roses to my cheeks and a brightness to my eyes that haven't been there in a long while.

A deep peace settles around me like a shawl. There's no need to answer his question as we both know that if the evening passes too quickly and we have to meet again, I'll be there. That this time I won't let him go so easily. Will fight for him if I have to.

Sometimes, you don't know a decision is wrong until it's too late to step back from it.

THIRTY-TWO

RACHEL

Lexi and I are kneeling at the edge of the pond. Next to us is a dripping net. An old margarine tub full of water, the squiggling black bodies of tadpoles appearing and disappearing as the pond weed moves.

'These things.' I point at the tub. 'When they grow up, they'll be frogs, Lexi. I've seen newts here too. Maybe we can see if we can find one next time.'

It's hot today, little movement in the air, and I wipe the sweat from my brow with my forearm. Beside me, Lexi pokes at the weed, stirring it up into a green soup. When she removes her finger from the water, it's wound around with wet green strands. She laughs and I laugh too, glad that I've found something that has not only kept her occupied but has given her enjoyment. It's unlikely she'd understood any of my improvised science lesson, but, even so, she'd sat on the grass, eyes lifted to me, like the perfect student.

'Pole.'

I look at her in astonishment. 'That's right, Lex. It's a tadpole. Clever girl.' In the weeks I've been looking after her, she's barely said a word and it's worried me.

The rush of pride I feel takes me by surprise. I taught her that.

I'd told James all about it the night we met up and he'd been sympathetic. Said I was right to be worried about Phillipa's children. To step in.

Now I have James in my mind, it's hard to get him out. When I'd got home from the restaurant after our meeting, Owen had already been in bed. The light off. The bedroom in darkness. I'd been thankful for that, worried he could be waiting up for me – sitting alone at the kitchen table where he could see the front door opening, or on the settee in the living room, the TV screen showing a programme he would have had no interest in watching. The sound turned down low. Ready to interrogate me.

And any questions, even one as simple as whether I'd had a nice time with my friend, would have spoiled the magic of the evening. Turned what had been beautiful into something sordid. Worthy of my shame.

Instead, he'd had his back to me, as he so often did, covers pulled up to his chin. Hadn't stirred as I'd climbed into bed, the pictures of the evening running on a continuous loop in my head. Not just images but sensations too. The sound of James's laugh. The earthy smell of his aftershave. How right his fingers had felt laced between mine. And, more importantly, the relief I'd felt as the weight that had been on my shoulders these last few months, had lifted as I'd told him the things I could never tell Owen.

Sleep had only come as the first light of dawn crept under the curtains. And when I'd finally woken, run my arm across the sheet to Owen's side of the bed, I'd found it empty.

I'd got up then, walked along the landing and pressed my ear to the study door. The rhythmic tap of his fingers on the keyboard the only sound in the house. A sound that left me feeling as though I was standing on the edge of something. A spectator who no longer knew the rules of the game. The need for them slowly but surely being erased.

A breeze sets the reeds rustling, and I turn my attention back to Lexi. The knees of her tights are stained green from the damp grass and rubbing at them only makes the stain worse. Why didn't I think to change her into something more sensible before taking her out? I look at my watch. It's two thirty. Plenty of time before Phillipa comes home from wherever she's been this afternoon. I've given up asking where she goes as the answers send a shot of irritation through me. Why have a child if you don't have any interest in them?

I bend down to Lexi and lift her. Settle her on my hip. 'Come on, sweetheart. Let's get you home.'

The little girl points to the margarine tub. 'Pole.'

'No, we can't take them with us, Lexi. They live here in the pond. It's their home.'

Holding Lexi tightly, I reach down and pick up the container of muddy water in my free hand. Empty it into the pond. I step back smartly so as not to get splashed and, together, Lexi and I watch the tadpoles disappear into the reeds. The ripples on the surface moving outwards towards the pond's edge. As my eyes follow them, I see something at the base of the birch tree, half-hidden by the long grass. It's a fresh bouquet of flowers: Baby's breath and tiny pink rosebuds. Placed there in memory of the child who drowned.

I shiver. Was it Chantelle whose hand had placed them there or someone else?

I'm contemplating this when I hear a sudden cry. The edges of it sharp. Cut through with panic. A woman's voice.

'Where is she? Where's my baby?'

I stiffen, my eyes fixed on the faded ribbon that now hangs limply against the silver bark of the tree. My heart thumps as I hold Lexi a little tighter. Hearing another voice. Kayla's? Julia's?

The shout comes again, and I remember myself. It's Phillipa's voice I'm hearing – Lexi's mother. Not ghosts from the past.

Hoisting Lexi higher on my hip, I reach around her and tap my watch, my heart sinking when I see it still says two thirty. It must have stopped while we were out here. Time racing away unchecked while we were fishing for tadpoles.

With no idea of the correct time, I hurry to the gate, fumble with the latch and let myself out. When I'm on the green, I raise my hand.

'It's all right, Phillipa,' I call. 'Lexi's safe. I've got her... she's with me.'

Phillipa is in her running gear: lime-green vest and cropped black leggings. A sports bag is discarded on the drive. Seeing me, she runs across the road. Meets me halfway across the green.

'What were you thinking?' She snatches Lexi from my arms, her voice rising. Her finger pointing at the pond. 'How the hell could you have taken her there? To that place?'

I look behind me. See the shivering silver birch leaves. A glint of water through the iron rails. 'We were looking for tadpoles. I didn't think you'd mind. I didn't mean to be so long, but my watch stopped. Look, she's fine. No harm done.'

Phillipa shakes her head. Looks at me with disdain, her voice carrying across the green. 'You really believe that, don't you? What you are, what you've done, is nothing short of irresponsible.'

'Phillipa, I—'

But she's not listening. Doesn't want to hear my explanation that Lexi had got bored of her toys. Pointed to the window when I'd picked her up and asked what she wanted to do instead. Phillipa turns away from me, one hand on the back of her daughter's head, and half jogs back across the green. When she reaches the house, she picks up the discarded bag, goes inside and slams the door behind her.

I stand there, alone on the green, humiliation coursing through me. I'd thought we were alone, that no one was there to witness Phillipa's tirade, but now the tiny hairs on the back of my neck are prickling as though alerted to something unseen.

Slowly, I turn. Chantelle is by her front door. It looks like she's been adjusting the position of the pushchair, but now she's straightened, one hand on the plastic-covered handle, watching me. Next door, Simone is reversing out of her drive. As her car passes me on the green, she slows, her face turned to me. I watch as she drives away... was that a shake of the head I'd seen?

Hot anger rushes through me. Anger I'm struggling to contain.

THIRTY-THREE

RACHEL

'Why don't you tell me exactly what happened?'

We're sitting on a bench by a lake. One I've never been to before. Far enough away from the town that the chance of meeting anyone I know is slim. The anger is still there, eating away at me. Anger at Phillipa. At Owen.

'James,' I say carefully. Not looking at him. 'Do you really want me to tell you? Do you really want to hear?'

His fingers are spread out on the worn wooden slats of the bench. Pinky finger touching mine. A deliberate touch. One that sends shivers up my arm. He leans in close. Warm breath on my ear.

'Of course I want to hear.'

I lean my head against his. His hair tickling my cheek. 'I thought I was doing something nice. Taking her daughter out. Showing her the living things in the pond. It was something I used to do with my dad when I was young. Our special time. At weekends, we'd go with a net to a lake or a river. See what we could find.'

I don't tell him about taking Jade to the pond at the bottom of our garden when we lived in our old house. How the silver ripples, when the wind blew, were so mesmerising I forgot she was with me.

'That's a sweet story.' He takes my hand in his. 'Go on. You took this little girl to the pond.'

'Her name's Lexi.'

'Lexi then. So, what happened? It must have been something pretty bad for you to have messaged me.'

'It was the way she spoke to me. As though I was incompetent. Not capable of looking after her daughter. I was desperate, and Owen didn't understand.' I stare out at the lake where two dragonflies are patrolling the margins, their iridescent wings catching the sunlight. Watch as one settles on a leaf. Beyond it, I can see the small weir, crafted from a mosaic of weathered stone, the rhythm of the water as it cascades over, a soothing background to our conversation. 'It's like he has this block. Something stopping him from engaging. From empathising with me.'

'I'm sorry.' James looks at me with sympathy. 'It must be hard for you.'

'It is.'

He twists towards me and with his free hand tucks a strand of hair behind my ear. I miss these small intimate things that make me feel I'm someone in my own right. Not just Owen the bestselling author's wife.

'After I ended things with you,' I say, 'I thought things would change. That he'd be different.'

I remember the sting of disappointment the first time Owen had turned away from me in bed. The humiliation. The ache in my heart from knowing he didn't want me any more. Didn't need me.

James squeezes my fingers. 'I know that's what you were hoping. You told me as much on that last evening we were together. But you still have *me*. Whatever you might have said, however you couched it, I never really believed you meant it. That it was really the end for us.'

I sigh heavily. 'I know.'

James looks out over the lake. 'I wish I could make this better for you. I love you, you know. More than I can say.'

He turns back to me, cups my face in his hands. The lids of his eyes half-closed. His lips parted as though he wants to kiss me, and I want it too... so desperately.

It takes every ounce of my willpower to turn my head away.

'Having you listen helps. It's all I need to make things feel a whole heap better.'

I haven't said I love him back, and if James is disappointed, he doesn't show it. 'Sometimes, words are not enough, Rachel. This woman, this Phillipa. It sounds like she takes pleasure in belittling you. Putting you down. You shouldn't let her get away with it.'

I run my hand over my hair. 'What choice do I have? She's my neighbour. I have to live with her. I don't want to stoop to her level. Make it into something bigger than it is.'

'You're a marvel, do you know that? There aren't many people who would be as tolerant as you. I know *I* wouldn't be.'

I turn to face him. Wondering if he's only saying it to make me feel better. To persuade me he's the man I want him to be. Not weak like Owen.

'You don't mean that.'

'Don't I?'

And I realise then that I don't know the answer. Despite all the times we met back then, I can't say I really know James. But, real or not, I like it when he talks like this. It makes me feel as though he's got my back, and it's a long time since I've had someone do that.

I look away. Feel the curve of my nails as they press into my palm. 'I don't trust Phillipa. There's some link between her and the little girl that drowned in the pond... I know there is. I just need to find out what.'

'What makes you think that?'

'It was something one of our neighbours said... Chantelle. Apparently, Phillipa was interviewed by the police, but no action was taken.'

'They wouldn't do that without cause.'

'That's what I thought. You know I found a photograph in her house of what I'm sure was the child when she was a baby. Except...' I swallow.

'Except what?'

I feel sick saying it. 'The baby's face was scrawled over with marker pen. Her mother, Kayla, was Phillipa's best friend, but I know they'd fallen out.'

'Really?' He looks surprised. 'How on earth would you know that? It could have been a photo of her own child.'

'No, it was in an album of photos taken long before her children were born. I know it sounds bad that I was snooping, but I needed to know what type of woman Phillipa was. Whether her daughter, Lexi, was safe in her care. As well as the photograph, I found a letter from Kayla. In it, she said she knew Phillipa was jealous of her little girl and didn't want her anywhere near her.'

'I see. Quite the sleuth.' He pauses, taking in what I've told him, then gives me a straight look. 'What does Owen think of all this?'

'He's not interested. Doesn't care what Phillipa might or might not have done or how she treats her children... or me for that matter. Can you believe he went to her house the other evening to give a talk to her book group?'

James drums his fingers on his knees. 'Goodness. How did that make you feel?'

'It made me feel worthless, if you must know. As though my feelings don't count for anything. Or my concerns.'

James bows his head. 'I'm sorry. That man needs his head

looking at. He'll lose you if he carries on like that.' His hand moves from his knee to mine. 'You know I'd never do that, don't you, Rachel?'

He pauses and I wonder what it is he wants me to say. Whether he's making it into some sort of competition between him and Owen. One that my husband can't win.

'Owen wouldn't have done it either, once upon a time.' But, even as I say it, I'm not so sure. It could simply be that the opportunity had never presented itself. A church bell chimes in the distance, and I look at my watch. Stand. 'I have to go. I'm sorry I've dragged you all the way out here.'

James reaches for my hand. 'You don't ever have to apologise.'

'Don't I?'

He stands too. Places a hand against my cheek. 'No, you don't.'

This time when he bends to kiss me, an urgent kiss that takes my breath away, I don't stop him. But I can't let it go any further. However much we both want it to.

'I have to go,' I say again, my hand against his chest. And I mean it. I don't trust myself to stay. 'It's Owen... I can't do this to him again.' I stop, knowing James understands. I search in my handbag for my keys and cross the grass to my car.

'That thing I said,' James calls after me, making me stop and turn. 'About Phillipa. I mean it... if you want me to do anything.'

I'm not really listening, too busy dissecting the things I've told him. Wondering if I've done the right thing in coming here today. In confiding in him. I'm also thinking about how I should be, how I should act, when I get home.

James sits back down, his legs stretched out in front of him. Arms wide across the back of the bench. As if he hasn't said anything of consequence.

If only I'd been paying more attention. Listened to him properly.

Really listened.

THIRTY-FOUR

RACHEL

Owen seems different today. Striding into the kitchen, his head held high. Exuding a confidence I haven't seen in a long time.

'It's going well, I presume?' I say, holding out the mug of coffee I've made.

He sits at the table, takes the coffee from me, a slant of sunlight that shines in through the kitchen window highlighting his sharp cheekbones. The cut he'd received from his fall on the patio steps now barely visible.

'It's getting there, Rachel.' He takes off his glasses and wipes them on a corner of his shirt. 'You know I think I have something. I feel it here.' He thumps his chest. 'Really feel it.'

I continue buttering the slice of toast that's in front of me. 'I'm glad. I just hope you're right.' I regret saying it even as the words are coming out of my mouth. See how Owen's face falls. 'Not that I doubt it for a minute,' I add quickly. Too quickly.

Owen puts his glasses back on, his pale eyes on me, magnified by the glass. He takes a sip of his coffee.

'The women at the book group certainly thought so. They were quite excited, truth be told, about having a real live author living in their close. I've promised them copies of the paperback when it comes out.'

I put down my knife. Put the lid back on the butter. 'Don't you think you're jumping the gun a bit? Shouldn't you at least have waited until you've shown it to your agent? Got her take on it?'

He shakes his head at me sadly. 'There you go again. The doubting Thomas. I would have expected more from my wife.'

He's right. I want to be that person, but we've had so many disappointments it's hard to remain positive. It's also hard to hear him talk about the book group. Surprised he's brought it up after what I told him.

I have to try and be upbeat, though, for my sake as well as his.

'I'm sure your novel will have the success it deserves. All I was doing was trying to be realistic in case—'

He thumps his mug down, coffee spilling onto the wooden table. 'In case what? Your award-winning husband fucks up again?'

'That's not what I meant. I just don't want you to be disappointed, that's all.' I push my plate away, no longer hungry. Desperate to change the subject, and with the image of Phillipa's book group still in my head, I find myself asking the question I'd promised myself I wouldn't ask. 'I was wondering, Owen. Did Phillipa mention anything about me when you were there?'

He frowns. 'Mention you? No, why would she? The evening wasn't about you.'

That much I know. I hadn't even been invited.

'I know, but I was worried she might have said something to the others. Told them she wasn't happy with my work, that she didn't trust me to look after Lexi properly. I would have hated that... not being able to give my side of the story.'

While I wait for Owen's response, I think about the moment Phillipa rebuked me over taking Lexi to the pond. I still haven't told him I'm no longer working for her. How Phillipa had cut me off when I'd tried to explain.

Since then, I've tried not to dwell on what happened with Lexi. Tried not to imagine how much she will be missing me – for I've little doubt she is. In the few short weeks I'd been working at Phillipa's, the little girl's smile, once rare and a thing to coax, had become commonplace. The two of us had formed a close bond, and I try not to think how Phillipa might be taking her frustration at her curtailed freedom out on the little girl.

Without my job, the days at Pond Close stretch endlessly ahead of me, and I wonder what I'm going to do with myself. Look for another job, I suppose. My last search turned up nothing that interested me, but whatever I end up with, I'll have the consolation that Phillipa won't be my employer. Phillipa... a woman who can fawn over my famous husband whilst treating me like something off the sole of her shoe.

Thank God for small mercies.

'As I said.' There's a note of irritation in Owen's voice. 'You weren't mentioned.'

'Were they all there?' I can't let go of the idea of him at the book group. In prime position to pick up more information about everything that's happened in the cul-de-sac – not just now, not just Kevin, but the things that went on before we'd even thought about moving here.

Owen links his fingers together. Elbows on the table. 'Who?'

'The neighbours? The wives?'

He takes another sip of his coffee. Thinks about my question. 'There were about eight people there, but, apart from Phillipa, only two from the close.'

'Which ones? Simone?' I steel myself to ask, even though

I'm sure she wouldn't have been with her husband missing. 'Kevin's wife.'

He pulls a face. 'No, not her. That common one from across the green, you know the footballer's wife, and Pam the other side of us. Except she left early. Maybe she isn't partial to thrillers.'

'Or maybe she's not partial to *us*. Have you seen the way she looks at us, Owen? Geoff too.'

Owen rubs the side of his face, his beard rasping under his palm. 'I can't say I've noticed.' But from the way he's said it, I know he's lying. He will have noticed but stored the information away somewhere. In the room in his head marked *Things to process later*, most likely. Where it will join the many other things that inhabit that space... mostly things I've said or done that he's misunderstood or not comprehended. Like my disappointment at leaving our old house and coming here.

Sometimes, I wonder what it must be like to see the world like my husband does – as if through the wrong end of a telescope. Everything shrunk to its lowest common denominator. Sequences of events stripped of emotion like a carcass picked clean by vultures. The flesh put back on them only when they become part of his novel. Reaction, feeling, response, passion – flowing from the part of his brain that's closed to me, to his fingers. Then from his fingers to the keyboard. The process giving his work the emotional depth that has become his trademark. What had pushed *Dead Air* into the bestseller list.

If only the reader knew what it had taken to put those emotions between the covers. Each one learnt rather than felt. I watch Owen sip the coffee I've made him. Even now, after everything, he's oblivious to the turmoil in my head. What I'm really feeling. If only I'd known, that day when I'd asked him to sign *Deep Breaths* for me, that the characters in his book would be more three-dimensional than him.

Yet, if I had that time again, I'd still have married him. Because, despite everything, despite James, the love I have for him is still strong. Probably always will be.

I try again. Desperate to find out more from Owen. Frustrated that I wasn't there to hear anything for myself. 'Did they talk about Kevin? Do you know what the others think has happened to him?' With Simone absent from the gathering, they might have talked freely, and I want to know what was said.

'They think, as I do, as the police do, that he's gone AWOL for a reason. Dodgy dealings I'm guessing. He always was a slippery fish.'

I take this in. Think about it. I don't say that it's odd no one mentioned he'd left behind a heavily pregnant wife. Clearly Owen hasn't thought about that.

'And what about the other thing?'

'What other thing?' He's no longer trying to hide his impatience with me.

'Did you get the chance to ask Pam about what happened all those years ago when Phillipa and Kayla fell out?'

'Yes, and I wish I bloody hadn't. She said it was a long time ago and no one else's business, then left without buying a book. Besides, she moved here in 1999 after it had all happened so was hardly a primary witness.' He shakes his head. 'I looked a right idiot. Thank God no one else heard me ask.'

I point to the jar of marmalade, defeated. 'Do you want some toast?'

Owen shakes his head. 'No, I need to get on.'

He pushes back his chair and takes his mug over to the sink. Leaves it on the side. When he's gone back upstairs, I take the mug and put it with mine in the dishwasher, then sit back down and open my laptop. My heart heavy at the thought of trawling through the job vacancies again.

I'm only on the first page when there's a knock on the front door. It's a small sound. Enough that I can hear it but not so loud it can be heard upstairs.

When I open the door, I'm surprised to see Simone standing there.

THIRTY-FIVE

RACHEL

'Hello, Rachel. Do you have a moment? There's something I need to talk to you about.' She hesitates, her voice lowering. 'In private. It's important.'

I take in her serious face, the strands of unruly hair that have escaped her band. I feel guilty for not having been round to see her since Kevin went missing, but something has stopped me.

'I'd ask you in but—'

'I don't want to come in.' Her face freezes into a frown. 'I just need to speak to you.'

I look back at the stairs. 'Now?'

'Yes. It won't take long. It's something you need to hear.'

'Is it about Kevin? Has he come home?'

She looks down. Sucks in her top lip. 'No. Look, Rachel. Come over to mine. What I have to tell you could be linked to it.'

I hesitate, but something tells me this time I need to hear what she has to say. What if she has information about our house? About Phillipa's connection to it... or the little girl, Maddie? I find my shoes and bag then, closing the door behind me as quietly as I can, I follow Simone down the drive.

'Let's not cut across the green,' I say, knowing Owen could see us if we did.

'No,' she replies, understanding.

We walk without speaking. Not as quickly as I'd like because Simone's pregnancy makes her slow. When we reach Simone's house, instead of going in the front door, we take the path around the side of the house. Simone unlocks the sliding patio doors that look identical to ours, and lets me into the large living room.

She slides the doors shut and lowers herself into the armchair next to the fireplace, but I remain standing.

'What's this about, Simone? Are you okay? I should have come over.'

'Please. I can't talk to you while you're hovering over me.' She gives a tight smile. 'Don't worry, I'm not about to try to force you to be my friend again, if that's what's bothering you.'

'Don't be silly.' But the hot rash of shame is already clawing its way up the skin of my neck. I know I treated her badly.

I sit on the settee opposite Simone, remembering how it had been the last time I was here. The belief I'd had that the seed of our friendship would develop into something more lasting. That warm feeling of belonging after years of it just being me and Owen. How quickly that had changed and all because of the stupid animosity between our husbands.

The silence expands. Simone is looking at me, and I'm unable to read her expression. It makes me nervous.

'Simone? What is this? What's going on?'

She strokes the hard bullet of her belly. It must only be a matter of weeks, days even, before her baby's due. 'This is awkward.'

It's obvious now, this has nothing to do with the little girl who died.

'Just tell me, okay?'

'All right.' She winces and adjusts her position. 'It's about Owen. You asked me if I could find out what went on with him and Kevin at university. The secret Kev mentioned... What it was. You wouldn't listen before but you have to know.'

I stare at her, not blinking. It seems a long time ago now. So much has happened since, and I'd almost forgotten I'd asked her. Forgotten how she'd tried to tell me before and I'd sent her away.

'Go on.' I'm here now, so I might as well hear it.

'Okay, but you might not like what I'm going to tell you. When I'd asked Kevin about Owen before, he'd been cagey. Had given me a potted version of their time at uni. It wasn't much but enough that I thought you should hear it, only I was pissed off that you'd dropped me without an explanation. But a night or two before he went missing, I asked again because I was curious. I must have caught him off guard because he told me.'

My heart is in my mouth. 'What did he say?'

Even though I'm nervous of what I might find out, I know I need to hear it. This secret Owen had at university has been bothering me since the day I overheard the two of them in his study.

Simone's eyes slide to a photograph that stands on a shelf above the fireplace – Kevin in a mortar board, a scroll in his hand. She pulls her cardigan around her as though she's cold. 'I don't know how much Owen has told you about his time at uni.'

I fold my arms against my discomfort. 'A little.' I look away from her, my eyes settling on the pile of baby clothing on the arm of the settee. On top is a bib, a letter M embroidered on it in pink thread. It's the same as the one I'd seen at Phillipa's house. I blink. Force myself to look back at Simone. 'What I *do* know is that Kevin wasn't a very good friend to him.'

Simone ignores my barb. Sits a little straighter, her eyes

avoiding mine as though she's trying to find the right words to tell her story. Something that won't have me running out of the door before she's finished.

'You're right, he wasn't. In fact, from what Kev's told me of that time, he was a bit of a dickhead... but Owen wasn't a saint either. There were things he did—'

I'm alert now. 'What things?'

Her eyes find mine again. 'There was this girl, Anna her name was. She was on his course, and they palled up quite quickly, even though they were very different.'

'How so?'

'Anna was outgoing, fun-loving. Always out at parties. Owen was pretty much the opposite. He was very studious and never quite understood the jokes people told... which often made him the brunt of them. He was different to the other students, and I think that's what Anna liked about him... that and his ambition. Apparently, he told everyone he'd be a successful crime novelist one day, that if Ian Rankin could do it, then anyone could. No one believed him of course – it wasn't as if he was even studying literature and was known for spouting a lot of nonsense back in those days.' She points at a copy of Owen's book that's on the table. One Owen would have signed with his pretentious flourish had she been at the book group. 'Little did they know.'

I lean forward in frustration. 'What about this girl then?'

Simone brushes a strand of hair from her eyes. 'Their friendship was purely platonic, she had a boyfriend apparently, but she and Owen were always together. In the lecture theatre. Around the campus. It seemed to work, but then something terrible happened. The boyfriend, Christian I think Kevin said his name was, was a bit of an idiot and didn't treat Anna very well. One night, on his way home from a party, he tripped and fell into the canal. He'd been drinking heavily, had taken a load of drugs too, they found out later. He was dead when they found him.'

'Jesus! Was Anna with him?'

She shakes her head. 'No. It was coming up to the end of year exams, and Owen must have gone on at her about their importance. Instead of going clubbing with Christian, she and Owen had been revising together.'

'So, what happened? What's any of this got to do with my husband?'

Simone clears her throat. 'After Christian died, it was a terrible time for Anna, but Owen was there for her. He'd call her a lot. Turn up at her halls of residence with gifts and food – things he thought she'd like. She'd thought it nice at first, but, after a few weeks, she started to complain to her friends about him, and it didn't take long for Kevin to hear about it. Owen was making her feel like she couldn't breathe. Was always there, always fussing, and she had no space to grieve. It wasn't only that, though. It was like Owen saw himself as her gatekeeper. He'd turn people away if they came to see her. Insisted Anna wasn't ready for visitors. It all became too much, and, eventually, she had to tell him it would be better if they didn't see so much of each other.'

Across the green, Owen will be sitting at his computer, unaware that he's being talked about. I wonder what he'd think if he knew.

'I don't see why you're telling me this. Okay, Owen went a bit too far, but I doubt he meant any harm. Knowing him, he would have thought he was doing the right thing. The poor girl had just lost her boyfriend. She—'

'He didn't stop, Rachel. That's the point.' Simone can't hide the frustration in her voice. 'He carried on going to Anna's halls of residence even after she'd told him not to. I know it's hard to hear, but in the end, she had to report him to the university authorities. It's a wonder he wasn't thrown out.'

'Says who?'

Simone looks awkward. 'Says Kevin.'

'I think that says it all, don't you?' I stand, aware of the push of blood through my veins. 'Owen was right. Your husband *is* poisonous. This is all second-hand information. Hearsay from the man who belittled and bullied someone simply because they were different. You don't know how the memories of it still hang over him, Simone. And you weren't even there when any of that stuff with Anna happened. Didn't even know Kevin then! What is it with that husband of yours? If I didn't know better, I'd say he was jealous.' I pick up my bag, realising the truth of what I've said. 'Yes, that will be it. He's pissed off with Owen's success. Miffed that the poor kid he bullied actually made something of himself. All this... this nastiness... you're only saying it to put the blame on Owen for his disappearance.' I spit out the words. 'For having *left* you.'

Simone pales. Her eyes are shiny with tears. 'That's not what this is about. But I need to tell you that if Kevin doesn't come home soon, the police will be back asking more questions. If they do, I'll have to tell them what I told you.'

'Then I will be happy to talk to them because as far as I'm concerned, it's *your* husband who has something to hide.'

'What are you talking about?'

We've come this far I might as well tell her my suspicions. 'A few nights ago, Owen was attacked. He said he slipped on the patio, but I don't believe him. He tried not to let me see, but he had bruises on his side... the marks made by a fist. Someone was waiting for him round the back of the house, and if the past's anything to go by, it's not hard to guess who was responsible, is it?'

I stop, knowing Simone will understand what I'm saying.

'You know that's impossible. Kevin went missing before that happened.'

'Exactly.' I've only just thought of this. 'Don't you see? He'd have known he'd never be suspected.'

Simone's expression hardens. 'They were kids back then, Rachel, but people change. You're right, I know I wasn't there when Owen and Kev were at uni, but I do know my husband. He might be many things, but he's not a liar and he's not violent.' With difficulty, she levers herself up from the chair, stands with her hand on her bump. 'Look, I'm just the messenger here. I'm only telling you this because you asked me to find out what Owen's secret was. I hoped you could talk to him and that maybe he'd be able to shed some light onto where Kevin might be, but, at the end of the day, it's up to you what you do with the information I've given you. You can believe what you like.'

I don't answer, scared of what I might say to this woman who I'd once hoped could be my friend. It's only when I get outside that I start to shake. I bend at the waist, hands on my knees, trying to stop the churning in my gut.

At first, I think it's the anger coursing through my veins that's caused these sensations, but then I see the gooseflesh that has risen on my arms. It's more than that. What my body is doing is reacting to the fear of the unimaginable. That what Simone has told me could be true.

I swallow hard. Straighten. I tell my legs to start walking. Across the road. Across the green. Along by the iron fence that was put there to stop another child drowning in that pond. Our house getting ever nearer. No longer caring if Owen sees me. That he'll guess where I've been.

The only thing I care about is the truth. Not Kevin's version of it. Not Owen's even. But the *real* truth. Because time is running out. Rumours have a habit of spreading, and if the rest of the close get wind of what Simone has told me, they'll turn against us, maybe agree with Phillipa that little Lexi isn't safe to be anywhere near us. They'll think I can't be trusted with a child's care, even though it's Phillipa they should be pointing the finger at.

My neighbour is linked in some way to Maddie's death, and I'll prove it. Even if the police couldn't.

THIRTY-SIX

RACHEL

When I get back home, Owen isn't in. He's taken the car, and I'm annoyed that he didn't tell me he was going out. But Owen's absence might work in my favour. It will give me the opportunity to have a thorough look around – something I haven't been able to do with him always in the house.

I let myself in. Stand in the hall and think. If people are going to believe me that Phillipa had something to do with the little girl's drowning, I need more than a photograph and a letter. And certainly more than gossip from a neighbour about her having been brought in for questioning after the incident.

In the kitchen, I stare at the wall which neither Owen nor I have had the heart or inclination to finish stripping, let alone repainting. Wondering if any more secrets lurk behind the vinyl tiles, I refill the bowl with warm water and, with the sponge, soak the frayed edges of paper around Phillipa's name. I'm too impatient to wait for it to soften and the result is I have to jab and shove at the paper with my scraper, frustrated at the way it comes off in tediously small pieces. But, despite my shoddy workmanship, it doesn't take long to see there is no more writing on the wall. Only what was there before: *Why Phillipa?*

I'd been crouching, but now I stand again, wiping my wet hands down the sides of my jeans. The kitchen isn't going to elicit anything new. I need to look somewhere else.

I climb the stairs, unsure of what I'm looking for and where to look for it. At the top of the stairs, I look at each of the rooms. There'll be nothing to see in our bedroom, I'm sure of it, and when I try the door of Owen's study, it's locked. I frown. Why is he wanting to keep me out? I'm his wife... what is it he doesn't want me to see?

The door of the spare bedroom stands open and I wander in. There's not a lot in the room, just a few packing boxes we haven't yet emptied and odd items of furniture that didn't fit in anywhere else. The room looks out onto the large lawn, the tall Leylandii at the end creating a dark hedge where anyone could hide from view if they wanted to.

Above my head is the loft hatch. I've never been up there, and now I'm wondering if this might be the place to start my search. I get the pole with the hook from the corner of the room and pull on the metal ring in the hatch. It swings down and, I pull again with the hook and drag the loft ladder into place.

The rungs of the ladder are hard under my socked feet as I climb up and poke my head into the dark space above me. I feel around with my hand, remembering how Owen had used a torch when he'd been up here before, and am rewarded when my fingertips touch it. I climb higher, push myself into the space so I'm sitting on the edge, my legs dangling, and turn on the torch. Light floods the attic.

There's not much to see, just a few of our empty packing boxes, a roll of dusty carpet and a couple of kitchen chairs with wobbly legs that the Brookners must have left. I'm disappointed, although I don't know what I'd been expecting. Bending at the waist so as not to bump my head on any of the rafters, I edge forward. The joists that run from end to end have been covered at some time by ill-fitting sheets of hardboard and, as I make my way over to the far end of the space, they move beneath my feet.

Something touches my face and I jump back before realising it's a strand of cobweb that's loosened from one of the rafters. I brush it away, feeling foolish. There's nothing to see here. Nothing to help me link the past to the present.

I'm above our bedroom now, and it's only as I'm turning, one hand on the rafters to steady myself, that I see it – a small white box half hidden in the shadows. I drop onto one knee, reach out a hand and lift it from between the joists then, cradling it in my hand, I cross the wobbling boards to the loft hatch and climb down.

Once I'm safely back in the spare bedroom, I turn the box over. The plastic looks new, and I can't imagine how this unrecognisable object has anything to do with Phillipa or the little girl who lived in our house. Yet, all the same, my instincts are telling me what I've found is significant.

Leaving the box on the table on the landing, I cross to our bedroom and lean my elbows on the windowsill. Is that Owen's car parked in the straight piece of road at the end of our close? It certainly looks like it. But why is he sitting there and where has he been?

Simone's words come back to me, *as far as I'm concerned, it's your husband who has something to hide*. I didn't believe her when she'd said it, but why then is he sitting in his car at the end of the street as though afraid to come in?

As though there's something he doesn't want to tell me.

THIRTY-SEVEN

OWEN

Owen sits in his car at the end of their road. It's been half an hour or so since he saw his wife stride across the green and let herself into their house, and he knows he should go in.

Rachel's been at the Wellbecks' house, but what he doesn't know is why. It makes him uneasy and the question he asks himself is what she and Simone have been talking about? Has she been telling her about James? Because surely he can't be the only one to have noticed the change in his wife these last few days. The flush of her cheeks. The look she has in her eyes as though harbouring a secret. One that pleases her. One that she really should keep to herself.

Except, maybe, as he's feared, she already has told someone. Her feelings for the man so great, so exciting, she's been unable to keep them to herself any longer. He thinks of the humiliation if he's right. The shame. Without realising it, his hand has found its way to his bruised side, but when his fingers press into the soft flesh, he no longer winces. It's healing well and, when he lifts the edge of his shirt to look, the bruise has faded to an almost imperceptible yellow.

He thinks of Kevin. How his worries about the past, the

threat of an embarrassing unveiling of his secret, have vanished with the man. It's better for him that he's gone, and he can't help wondering if they'll ever find him. Ever discover where he went. He tucks his shirt back in. With Kevin AWOL, he won't have to be forever looking over his shoulder. *He* won't be crying over him, that's for sure, but what he doesn't understand is how unconcerned Rachel has been.

Owen looks across at their house, scanning the windows for a sight of his wife. Wondering what Rachel's doing, before his thoughts turn back to Kevin and the question that must be on everyone's mind.

Is he alive or dead?

Owen starts the car and enters the cul-de-sac. He parks in the drive, then lets himself into the house. Rachel will have tried the door of his study. Found it locked and asked herself why. Still, no matter, he's made good progress today. Can feel the end is near... the big finale. The thrill he always gets at this stage is with him once more. He can't tell Rachel about it yet – not until he's made the final touches, tied up all the loose ends, but once he's done that, they'll be able to celebrate properly. She'll see how he's returned to being the man he was when she first met him. Worth a hundred of James.

'Rachel?'

The house is quiet, and, for a moment, he thinks she might not be there. But she must be. He saw her go in. Where is she and what is she doing?

He climbs the stairs and is surprised to see his wife leaning on the banisters at the top. Looking down at him.

'I need to talk to you.'

For the first time in a long while, Owen feels the flutter of anticipation behind his sternum. Blood stirs in his veins. He wants to write it down – that look on her face, the way her voice is tight with accusation – but something is playing on his mind.

Did he forget to lock the door of his study? Does Rachel know how close he is to the end?

'What's the matter?' He looks at her uncertainly. 'Has something happened? Is it about Kevin—'

A shadow passes across Rachel's face. 'It's not about him. What I need to talk to you about is more important than that.'

'Ask away. I'm all ears.'

He cups his ears and laughs, but Rachel doesn't laugh with him. 'This isn't a joke. I want you to tell me the truth, Owen. I mean it. I don't have the time for your bullshit.'

'Now I'm intrigued.'

It's the truth. She's going to talk to him about James – that's what this is about, isn't it? But there's no guilt in her eyes, not any he can recognise anyway, and he's surprised to find he's glad. He's not ready for that conversation. If they don't talk about it, it means he can pretend it isn't happening. Can trick himself into believing they're okay. That it's still *him* she loves.

Owen unlocks the door of his study. The room is his sanctuary, the place where he feels most in control – the solid desk, the computer, his novels standing side by side on the shelf, giving him comfort. And, if ever there was a need for that comfort, it's now, because he's seen the white plastic box on the table on the landing. The sight of it sending spears of ice through his veins. How had she found it?

He stands back to let her in. Dreading what will come next. 'Let's talk in here. What did you want to know?'

Rachel spins the swivel chair round and sits, leaving him standing redundantly in the middle of the room. He doesn't like anyone else sitting in that chair and the sight of her in it makes him feel untethered.

Her shoulders are tense as though she's had to psych herself up to speak.

'Who was Anna?'

The question, so head-on, so direct, isn't the one Owen's been expecting and it confuses him.

'Anna?'

Rachel shakes her head in frustration. 'Your old friend, Owen. The one from university. It was a long time ago, I know, but there's no way you can have forgotten her.' She folds her arms. 'And if you say you have, I won't believe you.'

A picture of Anna drops into Owen's head. Clear. Cinematic. Dyed blonde hair cut into what she told him were Rachel Green layers. Tartan flannel shirt and low-slung stonewashed jeans. He pushes the image away.

'What about her?'

'You tell *me*. She was *your* friend, not mine.'

Owen pushes his hands into the pockets of his cords. Jingles his keys and loose change. Thinks. What is it she's *really* asking him?

'I don't know what you want me to say. Yes, she was my friend. She was on my course and we hung out together in the first year. Why are you asking me about her, Rachel? Has someone been saying something?'

But he knows that they must have and it's obvious who. He's not the only person in the close who knew Anna.

Rachel doesn't answer his question but asks another of her own. 'Is it true that after her boyfriend died, you kept on seeing her... even after she asked you not to?' She closes her eyes, pained. 'There's a name for that, Owen. Stalking.'

Owen's mouth slackens in disbelief. 'I never stalked her. What sort of nonsense is that?'

Why is Rachel saying this? He'd explained it all to the Student Support Officer. Surely he didn't now have to explain it to his wife. But he knows he has no choice.

'It was all a misunderstanding. Made worse by Kevin and his idiot friends.'

Rachel swivels the office chair so it's directly facing him. The squeak as it turns on its metal spindle grates on his nerves.

She fixes him with a stare. 'How so?'

'Isn't it obvious? He wanted me gone. Wanted them to chuck me out so he could have a crack at her. Look, Anna was grieving. I only wanted to help her, but Kevin got to her first. Messed with her head and made her think my concern was something else. Something it wasn't.'

'Why on earth would he do something as awful as that?' She looks at him in disbelief. 'What did he hope to get out of it?'

'I told you. He wanted *her*. It's what Kevin did back then. Turned people against one another. Made people believe his rubbish.'

Rachel looks uncertain now. 'So you're saying what Simone told me is untrue?'

'I'm saying Kevin's always had it in for me.' He feels again the hardness of the wall of the halls of residence as his body was pushed back against the brick. Kevin's voice in his ear. *What are you going to do, Two-Pack? Cry?*

A pointless thing to say as Owen never cried. His mother had seen to that.

How disappointed Kevin must have been when he'd been allowed to stay on the course with the proviso that he kept away from Anna. He knows how lucky he'd been as if the same complaint had been made today, things would have ended very differently. His time at university would have been cut short. His writing career a non-starter.

All because of Kevin. All because of that bastard.

'You have to believe me, Rachel. You don't know him like I do.'

Rachel looks at him, assessing him, and he has an over-whelming urge to ask her about James – whether she knows what she's doing. But he fights it, knowing that no good will come of it if he does. James is a different problem. One he needs to deal with on his own. When the time is right. When he has the energy.

He watches as Rachel gets up from his chair and moves to the window. She looks out, her hands on her hips.

'If you're right, if he really is as bad as you say, then these things that have been happening here – the card, that bruise on your side from the night I found you by the patio steps – are down to him.' She doesn't look at him, an odd expression on her face. 'If you ask me, it's a good thing he's gone. A very good thing.'

'I fell, Rachel.'

She turns on him. 'Stop it! Stop shielding him. I'm not stupid. Bruises like that don't come from falls. Someone attacked you and it was Kevin. I know it was. And those blood-stains on the wall... the writing. Didn't you see how quickly he dismissed it?' Her voice is rising now, like it had that time when he'd tried to question her about Jade. Like she's trying to convince herself, or him. 'He was covering for Phillipa. For whatever it is she did back then. No one threatens our family, no one, and I told him as much.'

She stops, looks down at her hands, and he senses she didn't want him to know that. It explains what he'd seen; Rachel had taken matters into her own hands.

Owen looks at his wife's flushed face and, not for the first time, wonders what she's capable of. This wife on whom he's come to depend. 'Please, Rachel. You're getting hysterical. That business with Jade has—'

She looks up at him as a child would. Her eyes wide. Pupils dilated. 'You know I hear her. Her cry. Something bad happened in this house, and she's trying to tell me what it was.' She steps back. Takes her phone out of her pocket. 'Maybe we should phone the police.'

'What?' Owen's mind is racing. This is not what he needs right now – Rachel freaking out, telling the police a load of nonsense. Not when the man's gone, out of their hair for good, hopefully. Not when the book is so nearly finished.

'Why won't you listen? I told you I fell and those dreams you've been having... they're simply your imagination.'

Rachel presses her palms to the side of her head in frustration. 'But why else would I wake to hear her crying? She's trying to warn me. Warn *us*.'

Owen steps back, away from her. Thinks quickly, knowing he can't let her spiral. What he's about to do could ruin everything, but he has no choice.

'Come with me.' He turns his back on her and goes out of the room. Picks the white box from the table and holds it out to her.

Rachel's looking at him strangely. 'I found that in the attic. Do you know something about it?' She takes the box from him. Turns it over in her hands. 'Owen?'

'Of course I know. It's a portable sound machine.'

'What's it for?' It's clear from Rachel's face that she has no idea what he's talking about.

Owen knows this is a pivotal moment in their relationship – one from which they might never recover. He has to tell her, though. Must stop her believing the very thing he's put into her head... that the ghost of the child who drowned, or Jade even, is trying to tell her something. He has to stop her from going to the police.

'Wait here.' He leaves her on the landing and goes into their bedroom. Rummages in the drawer of his bedside table until he finds the small controller. He presses one of the buttons and a child's cry breaks the silence.

There's a scream, and he hurries back to find Rachel with her hands pressed to her ears. The sound machine on the floor.

'Make it stop!' Rachel backs away from the noise that fills the landing. So loud there's nowhere to hide from it.

Owen silences the machine. He goes over to Rachel and

puts an awkward arm around her shoulders. 'Look, I'm sorry. I was doing it to help my book. When you told me Lisa Brookner imagined she heard crying in the house at night, it intrigued me. I thought if I could recreate that sound, see how you reacted when you heard it, I could use those feelings, those emotions, in my next project.'

He realises how stupid he'd been, how impetuous. All he'd ever wanted was for Rachel to be happy here. How had he imagined this would help?

Rachel is looking at him in a way she never has before. As though seeing him for the first time, *really* seeing him, and it's disconcerting. Her face is set glass-hard, the colour not yet returned to it. She pulls away from him.

'Are you trying to tell me I was an experiment for your bloody book!'

He bends and picks up the small plastic-cased box. 'You're always telling me I don't feel things enough. Not in the way you do anyway. I thought if I studied—'

Rachel shakes her head in disbelief. 'I'm your wife, not an object to be used in your pathetic attempt to awaken your *feelings*.' She spits out the word and his eyes move from her pinched white lips to the tight cords of her neck where red blotches are blooming against the white skin.

Such anger. It takes him back to the house he'd lived in as a child – the one Rachel had made him take her to. He sees himself at the top of the stairs, chin pressed to the banister. Hears again his mother's fists as they beat against his father's chest. The shrill cut of her voice. *You fucking bastard. Get the hell out of my house.* Then his father gone, the front door slamming behind him. His mother's head tilting back as she looks up the stairs and sees him. The same red blotches on her neck as his wife's. The same flashing eyes. *What are* you *gawping at?*

But this isn't his mother, this is Rachel, and he loves her more than life itself. For the first time in his marriage, he truly believes she might leave him, that his stupidity has caused it, and he doesn't know what to do with this knowledge.

He takes off his glasses and wipes them on the bottom of his T-shirt. 'I'm sorry, Rachel. You have to believe me, I meant no harm. I see now how stupid it was. How thoughtless.'

Colour is returning to her cheeks. She closes her eyes, and he counts the rise and fall of her chest before she opens them again. *Six, seven, eight.*

'Please forgive me, Rachel.' He's pleading. Something he's never done before.

She covers her face with her hands. 'You made me believe it was real. Made me believe my own delusions.' She thumps her forehead with the heel of her hand. 'It was all in my head. Everything.' She looks at him accusingly. 'And you put it there.'

'I'm sorry. I don't know how many times I can say it.'

She gets up. Goes to the door. 'I need some space, Owen. Time to think.'

'I understand.'

She's about to leave when she thinks of something, turns back to him. 'The congratulations card that came through the door when we first moved in. I suppose that was your doing too. More grist for the mill. Another prop to see how I might react.' She paints quotes in the air. 'Emotional research.'

Owen doesn't answer. After his mother had died, he'd found the card at the back of a drawer along with condolence cards for the loss of his baby sister. He'd thought that by sending the card, Rachel would take it as a good omen. A sign that one day she would have a baby. But it had backfired. Rather than helping Rachel feel settled in the house, she thinks he did it to provoke an emotion that he could harvest and use in his books. It is, after all, what he'd done with the sound machine and now he wonders if maybe she's right. If somewhere, deep down in his subconscious, it was what he'd always intended. What an idiot he's been. What a fucking *idiot*. Putting his book before his wife.

Rachel shakes her head and turns away from him. Leaving him on the landing, she goes downstairs and soon he hears the slam of the front door.

He goes to the window – it's starting to rain, tears of it running down the pane. Rachel didn't take a coat; she'll get wet. He can no longer see her, but he can guess where she's gone. Today is the day she'll sleep with James, he can feel it, the certainty hitting him with the force of a wrecking ball. And he's driven her to it. He pats the pocket of his jeans, feels the car key's solid shape. Lack of a car won't stop her, though – it never has before. She'll phone for a taxi.

He takes the car key out of his pocket and looks at it. Goes downstairs and steps out of the house. Hoping he's not too late. Wondering what he'll do if he is.

THIRTY-EIGHT

RACHEL

James takes the bag I'm carrying from me and hooks it over his arm.

'Thank you,' he says.

I walk beside him, our arms brushing. Though whether it's deliberate or not, I'm unsure. 'For what?'

James smiles. 'For messaging me. For suggesting this outing.'

'It's nothing to get excited about. Just some sandwiches and some crisps I picked up on the way. Thank goodness the rain stopped... I hope you like coronation chicken.'

'I like anything if it's with you.'

We've left the lake and the weir behind us and have taken the narrow path between the trees. There's a tangle of undergrowth and thin branches that we have to push our way through, but now the rough path has widened again to a clearing. I stop at the edge of the trees, smiling at how the sun brightens the long, wet grass.

I take James's hand. 'Do you think anyone ever comes here?'

'It doesn't look like it.'

At the edge of the clearing, sheltered by the trees, is a semi-circle of cut logs. They're positioned horizontally on the pine-strewn ground, and after testing one with my hand to check it's dry, I sit. Look up at James and pat the rough bark beside me. It feels a million miles away from the still lake. The rush of water from the weir no longer audible.

James sits next to me. Places the bag of food between us and waits, sensing I have something to say.

I turn to him. 'I feel like I'm going out of my mind. Am scared my head will explode if I don't talk things through. I'm sorry, James. I had no one else.'

He laughs. 'Thanks.'

'You know what I mean.'

He doesn't answer but digs into the bag between us and takes out a packet of sandwiches. 'I'll let you do the honours.'

James has this way about him. A certain calmness and knack of making things feel ordinary, not quite so bad, even when my headspace is filled with a writhing mass of serpents. Our fingers touch as he hands me the packet and the serpents still. If I hadn't ended our relationship, maybe things would never have got so bad in the years that followed. I would have had someone to open up to, and, in turn, I might have been a stronger support for Owen.

Instead, we'd kept our feelings tightly to ourselves, and Owen had slid into a depression that had made it impossible for him to write as he once had – the words that would have given life to his novel, hidden from him. Was it any wonder his last book, *Tight Spaces*, had flopped? Was it any wonder we'd had to leave our beautiful home and move to Pond Close?

'So, what is it I need to know, Rachel?'

The plastic crinkles beneath my fingers as I open the sandwiches on my lap. I take in a deep lungful of pine-scented air. 'Owen did something unacceptable.'

'That doesn't sound good.'

'It wasn't... isn't,' I say, handing him a sandwich.

Usually, I feel guilty talking to James about Owen's failings, but today I don't care. Whether he knows it or not, this time he went too far.

James takes a bite of his sandwich. 'So, what did he do? Don't keep anything from me.'

I'm used to this. James likes to know everything, even when it's about my husband, and the ease with which I can talk to him makes me wonder, sometimes, if perhaps I tell him too much. Wasn't it for that very reason I ended it the first time? That feeling of overtelling swelling and stretching the guilt that was already there. Making me feel like the worst wife in the world.

But I can't keep this to myself, so I tell him about the card Owen sent and the sound machine.

James places the sandwich on the log beside him. 'You thought it was a real child in your house or, what, a ghost?'

'I don't know.' I've never talked to him about Jade and I don't mention her now. 'But, whatever I thought, I'm not sure I can forgive him.'

Because, even now, I find it almost impossible to believe he could do such a thing. That he'd really had no idea how it would affect me.

'Well, that was clearly very thoughtless of the man.'

I take a bite of my sandwich in a bid to cover my disappointment. *Thoughtless.* I'd expected more of James. The word is too mild. Weak. Where is his disgust? His repulsion at what Owen had done?

'You think I'm overreacting?' Not him too. Please let that not be the case.

'I didn't say that. It was wrong of him, shocking, and I'm glad you told me.' James takes my hand and brushes his thumb across the back of it, making my skin shiver. 'You have every right to be angry. The man's an idiot and can't see what's under his nose. Are you going to leave him, Rachel? Has it come to that?'

I try to read his voice. What is he hoping? I'd made it clear, right from the early days, that I'd never leave Owen and I'd thought James had accepted that. My being married had given us the freedom to be honest with one another in a way we might not have, had I been single.

I'm wondering now if he's changed his mind. If *I* have.

I slip my hand from beneath his. 'I admit that I thought about it. Came to the conclusion that I'd never be able to be in the same room as him again, let alone stay married to him.' I remember the rain plastering my hair to my face. Drenching my clothes. Not caring. 'I felt so sick that he could do that to me.'

I look at the sandwich. The dressing from the coronation chicken has stained the bread yellow and my hunger has left me. James's sandwich lies untouched on the log beside him, and I know he feels the same.

'I'm going to tell you something I haven't told you before, James.'

'Yes?' He looks at me with interest.

I keep my tone light. 'That's if you think you can handle another revelation.'

'It depends on whether you're all right with me knowing.'

Am I? I no longer know.

'It's something that happened before I met you – I wasn't ready to talk about it before, but I am now. Do you remember how I told you we had started a round of IVF after failing to fall pregnant? How when it didn't work, we were told another round would be unlikely to be any more successful?' He nods and I stop, unexpected tears blurring my eyes. Making the trees swim. 'Well, there's something I left out.'

James's eyes widen slightly. 'You don't have to tell me if you'd rather not. I'd understand.'

'I know that, but you need to hear this, James, as it affects you too. If it hadn't happened, you and I would never have met. Never have started this *thing* we have.'

'I see.' Is that sadness I hear? I'm not sure.

I carry on, unable to look at him. 'What I never said was that I wanted to go for it, even though the odds were against us, but Owen didn't. He thought it would be wasting everyone's time... ours and the hospital's.' The log is hard, small twigs sticking into my legs, even though I'm wearing jeans. A weak sun filters into the clearing where we sit, but behind the tall pines that surround us, there is only darkness. I adjust my position to get more comfortable. 'I've never told anyone this, and I guess I hide it well, but the cold hard truth is I resent Owen for saying that. For not having had enough faith. For not putting my feelings first.'

Sunlight throws a black and white patchwork of patterns across James's legs. His voice has turned serious. 'So, he never knew how you felt?'

'No, he never did. I think now I should have fought harder for what I wanted, but perhaps it's for the best.'

He puts his head on one side. 'How do you make that out?'

'Because I'm no longer sure who Owen is.' I touch my fingertips to my forehead. 'I'm frightened he's not the man I thought he was when I married him. He's so distant. Doesn't want to touch me... hold me. Living in Pond Close has made it worse, and I think it's because being in a cul-de-sac of families has made him resentful that I haven't been able to give him a child.'

James's voice is dry, matter-of-fact. 'Or the other way around.'

'Maybe.'

'And you think that if you'd been successful, if the IVF had worked and you'd had a child together, things would be different.'

'I think they might.' I stop, choking on the words. Hating the image it brings up... me a mother. Something I'll never now be. A child asleep on my lap. The heavy weight of her head on my shoulder as I carry her up to bed.

Her. Never him. A child like Jade. Like Lexi.

James turns to me. 'So you'll leave him. You've decided.'

There's something in his expression that makes me think my instinct was right. He prefers that Owen and I are married. Doesn't want anything to happen that will upset the status quo. Change what we have.

I feel a flash of panic. 'I don't know.'

'Your husband is a thoughtless bastard, but, from what you've told me, it's how he's always been.' He spreads his fingers out on his knees. 'You're the only one who can make the decision, but you need to think, honestly, about what it was that attracted you to him in the first place. Maybe, deep down, whatever it was is still there.' He smiles at me. 'What I will say is what you're doing now is a good thing. It's important you feel you can talk freely. About your feelings. Your fears. Even if only with me. Your loyalty is to be commended, but what you need to ask yourself is whether Owen is deserving of your love.'

James gets up. He stands in front of me and holds out his hands. When I take hold of them, he pulls me up so our bodies are pressed together. He puts his arms around me so we're closer still and runs his hand up my back, his fingers sliding into my hair, tangling with the strands.

Our faces are inches apart, our eyes locked, and I drink him in. Try to supress the butterfly wings of anticipation that I know are wrong but won't be stilled.

'The question you need to ask yourself is does Owen make you feel like this?' James dips his head and kisses my neck. My heart falters and I close my eyes.

'Please, James. Don't.'

It was only ever words before. Nothing physical.

'Or this?' His lips draw lower, to my collar bone, my throat, before rising again to meet my own.

I fight to tame the wild rhythm of my heart. This is how it should be with Owen. How I've always *wanted* it to be. But this isn't Owen, it's James. I pull back, scared he won't believe what I'm about to say. 'I don't love you, James. It's Owen I love.'

He cups my face in his hands, his eyes roving my face. 'It's all right. You don't have to love me. This is enough.'

'Are you sure?'

'I'm sure.'

He brings his lips to mine again and, this time, I don't resist. We both know what's going to happen, and I no longer care. It's what I want, and that's all there is to it.

Three years ago, I'd thought I'd been ready to give James up.

I'd been wrong.

THIRTY-NINE

RACHEL

Owen is in the back garden, cutting the grass. It's a rare sight to behold as gardening has always been *my* thing, not his, but today I'm feeling under the weather, a sore throat starting. The grass, both front and back, has grown long again, and the last thing I want is for Phillipa to have an excuse to come round. Not because I care what she thinks of us any more, but because I can't bear the thought of seeing Lexi. What it would do to me. The spare key Phillipa gave me is still in the pot beside the front door, and I've decided to post it through her letterbox rather than give it to her. It's better that way – for all of us.

Over the last couple of days, when I've gone outside, I've heard Lexi crying. The hopeless cry of a child who knows their mother isn't coming to pick them up. It breaks my heart not knowing what's going on at Number 3, and I can't help wondering whether Phillipa has gone back to her old ways: leaving her in her cot or playpen for her own convenience. Ignoring her when she's hungry. Once or twice, I've tried to catch Talia when I've seen her outside, but although she's given me a shy smile, the older girl has clearly been told not to speak to me. Neil too – the boy no longer returning my wave when he goes out on his bike.

I've been stripping the beds and am in the spare bedroom where the duvet covers and sheets are still in boxes, yet to be unpacked. From here the whine and rumble of the lawnmower is louder, cutting through my thoughts.

I take a sheet from the box and go to the window. With my forehead pressed to the glass, I look down on Owen as he walks the mower up to the Leylandii then back down again, keeping the stripes even. He's right below me now, and I can't help but notice how thin his fine hair has got and how long. He'd rejected my offer to find him the number of a hairdresser, one who'd come to the house, with a curt reply that he'd deal with it in his own good time. His book was his priority and anything else could wait. But it makes him look older, slightly unsavoury, and I don't like it.

As I watch him, I try to do what James suggested – not focus on the hair, the old baggy clothes Owen insists on wearing, but remembering what it was about the man that had first attracted me to him. Had made me fall in love with him.

I close my eyes, press the sheet to my lips, and force myself to remember. Surprised when the image comes back quickly. Filling my head. Making my heart quicken. Not Owen how he is now but how he'd been back then. The night we'd met.

I picture again how his face had glowed with an inner light – nothing to do with the spotlight that had lit the stage but all to do with the pride he'd felt in what he had accomplished. Hear once more the command in his voice as he'd read an extract from *Deep Breaths*. Owen looked like a man who had everything he'd ever dreamt of. His career on the up, any troubles he'd once had, behind him.

I open my eyes again, the image fading. How on earth am I supposed to keep hold of the feelings I had for him back then when he's played such a terrible trick on me?

Above my head is the loft hatch and the metal steps Owen climbed up in order to secrete the sound machine between the joists above our bedroom. I clutch the sheet tighter, remembering how the terrible sound had echoed when he'd pressed the button on the control. Bringing back memories of the nights I'd woken in the dark. The child's cry calling to me.

He'd begged me to forgive him, but can I? Could anyone?

Below me, Owen walks with a heavy tread. Up and down. His head bowed. The buoyant mood of a few days ago, when he'd told me his book was going well, deflated after the argument we'd had. The one instigated by the ridiculous stunt he'd pulled in the name of his art. Since then, we've been avoiding each other, taking it in turns to have the car... to leave the close. Anything rather than face up to the truth. That we've never really known each other. Or ourselves, if I'm being honest.

I still don't know if I'll leave him. If I could bring myself to do it. I push away the memory of James's hands, his lips, not wanting to confuse my thoughts further. I need to concentrate on Owen. Decide what I want.

That bloody book he's writing! It's taken over Owen's life, mine too, and I have a sudden desperate need to read it. To find out what Owen's done. How he's taken my emotions – my anxiety, fear and anger – and used them to flesh out his work.

A part of me is in that book and I have a right to see it.

The mower rumbles on, and I know I have to take the chance. Dropping the sheet onto one of the packing cases, I hurry out of the room and try the handle of his study. To my surprise, the door opens and I go in, leaving the door ajar so that I'll hear if the mower stops.

I go to Owen's computer, wake it up with the hope that his novel will still be open on the screen, but it isn't. And when I click on the file titled *Book 7*, a message comes up telling me that I need to put in a password.

This is new.

I stare at the screen in frustration, desperately trying to think what the password might be, but Owen isn't stupid. It will be something I'd never think of.

Leaving the computer to go back into standby, I slide open the drawer of the desk instead. Rummage around to see if there is anything new in there. Notes he's made, something linked to me perhaps. Surprised when I find there is.

The card is there, the one with the baby in the crib. A card which, despite his protestations, I'm convinced Owen sent to our house to gauge my reaction. Watching me. Harvesting my emotions for his book.

The sight of it fills me with disgust... that he'd kept it.

But there's something else. It drops from inside the card and floats to the floor, its edges fluttering in the draught from the door. Picking it up, I see it's an article cut from a newspaper. Only a column or two with a photograph. I place it on Owen's desk and smooth it out, my heart beating loudly in my ears as I realise what it is.

The article about the dead child, Maddie.

Why the hell has Owen got this?

I remember the question I'd asked him when Simone had first told me about the tragedy. *Did you know about this?* And his answer, *Of course not.* Yet here is the article in his desk drawer – not printed off from the internet but torn from a newspaper.

'What are you doing?'

I turn. Owen is behind me, his face set. I'd been too engrossed in my thoughts to listen out for the lawnmower. Hadn't heard it stop.

'I found this.' I point at the article that's on Owen's desk, not bothering to explain how it came to be there as we both know I've been snooping. There's no point in denying it.

Owen freezes. Recovers. He comes to my side and studies the photograph. 'It's the little girl who drowned.'

'I know. But why do you have it, Owen?' I pick it up and shake it at him. 'What was it doing in your drawer?'

'You know the answer to that.' He picks the page up and folds it neatly. Puts it back inside the card.

I stare at him, wondering what I'm missing. 'You're wrong. I have no idea. You said you knew nothing about what happened in this house. You lied to me.'

'You're right, I did and I'm sorry.' It's said without emotion.

Owen drops the card into the open drawer and slides it shut. 'It happened because I was desperate, Rachel. At rock bottom. My life spinning out of control. The IVF, James, *Tight Spaces* failing to get onto any bestseller list. I needed something to stimulate me. Get the creative juices going again. Growing up near here in the eighties and nineties I'd known about what had happened in Pond Close. Had read about it in the paper. When, quite by chance, this house was sent to us by the estate agent, it was like manna from heaven.'

'Manna from heaven,' I repeat, hardly believing what I'm hearing.

'Exactly. I knew that if I could imbibe some of the atmosphere, the sadness of the place, I would recover. My writing would recover. I had no thought that we would actually buy the place, just wanted to go and look at it.' His eyes search mine as though willing me to understand. 'But, as soon as I stepped through that front door, I knew I had to have it. The aura... it was too strong to resist. You feel it too... I know you do. I managed to persuade you that it was the perfect house in the perfect close and we moved here. Except, once we'd actually moved in, the place wasn't the muse I thought it would be. My writing stalled even before it had started.'

I'm trying hard to grasp it all.

'Which was why you moved it up a notch. The sound box. The card.'

'Not the card, I really did think that you'd see it as a good omen, but the other thing... yes, I'm afraid so. I did it for my writing, but I did it for you too – for our financial security. I didn't think beyond how it would make my books better. Didn't realise it would make you hate the house.' His voice breaks and he sinks to his haunches, his hands covering his face. 'Don't leave me, Rachel. I don't know what I'd do without you.'

I stare at him wide-eyed. I've never seen him cry before. Didn't know he was capable of it. The sight of those tears sends a stab of pain through my heart, and I realise it's because I still love him. But he needs help, and I'm not sure I can be the one to give it to him.

'We can't go on like this... You know that, don't you?' I squat beside him, put a hand on his back, hating to see him in such pain. 'Opening up is a good thing.' I think of my talks with James. 'I know that.'

Owen lowers his hands. The whites of his eyes are red and his cheeks damp with tears. 'I'm not so sure.' He closes his eyes as though seeing something he doesn't want to see, then opens them again. 'You've been seeing James. You've slept with him.'

The shock of his words hits me like a fist. The guilt that follows closely on its heels, rendering me speechless.

'I can't blame you,' he continues. 'Like everything else, I drove you to it.'

I can't look at him. Can't lie either.

'I'm sorry. But it's over now. You have to believe me, it's true. Get up, Owen. Please.'

Owen does as I ask. He walks to his office chair and slumps into it. 'This is such a mess. Such a bloody awful mess.'

I'm not sure what to do now. What to say. It has been a day of revelations, to say the least, and I'm not sure how to deal with any of them.

'Look, Owen. Why don't you lie down... have a rest? You look done in. I'll go downstairs, and when you're ready, we'll have some tea and talk about it. For the moment, though, I think we both need space to think, don't you?'

Owen fumbles in his pocket for his handkerchief. Blows his nose.

'Perhaps you're right.'

I place a tentative hand on his arm. 'I am.'

Leaving him in his study, I go down to the kitchen and am surprised when, a few minutes later, I hear him on the stairs. When he comes into the room, his eyes are bright and he can't keep still.

'I've been thinking, Rachel. It's a long time since we've been out anywhere. How about I book somewhere for dinner tomorrow night? My surprise. It will be easier to talk somewhere neutral rather than in this place.' His arm gesture encompasses the whole room. 'Especially after everything.'

I'm not sure what to say. The last hour or so has left me with little appetite, and I can't imagine it ever returning. But it's not just that. If I'm honest, I'm suddenly scared of how it might be. The two of us trapped by a table, ordering food we have no stomach for. Attempting to talk about things we should have talked about a long time ago.

'Please, Rachel.' He looks at me with pleading eyes. 'I'm really trying here, and I think you owe it to me, to *us*, to try too. I'll find a nice place. Somewhere you'll like.'

I give a weary sigh. 'All right.'

He smiles at me. 'That's great.' There's a pause and the smile slips a little. 'I need one thing from you, though.'

'What's that?'

'Your word that you'll tell him.'

'Tell him?'

'That it's over.'

I nod. 'You have my word, Owen.'

'Then I'll go and make that booking.'

He goes back to his study, and I stand at the bottom of the

stairs, waiting until I hear the door shut. Only then do I take out my phone.

I'm sorry, James, I type. *It's over.*

It's not hard to do. Since I had sex with James, I've felt the heavy weight of guilt because I'd never meant for it to go so far. Had only wanted to be close to him. Open up to him. But I'm worried now I've opened up too much. Those things I'd said about the IVF, how I'd resented Owen for not giving it another try, maybe I should have kept them to myself. Will he accept my decision?

Now I've typed the words and pressed send, I should feel guilt's release, but I don't. It's only when I'm back in the kitchen filling the kettle that I realise why. It's because of two things... two very different things.

The first is it's come to me that Owen never explained how it was he had the newspaper article in his possession. The second is that, with those few words from my husband, *I know you slept with James*, our roles have reversed.

I am no longer the accuser. I am the accused.

FORTY

RACHEL

Despite the sleeping tablets I took last night, I've woken up early, my head groggy, a crowd of faces filling my head: Kevin, Phillipa, Maddie, James. And when Jade's face joins them, I make myself get up, leaving Owen snoring softly to go downstairs and make some tea.

My throat feels thick, my eyes sore, and even though I try, I can't stop the thoughts that keep pressing in. Whether Lexi is safe with Phillipa now I'm no longer there to watch over her, whether I can trust Owen after what he's done, whether James will accept that it's over. If only I had a crystal ball to show me the future because, in the past, as Owen likes to tell me, my judgement has been skewed. The decisions I've made questionable.

I drink my tea at the kitchen table, watching as the sky through the window lightens, and when I finish it, it's still only six.

Not wanting to go back to bed, I take a box of cereal from the cupboard and pour the remains into a bowl. I pour milk over it, then squash my feet into the gardening shoes I've left by the front door and take the empty box to the recycling bin round the side of the house.

I'm just coming back when I see a movement, hear the sound of an engine. A police car is turning into our cul-de-sac, and I stand in my dressing gown watching it. Is it Kevin? Have they found him?

But the car doesn't continue around the green. Instead, it stops in front of Phillipa's house. I don't have time to question what I'm seeing as, before the officers have had a chance to get out, Phillipa has burst through her front door. Her silk dressing gown flowing behind her, she runs down the drive, oblivious to the small stones on the drive that must be jabbing at her bare feet.

'She's gone!' She throws herself at the car, her palms slapping at the passenger window. 'She was in her cot and now she's not there!'

A female police officer has got out of the driver's side. With a solemn face, she goes round the other side of the car and puts an arm around Phillipa. 'It's all right, Mrs Druce. We're here now. Let's go inside and you can tell us what happened.'

She leads her away from the car and back up the drive to the front door where Carl and the two older children are now gathered. The officer who had been in the passenger seat, a young man with an acne-scarred face, gets out now. No one has noticed me yet, but as he approaches the others, he turns suddenly, and I'm caught in his gaze: a rabbit in the headlights.

He looks at me a moment, then away again. Without saying anything, he follows the others into Phillipa's house and the door closes, leaving me standing on my porch, dread filling every part of my body. Because what I've witnessed has dragged back a memory of Jade's mother, Julie. How she'd run across the damp grass of my back garden towards the pond where Jade and I were standing, shouting her little girl's name. And this memory is quickly followed by another – the police questioning me in my living room. The answers I'd struggled to give.

Jade hadn't been missing, but Lexi is, the truth of it written across Phillipa's face as her palm had made contact with the window of the police car. I stare at the thin yellow strips of light between the shutters at her window. I start to shiver uncontrollably. What will Phillipa be saying to them?

Wrapping my dressing gown tighter around me, I go back into my house, for what else can I do? My cereal is now soggy, so I pick it up and empty it into the bin – no longer hungry after what I've witnessed.

Little Maddie drowned and now Lexi has disappeared. Soon the police will be round here, and I'll need to tell them what I know about Phillipa. I sit down and go through everything. Teenage Phillipa had been Kayla's best friend. I'd found a lock of Maddie's hair and a photograph of her as a baby with her face scrawled over in marker pen. Then there was the letter – the one where Kayla had said she knew Phillipa was resentful of her daughter, believing her presence left no space for their friendship, and that she no longer wanted to see her. It's woefully little, I know.

I chew on my bottom lip. What if I told them about the handprint I'd seen on Lexi's leg? The way she clearly neglected her own child. Would it be enough for them to believe her? If Phillipa had been responsible for Maddie's drowning, it wouldn't be a huge leap to come to the conclusion she might have harmed her own child for the same reason.

Maybe she felt Lexi had come between her and her husband. That the child, conceived so unexpectedly, so inconveniently, had been the reason Carl had run into the arms of Chantelle.

My thoughts are getting muddled – just the idea of the police and their questions filling me with panic. What I need is more evidence to link Phillipa not only to Maddie's death but to her own child's disappearance. I look around me, my eyes stopping at the wall with its writing. I can show them that, but I need to know more about Phillipa and the people who once lived in my house, for if Kayla had been a teenager when she'd had Maddie, her parents would have been living in this house too. Who were they and what did they know of the events that happened under their roof? Because no one in this bloody close seems to want to talk about it.

My brain is working feverishly. If only I could find them. Ask them what they thought happened. What they thought of Phillipa.

Reaching for my laptop, I google the information I'm after and click on the link that's given. It takes me to the Land Registry Search, and I read that, for a fee, I can have the Title Register emailed to me. I find my credit card, enter the details of our property and pay. I want to know more about Maddie's family. My heart is beating quickly as I click to confirm. Hopefully, it won't take too long to find out because time is something I don't have.

I wrap my arms around me. More than ever, I feel Maddie's presence in the house. Owen was behind the child's cry that woke me, but I know that the little girl is calling out to me from beyond the grave.

Wanting me to hear her.

Wanting me to know the truth.

FORTY-ONE

OWEN

Owen sits on the end of his bed, his head in his hands. He'd heard Rachel get up. Had stood at the window and watched her stamp around to the side of the house, a cereal box clutched to her chest. Feet clad in her old gardening shoes.

As the police car had rounded the corner of their close and stopped outside their neighbours' house, he'd seen her freeze. Take a step back into the shadow of the porch.

He'd watched, curious, as Phillipa had run out. Thrown herself at the car, her lips moving soundlessly. He could guess what she was saying, though. Could deduce it from the way she turned and pointed to her small daughter's window. The way the female police officer had put her arm around her and escorted her back to the house. That look on Phillipa's face – he'd seen it before on Jade's mother. He sifts through the list of emotions he stores in his head until he makes a match. Is floored by it. That look is the same one his wife wore when the consultant had told them they'd never have a child of their own.

Despair.
Desperation.

Owen lowers his hands and grips his knees. He thinks of his wife who has not yet come back to bed.

Oh, Rachel. He stares at his reflection in the mirror on the chest of drawers. *My darling wife. What have you done?*

FORTY-TWO

RACHEL

Owen pulls out a chair. 'I hope you like it here. It's had some good reviews.'

'It's very nice.'

I take my seat and look around me, taking in the modern paintings with their little white stickers in the corners. The wide windows looking out onto the car park. I can't believe that I'm in the same restaurant I'd been to with James. What hand of fate has brought me here? I watch Owen as he takes off his coat and drapes it over the back of his chair. Is this deliberate?

We are at a different table, thank goodness, to the one I'd sat at with James, but the waitress is the same one I'd had before. I don't look at her, not wanting to know what she'll think of the man who takes his place opposite me. His hair draping over the collar of his shirt. His glasses misting in the heat of the room.

I dip my head to the menu, trying to find something I'll be able to eat, for my appetite hasn't returned. Has shrunk further since Lexi's disappearance and the visit we'd had from the police this morning.

Unable to choose, I look up at Owen. 'What are you going to have?'

'Let me see.' I watch his finger run down the menu, and for a horrible moment, I think he's going to choose the seafood risotto, the meal James had chosen, but he doesn't.

'I fancy a steak.' He places the menu on the table. 'Yes, a steak... with peppercorn sauce. Want the same?'

I shake my head. My throat is still sore and I'm feeling hot. I should have taken some paracetamol before I came out.

'I'll have the seafood risotto.' It's out before I can stop it. My treacherous brain wanting to take me back to that first meeting I'd had with James after he'd contacted me again.

I feel the heat burn my cheeks, but Owen doesn't seem to notice. 'Good choice.'

The waitress comes over. She looks at me curiously as she takes our order, and I notice how she doesn't linger at Owen's side as she'd done with James. Simply taps on her screen and nods.

She turns to go, but Owen clicks his fingers, the action making me cringe with embarrassment.

'I'd like to change our drink order, if I may.' He adjusts his tie. 'We'll have a bottle of the Moet.'

I stare at him. Lean towards him, my voice a hoarse whisper. 'No, Owen. It's too much and what's there to celebrate? Lexi could be dead for all we know. Drowned.'

My voice catches and I cover my face with my hands. Today, Simone told me they'd found Lexi's little pink coat by the weir. The shock of it still hasn't left me. Only a few days ago, I'd been sitting on the bench opposite the rushing water, talking to James – something I'd failed to mention to the police.

'Lexi isn't our responsibility, Rachel. We shouldn't let it spoil our night out. We've told the police everything we know, and I can't believe they hadn't thought that there might be a link between her disappearance and the Wellbecks. I wouldn't put it past the bastard to have crept back to the close last night and snatched the child. They were idiots to dismiss my concerns.

Anyway...' He sits back, fingers laced behind his head. 'We *do* have something to celebrate.'

I stare at him blankly. Owen's idea that it could be Kevin who took Lexi is ridiculous for what reason would he have to harm her? The police will be back, I know it, because although neither of us had mentioned Jade, it won't take long for them to find out.

No, I can't think there's anything to celebrate, unless it's me ending it with James.

The waitress has returned with the bottle in its silver ice bucket. She lifts it out, starts to twist the wire that holds the cork in place, but Owen waves her away with his hand. 'It's all right. I'll do it. I've opened enough champagne bottles in my time. Especially when *Dead Air* made the *Sunday Times* bestseller list.'

He beams, looks at the waitress for her reaction, but she only looks confused.

Owen hides his disappointment with a smile. Waits until she's moved away. 'Probably not my audience... too young. She would have been only a kid when it came out.'

'You're right. She can't be more than eighteen.' I watch as he presses his two thumbs to the cork. Try to sound enthusiastic despite all that's happened. 'So, what are we celebrating? I need to know if I'm to clink your glass.'

Owen gives a smug smile. 'We're celebrating the completion of my next book.'

I look at him in surprise. 'It's finished?'

'Well, only the first draft, but I've written The End, if that's what you mean.'

A group of people have come into the restaurant, and I wait for them to pass. 'I had no idea you'd got so far with it.'

The pop of the champagne cork makes the couple at the next table look up. The girl cranes her neck to see what's going on, and Owen lifts the bottle proudly. Pours the pale amber liquid into my glass, then his. He hands me mine. 'I worked on it yesterday evening and half the night too. Then all of today.'

'I see.' That explains why his side of the bed had been empty when I'd woken at two the last couple of nights.

Owen takes a long drink of his champagne, his Adam's apple working as he swallows. He puts his glass down and dabs at his mouth with his serviette.

'It has a name too.'

'Really? Can you tell me?'

He laughs. 'Certainly not. Bad luck and all that.'

'Then can I read it?'

He runs his fingers through his hair, drawing the fine strands back. 'I don't think so.'

'What about your agent then? Did you show it to her?' He'd had a meeting with her this morning, leaving after the police had left, but hadn't told me why.

'No, I decided it wasn't the right time. In fact, having given it some thought, I'm not sure I want to at all. I'm well-known enough to my readership to self-publish. Why should I share the profit? The glory? And besides, I don't want them meddling.'

'It's not meddling, Owen. It's making your book stronger. I'm not sure this is wise. Why not think about it?'

But he's not listening. His mind is somewhere else: at his next book launch, at the dinner to celebrate his rise back onto the bestseller lists, at the talk he'll give at next year's crime festival.

Already the old Owen is returning. The confident one with that hint of vulnerability. The one I fell in love with. If only I could appreciate it, but, at this minute, all I can think about is Lexi.

I put down my glass, reach across the table and take his hand. 'I'm pleased for you, really I am, but being here in this restaurant,' – I hold up my glass – 'drinking champagne, feels wrong when back in Pond Close a mother is grieving.'

I expect him to pull his hand away, but he doesn't. It's as though he hasn't heard me. Instead, he gives me his brightest smile. 'I wrote this one for you, Rachel. Because I love you. There's even a dedication to you at the front.'

Despite my worry about what's going on at home, I'm moved. Owen has never dedicated a book to me before. In fact, he doesn't use dedications at all, saying they're a waste of time.

'Thank you. That means a lot.'

His chest puffs out. He's glowing. And it's hard to reconcile him with the man who was crouched in his study, hands covering his eyes, tears dampening his collar. I'm relieved. Having the old Owen back is something I've prayed for.

We drink our champagne, and our meals arrive. My hunger has miraculously returned, and the seafood risotto tastes even better than I remember. So much so, I finish it all. Owen is good company: complimenting me, telling me anecdotes from his childhood that I never knew – things that make me laugh, talking about what we'll do together once his book is out and the first royalties come in.

I'm light-headed with the drink and relief that the evening is going so well. The look on Phillipa's face is fading. My worry over the police officers' visit, and the knowledge that Lexi's little coat was found at a place where I'd been with James, receding to a distant corner of my mind. If only we could keep this, bottle whatever it is that has brought us back to being the people we used to be. In fact, it's so perfect, I can almost forget that only recently I was sitting here with James.

Owen drains the last of his glass. The champagne bottle is empty.

'Just as well we got a taxi,' I say.

He reaches over. Tucks a strand of my hair behind my ear. 'I thought it wise. We've a lot to celebrate.' His face turns serious.

'I know it must have taken a lot to end it with James. I won't let you regret it.'

I bite my lip, James's name bringing back images of sunlight flickering through trees onto bare skin. The words he'd whispered in my ear, as we'd made love, making me forget everything that had made my life intolerable: Simone's face as she'd told me about Owen's past, the way my husband had distanced himself from me, Phillipa's insensitivity in the face of my childlessness.

'I don't regret it, Owen.'

And, despite the heady memory, I don't. Sex with James had been a mistake, and now my life is changing for the better, I no longer need him.

When the taxi drops us off at the house later, the upbeat vibe stays with us and as I walk up to the door, I hardly give a thought to the police car that had been parked outside earlier. Wondering, instead, if tonight will be the night Owen will reach for me once we've turned off the light.

Owen makes us a coffee, humming to himself as he lifts the mugs from the shelf. He grins. 'Maybe once the book's published, we can have a little party. Invite the neighbours for a signing.'

I frown, my good mood slipping away. 'I don't want that woman in my house.'

'What woman?'

'Phillipa.' My words slur slightly, my sympathy for her ebbing away. 'She doesn't deserve to call herself a neighbour... or a mother. You should have heard how she talked to me. The way she rubbed my childlessness in my face. If you invite her, Owen, I swear to God I won't be there.' It's as though I've forgotten that Lexi is missing. That, at this very moment, Phillipa will be crying into her pillow.

Owen puts the kettle down and comes over to me. 'Then I

won't, my love. Not if you don't want me to. Anyway, enough of her. I have a present for you.'

'Really?' I can't remember the last time Owen gave me a present, unless it was for my birthday. 'What is it?'

He presses a finger to my lips. 'Hush or you'll spoil the surprise. You'll find out in the morning, and I know you won't be disappointed. Let's forget about the coffee. I'm tired and bed seems a very good idea.'

There's a hint of something in the way he says it, an invitation, and I hug it to me. Tonight, Owen won't turn away from me or push my hand away when I rest my palm on his chest. I know it. He has forgiven me, and, because of that, I can forgive him too. We'll start again, just the two of us, and James will be no more than a memory. Insignificant. Inconsequential. Consigned to a past I would rather not remember.

Before I go to bed, I check my phone. I haven't looked at it all day, and there's an email I haven't seen. It's from the Land Registry and I'm surprised. I hadn't expected to hear back so quickly. Thought it might take days... weeks even. With a racing heart, I open it and scan the Title Register, searching for the name of the person who owned 2 Pond Close in 1998.

I frown and read it again, thinking my eyes have played tricks on me. But the name is the same as it was when I first looked. A name I know.

Mr Geoff Ford. Pam's husband.

Our neighbour.

FORTY-THREE

OWEN

Owen hasn't been able to sleep. His mind is too full... his heart too. He looks at his sleeping wife, the bedclothes rucked around her waist, and wonders, as he has a million times, what she sees in him. Last night, in the taxi home, buoyed up by how well the evening had gone, he'd imagined that he'd make love to Rachel for the first time since they'd moved to Pond Close. That it would be perfect. But the champagne, while working its magic at the restaurant, had turned on him once they'd got home. Sending him to sleep as soon as his head had hit the pillow.

And now that he's awake, his head beginning to ache from the drink, the doubts about Rachel have started to creep in. What if he'd made a mistake again? What if she'd never loved him? Had simply felt sorry for him.

He swings his legs out of the bed. Feels across the floor with his bare feet for his slippers. Rachel thinks he's told her everything, but he hasn't. Because there's something he's kept from her all these weeks. The day the estate agent showed them around the house had not been the first time he'd set foot in it.

He reaches out a hand to touch his wife's smooth shoulder but removes it again before he can feel the sweet softness of her skin. Would she forgive him if she knew? Would she understand?

He's been to Pond Close before. Been inside the walls of this house. Many years ago.

Owen walks across the bedroom, puts on his robe. He looks back at his wife, her hair spread across the pillow. Her eyelids flickering softly in the strip of moonlight that slips through the gap between the curtains. Poor thing. In this house, God's miracles hadn't worked their magic for *her*.

Last evening, he had been certain about their future, but now the doubts are creeping in again. He goes to the chest of drawers and slides open the top one. Under his neatly pressed T-shirts is a box. Rachel's present. He lifts it out and opens the lid. Inside is an eternity ring, one he knows they can't afford. He wants his wife to stay with him for ever, but something is haunting him.

He pulls open the drawer below, slowly so as not to wake Rachel, and places his hand on the faded jeans that lie there. Then he lifts out a short-sleeved black shirt and holds it up against him. In the darkened room, he draws his hair back from his face, his hand acting as a band.

Would she prefer him like this? *Would* she?

She'd slept with James when she'd sworn she never would. Not Owen. *James.* Just as he knew she would.

Last night, after too much champagne, they had fallen straight to sleep. As his eyes had closed, his forehead touching hers, it hadn't bothered him... but now it does and the memory he has of his wife having sex with James now feels like an infidelity. The taste of her, the sounds she'd made in that wooded clearing, instead of exciting him again, turns him cold.

He lets his hair fall from his fingers. Closes the drawer, then, with a last look at his sleeping wife, carries the jeans and black shirt onto the landing.

What Rachel had done with James in that woodland

clearing was proof enough. She can't be trusted. It would take only one look, one question, one smile from a stranger to turn her head. To make her leave.

He unbuttons his pyjama top, shrugs it off and lets it drop to the floor. He's in danger of losing his wife, and he can't allow that to happen.

FORTY-FOUR

RACHEL

My eyes shoot open, and I blink into the darkness. Last night when I'd gone to bed, even though Owen thought I was asleep, I'd lain awake worrying about Lexi. My head filled with the sound of the water that cascaded over the weir as it had that day with James, making me wonder if she was there somewhere beneath the water.

The sound I've woken to is a different one. A child crying.

I lie still, as I did all those nights before, but the house is quiet now. The only noise the beating of my heart in my chest. The blood pulsing in my ears.

'For God's sake, Owen!' I prop myself on my elbow. Reach over to him. 'This isn't funny.'

But my hand meets nothing except the bunched-up duvet, the light that floods the bedroom, when I switch on the bedside light, confirming it – Owen's not there. And from the feel of the cool sheet on his side of the bed, he's been up a while.

As my heart rate starts to return to normal, the fear I'd felt on waking is nudged aside by the anger that has started to build inside me. What the hell is Owen playing at? What new book material can he possibly think he'll gain from me, when I know

now that the sound I'd woken to all those nights had never been real?

What on earth was the point of it? Hasn't he learnt anything?

That bloody machine!

Shifting over to Owen's side of the bed, I open the drawer in his bedside table. Rummage around. There, underneath an empty wallet and a neatly folded handkerchief, is the small box Owen had hidden in the roof space. The controller is there too. Would he really have been so stupid as to have activated it?

I stare at the hated thing, knowing I have to be sure.

With my heart beating high and hard in my chest, I press the button on the remote, dropping it onto the floor as the loud wailing I'd heard the other day fills the room. I press my hands to my ears, but it makes little difference. The volume's been set so that I'd hear it through the ceiling, and there's no way it could be this that had woken me. The cry I'd heard had been distant. Merging with the dream I'd been having. Making me believe it was real.

But now I wonder if it had simply been the drink from last night stimulating my overactive imagination. The stress of the last few weeks making my brain replay the sound I'd woken to so many times in those early weeks. Like an echo of the past.

The child is still wailing, the sound shredding my nerves. Needing it to stop, I stamp on the remote with my foot to shut it off, and, immediately, the bedroom is filled with a merciful silence.

'Owen?'

I come out of the bedroom, bending to retrieve the soft thing I've just stepped on. Surprised when I find it's Owen's pyjamas. What the hell's going on? I look along the landing. The door to the spare bedroom is shut, and when I lean on the banister and look down to the hall, it's in darkness. A light is on in Owen's

study, though, the door ajar. I go up to it and knock quietly with
the back of my knuckles.

'Owen? Are you in there?'

When there's no answer, I step into the bright room. See it's
empty.

The curtains are closed, and when I pull one aside and look
down, our car is still parked in the drive. Not that Owen would
have had anywhere to go at this time of night. It's a moonless,
windy night, rain sleeting diagonally across the windowpane,
the pavements dark and glistening under the street lights that
are positioned outside each house. For some reason, it makes
Pond Close look like a cheap stage set waiting for the first characters to appear, but there's no movement save for the rain and
the swaying branches of the birch in the fenced-off area of the
green.

I drop the curtain, hoping Owen hasn't gone outside and
isn't round the back of the house – the place I'd found him
before. Blood from his cheek staining the step.

I rub at my arms. The room's cold and I'm unsure what to
do. Everything about the previous evening at the restaurant now
feels unreal. Had it really been that easy for me and Owen to
reconnect? Could something as simple as a bottle of champagne
and a nice meal really fix our marriage? Now, standing in
Owen's study, the effects of the alcohol wearing off, I'm not so
sure.

I switch the study light off and am about to leave the room
when something catches my eye in the darkness – the amber
light on Owen's computer that tells me it's in standby mode. I
stand with my hand on the door frame, looking at it. It's not like
Owen to leave his computer on. Had something disturbed him
while he was using it?

I go back into the room. Without bothering to turn the light
back on, I walk over to the computer and reach across the swivel
chair to move the mouse across the desk's shiny surface. The

computer springs to life, and my body is flooded with adrenaline as the screen lights up to reveal a page of writing. When I'd tried to view it before, it had been password protected, but now here it is!

Greedily, my eyes devour the words, but I'm only a third of the way down the page when I stop. I've read this before. Disappointment replaces the excitement I'd felt at the prospect of reading Owen's new work for the first time. This isn't it... it's the opening chapter of *Deep Breaths*. The book Owen had signed for me the night we met.

I stand back, my fingers gripping the top of the swivel chair in disappointment and frustration. Why had he been looking at it and where on earth *is* he?

The printer light's on too, which means the new book is finished. He only prints it when he's happy, and he hides it high above on a bookshelf to keep from prying eyes. Working up the courage to submit it. He thinks I don't know, but I do.

There's a small stepladder beside the bookcase, and I pull it towards me. Climb up its three steps. The shelf of the bookcase digs into my ribs as I lean forward and slide my hand between the top of the wooden cornice and the ceiling. My fingers stretching and reaching, moving from one side to the other until they meet with something.

My heart races as I lift the thick wodge of pages from their hiding place and carefully climb back down. The pages are loose, and I put them on the desk to ensure I don't drop them and get them out of order. There, on the front page, as Owen said it would be, is the title. Not *Book 7* as the file on his computer had been called, but a proper name.

I Did It For You.

Slowly, I turn the page. Find the dedication. *For my beloved wife, Rachel. My muse.*

There's a sound from downstairs, and I freeze. It comes again, and my body responds, fingers grabbing at the manuscript. But my hands are shaking so much, I lose half of the pages and watch in despair as they float to the floor. Because what I've just heard is a child's cry. What the hell is going on?

I run downstairs to find the kitchen in darkness and am going back into the hall when I hear the cry again. I can't move, fear blocking the desperate messages my brain is sending to my legs. This isn't my imagination, that cry was real and it's coming from the living room.

'Mumma.' The sob turns into a hiccup. I know that voice. Would know it anywhere.

'Oh, my God. Lexi!' I run into the living room and see the little girl pressed into the corner by the sliding doors. One of the dining room chairs is on its side where she must have knocked it over in the dark. 'It's all right, sweetie. It's me, Rachel. I'm here now and everything's going to be okay.'

I switch the light on, hurry over to her and take her in my arms. She doesn't appear to be hurt, just frightened. Cold too as her feet are bare. Strands of wet hair dampening her pyjama top. Despite my shock at seeing her, my heart is singing. Lexi's alive. *Alive!*

Outside, the rain lashes against the window. I can't get my head around it. Why is Lexi in our house? How did she get here?

Suddenly, the security light at the back of the house comes on. The patio door slides open, and I press my hand to my mouth. My chest tightening at the sight of the man standing there. Rain dripping from his hair. His eyelashes. The man I'd once thought myself in love with.

I stare dumbly at the bottoms of his wet jeans, at the wet black shirt sticking to his chest. Wondering how I could have been so stupid. Gone along with the ridiculous charade.

'James.' My voice has dropped to a whisper.

Not because I'm shocked, but because I can't, for the life of me, imagine how this will end.

FORTY-FIVE

RACHEL

'What have you done?'

I stare at the man to whom I'd told everything, like a penitent at a confessional: how Phillipa had made me feel so small. How she'd rubbed my childlessness in my face and how I believed she'd been mistreating Lexi.

But that hadn't been all. I'd also told him how I resented Owen for not letting us try another round of IVF. For not understanding my need to keep trying and my belief that things might have been different between us if we'd had a child together.

I look at him now, his hair plastered to his face. Remember the kiss we'd shared that day at the lake and the words I should have taken more notice of as I'd left to go home. *If you want me to do anything...* Well, he's certainly done something, and I'm struggling to see how we can put it right.

'For God's sake, shut the patio door.'

He does as I ask, then waits. What is it he's expecting? For me to tell him how grateful I am? How indebted? I never thought I'd see James again, hadn't thought I'd need to, but now he's standing in my living room, and I have no idea what to do.

Lexi's thumb has slid into her mouth and her head leans against my chest.

'How did you get her?'

But of course, I know. He'd used the key Phillipa had given me when I was working for her, the one I'd never got around to giving back. He'd sneaked into Phillipa's house and snatched Lexi from her bed.

'I love you, Rachel.' He takes a step towards me, hands outstretched.

'This isn't funny. I told you it was over, and this charade has to stop now. It's gone too far.'

It's true. This game we've played, the one Owen thought up to help me through the darker days after the IVF and Jade, is no longer what I want. Something has gone wrong, and if I don't do the right thing now, act in the right way, the repercussions could last a lifetime.

James is looking at me, pupils dilated. Proud of himself.

He doesn't need to speak, his expression tells me everything. *I did it for you.*

I press a hand to Lexi's head, smoothing the curls. Calming her.

'Owen...'

My husband smiles at me. Pushes his hands deep into his jeans pockets. 'What is it?'

'What were you thinking? We have to take her back. You know that, don't you?'

My heart beats into the silence. I want him to answer, but I'm afraid of what he might say.

Owen's face changes. Gone is the look of satisfaction. The self-assurance. His shoulders slump. His eyes meet mine and holds them.

'You said it was what you wanted.'

I shake my head and rock Lexi on my hip to soothe her. 'I

didn't say that. Why would I? Lexi's not my child. She's Phillipa's.'

'You told me Phillipa didn't deserve to be a mother.' He steps forward. 'Don't do this to me, Rachel.'

'They were just words. I didn't mean anything by them. People do that... say things they don't mean.'

'Like you said you'd never sleep with James.'

I stare at him as though I don't know him. 'Owen, you *are* James.'

That brighter version of himself. The one he'd invented in order to connect with me when the disappointment of the failed IVF and its consequences had widened the cracks in our marriage. When he knew that he wasn't enough and that, as himself, he could never reach that emotional core of me. Could never help me.

'You know what I mean. You fell in love with him... the *idea* of him. This man who listened to you. Who let you offload your problems. Your *feelings*.' He says the word as if it disgusts him, and I'm hurt by it.

'It was your idea, Owen. Not mine. Why suggest inventing James if you didn't believe in him? You made it feel so real.' I stop, remembering the shock of seeing him in that coffee shop and the realisation of what he was doing. The way he'd looked at me across the table as we'd drunk our coffee. The questions he'd asked. The way he'd reacted to my answers... to the truth.

It was role-play, he'd said. It wasn't cheating.

Owen points a finger at me. 'You slept with him, and it would only have been one small step further to sleep with someone else. I couldn't have you leave me, Rachel. I couldn't let you ruin my work.'

I can't believe what I'm hearing. 'What? Your novel?'

I right the chair Lexi had knocked over and sit. Lexi's face buried in my neck.

'This isn't how things are supposed to go, Rachel. In the story you're happy I've done this.'

I look at him in shock. Think of the papers scattered all over the floor. Can it be true that he's written all of this into his novel? Taken my feelings about Lexi and Phillipa, the baby we couldn't have, James even, and put them in his book? What was his plan now?

'I don't know what fantasy world you think you're living in, but it has to stop. You've taken someone's child, and we have to give her back right away. Phillipa is distraught.' Lexi's face is grubby with snot and tears and a sudden thought comes to me. 'Where on earth did you keep her?'

He gives a smug smile. 'Why, at my mother's old house, of course. That day I took you to see it, I noted the *For Sale* board. It was a vacant possession and the obvious place. Luckily, the people who bought it from me after she died never changed the locks.'

'But you were with me last night. How could you...? How did you...?'

'There's no need to make so much fuss, Rachel. It was only a couple of nights. I bought a playpen from a second-hand shop. Made her a bed in it with a duvet and a pillow. Left her a bottle and some snacks and popped by yesterday when I said I was seeing my agent. As you can see, she's quite all right.'

I stare at him in disbelief. Knowing how terrified Lexi must have been alone in that house. All the things that could have happened. Not wanting to dwell on it for fear it will send me crazy, I focus instead on the fact that she is here. That she's alive.

'Her pink coat. It was at the lake... why?'

He gives a nonchalant lift of his shoulders. 'Isn't it obvious? I needed the police to believe she was dead. So we could start our new lives with Lexi.' He beams at her. 'With our little girl.'

'This is madness. It's all right, Lexi. I'm taking you home.' I hold out my palm to Owen. 'Give me the key.'

'The key?' He looks at me blankly as though I've asked him for the moon.

'To Phillipa's house. Come on, Owen. This has to end here. We have to fix this mess.'

'This *mess*.' Owen's face twists. His tone alters. 'Is that what you think this is?'

'What would *you* call it?' I can't believe we're having this conversation.

He'd been looking at the floor, but now he strides over to us. Snatches Lexi from my grasp. 'You ungrateful bitch.'

Lexi starts to cry, but he holds her to him, his arms crossed around her chest. It's when I realise that to Owen this is real. No longer in his head. No longer fiction.

FORTY-SIX

OWEN

Owen looks at Rachel. The wife he'd thought had loved him unconditionally. Who would never be unfaithful to him. Never leave him.

Her face is pale, her lips pinched, and he sees now, what he hadn't before.

'You're no better than the others.' How could he not have known? Been so blind to it. 'No fucking different.'

Rachel's eyes widen, and he knows it's because he's never sworn at her before. Has always been courteous and polite to her. Like his mother had taught him. But his mother isn't here to see him. Hear him. His mother had *never* been there for him... not until his dad had pissed off and she'd got sick. Then it was even worse; she'd never left him alone. Never let him breathe.

Owen come and massage my feet. Owen come and read to me.

He laughs at the irony.

'What are you talking about? What others?' Rachel stretches out her hand. Her face is white. 'Let me have Lexi, Owen. She needs to go home.'

He'd done this for her. Everything he did was for her. Stupid ungrateful bitches, all of them. Leading him on. Letting him believe they loved him.

'You women are never satisfied, that's the problem.' He points a finger at her, his other hand pressing Lexi against him. 'It's take, take, take. Saying one thing. Meaning another. Never happy, even when you're doing something for them to make their life better. You wanted a baby and I give you one. Anna wanted shot of her arsehole boyfriend and I obliged. No, *thank you, Owen*. No, *what can I do for you in return?* Just the cold shoulder. An epidemic of lies and gossip to contend with.'

'What are you talking about?'

He looks at her in surprise, forgetting she doesn't know the truth.

'Why Anna, of course. She hadn't wanted to see me after the bastard had been pulled out of the canal. Said I was crowding her. No appreciation for what I'd had to go through to give her what she wanted. Not that I told her everything.' He looks down at Lexi. 'Like a well-written book, it's not the process that's important, the path to getting there, but the end result, don't you think?'

Rachel is shaking her head as though trying to rid herself of some image that's stuck there. She stares at him in horror.

'What did you do, Owen? You have to tell me.'

'I don't know what you want me to say. He was a drunk waste of space. Off his head on drugs by all accounts. He wasn't good for her. Didn't treat her well... not the way I would have if she'd chosen me. If I hadn't met him on my way home from Anna's, hadn't given him a helping hand, he would have ended up in that canal anyway. It was a mercy for everyone. No great loss, especially not to Anna, but some people are never happy.'

He thinks back to that time. Anna sitting white-faced on the bed in her student accommodation. Not wanting to speak to him. Not wanting him to comfort her. It had taken him back to another time, another place. His eyes sweep the living room, stopping at the open door that gives a glimpse of the dark hall. The kitchen. Memories returning. But he doesn't want to think of that now.

A wariness has crept into Rachel's face, and Owen puts his head on one side as he considers the observation. She's frightened of him, and it's something he would be interested in investigating further. Something that could be useful for the sequel to *I Did It For You.*

'I believe it's a good death, drowning. A kind one. After the panic, the fear of the first few minutes, there comes a numbness. A moment when you have an almost out of body experience.'

He closes his eyes. Feels the press of his mother's hands on his shoulders. Sees the bubbles of air that escape his mouth like pearls. The way the bathroom light fractures on the surface of the water, splintering her face. Distorting it. He remembers the peace that followed. The painful disappointment as larger hands had grabbed him under his armpits. Hauling him from the water like a prize fish.

Then his father's raised voice, *What the hell are you doing, you mad bitch?*

It was something he and his mother had never talked about, and sometimes, he wonders if he had, in fact, dreamt it. They'd never talked about the sister he'd lost either. The colicky child slipping beneath the water of the bathtub when his mother's back was turned. An accident, they'd called it. A tragic accident.

He smiles at Rachel. 'I did them a kindness. Everyone dies in the end. A heart attack, a stroke, cancer. I saved them from that.'

Is that what his mother had been thinking as she'd pressed down on his shoulders? He'll never know.

Rachel's mouth has fallen open. Her arms are wrapped

around her body as though she's defending herself from something.

She squeezes her eyes shut.

'You said *them*, Owen.' Her voice cracks. 'I don't understand. You said *them*.'

FORTY-SEVEN

RACHEL

I feel as though the air has been sucked out of the room. Out of my lungs. Nothing is the same as it was and will never be again – the real world there but out of reach. I no longer know the man who stands in front of me. No longer want to.

Lexi is scared. She struggles in Owen's arms, her face red and wet with tears, a snail-trail of snot running down her upper lip, but he holds her firm.

'Who else, Owen?' Fear blooms in my chest at the thought of his answer. Kevin had been right about him all along. Our neighbour clearly hadn't been a saint at university, that much is obvious from the things Owen had told me, had bullied and victimised others. But Owen? His crime in comparison, if he's telling me the truth, is somewhere off the scale.

'She pretended she loved me.' Owen's expression is closed. Defensive. 'That's what they all do. They say one thing and mean another. My mother, Kayla, Anna. Never grateful. Always wanting more.'

There's hard steel in his voice, and I'm afraid of it. Of him.

'You knew her? You knew Kayla, the girl who lived here? The one whose child drowned?'

'What difference does it make?' His irritation with me is evident in his tone.

'How did you know her? Don't lie to me, Owen. Tell me the truth.'

His mouth twists as though disapproving of the memory.

'I was fifteen. I thought she loved me.' There's a rare note of vulnerability in his voice. 'She was a couple of years older and was kind to me. Waved to me from the window when I was doing my paper round and let me come into the house when I was drenched from the rain. She saw something in me that others didn't. Sometimes, she was there, but sometimes she wasn't, but on the days when I'd see her, I'd go home with my heart full. Ours was a special friendship. One to be prized, something no one else would understand – like Romeo and Juliet. Okay, I was only fifteen, with a face full of acne, but we were meant to be together. "*Love looks not with the eyes but with the mind.*"' He laughs. 'We'd been studying *A Midsummer Night's Dream* in English, and it was my favourite quote. Shakespeare certainly knew his stuff.' He places a hand on Lexi's head. 'Yes, she was very kind.'

I note the repetition of the word kind. Would find it poignant were it not for the path I fear it's leading me down. A path to the terrible poisonous truth.

'Give me Lexi and you can tell me about it.' I take a step closer. The child he's holding so tightly is my priority. 'Kayla sounds like she was a nice girl.'

Owen looks at me as if I'm mad. Ignores my request to take Lexi.

'She was a whore like the others. Leading me on. Pretending she was in love with me when all the time she felt sorry for me.' He spits out the words. 'She thought she was better than me.'

I look at Lexi. The sound of her crying fills the room,

reminding me of the nights I'd lain awake in bed, my head filled with the same sound. Had little Maddie cried like that?

Little Maddie.

Lexi's face is screwed up with fear. Owen's hands pressing her against him, keeping her prisoner, and a terrible thought occurs to me. Might Owen have done something to Maddie? Played some part in her death? But what? He was just a teenager. Barely more than a child himself at the time.

'Was Kayla pregnant when you knew her?' I need to keep him talking. Need time to think of how I can get Lexi away from him.

Owen nods, his face wistful. 'I used to help her when she got so big she couldn't even tie her shoelaces. Do bits and pieces around the house.'

'And you never saw her parents... those times you were there?'

'I never saw them. Never met them. She lived with her mum and stepdad, that's all I know. Hadn't seen her real dad in years and couldn't care less. Her stepdad had practically brought her up and she was close to him. That's what she told me anyway.'

It's like someone has stepped over my grave. Without being aware, Owen has handed me another piece of the puzzle. Geoff was Kayla's stepfather, hence the different surname, so Pam would have been her mother. The newspaper article had only mentioned that her grandfather had found Maddie, hadn't mentioned his name.

I think of the bibs embroidered with the letter M in my neighbours' houses, the blanket that had been around Chantelle's baby when I'd met her by the pond. Seeing them now for what they probably are. Not suspicious or sinister but humble offerings from bereaved grandparents who would prefer to see their friends' children use their beautiful granddaughter's things than take them to a charity shop or the landfill. I imagine them bagged up in the loft in the house next to ours. Geoff handing them down to Pam. *Let's give them to our friends. It will keep Maddie's memory alive.*

The question is, did Pam and Geoff know anything about the teenage boy who visited their pregnant daughter? And if they did, do they have any idea that he and the man who now lives in their old family house are one and the same person?

The whole idea is preposterous. Ludicrous.

'Pam and Geoff were Maddie's grandparents, Owen. Did you know that?'

Owen stares at me. 'Don't be ridiculous.'

He doesn't know. I can see it in his eyes.

I shove my phone at him. 'It's here on the Title Register I sent for. Geoff Ford... he owned the house at the time you were doing your paper round. When you were visiting with Kayla.'

Owen looks. Blinks at the screen. 'How can it be?'

'I don't know, but it's true.' I'm fighting to keep control. Owen has Lexi, and my fear for her is crowding everything else out. He'd taken her from her bed and brought her here because he thought it was what I'd wanted, had pushed Christian into the canal because it was what he'd thought Anna had wanted. What had Kayla, Owen's first crush, and Maddie's mum, wanted?

I'm terrified of what he'll say, but it's something I have to ask.

Something I have to know.

FORTY-EIGHT

RACHEL

'And when the baby was born, what then? Did you still see Kayla?'

I've been afraid that Owen will lose his patience with my questioning and Lexi will be in more danger, but I don't know what else to do. I'm in luck, though, as I'd forgotten how much he misses it: the panel talks, the radio and newspaper interviews each time a new thriller came out. As long as it doesn't involve emotions, he's never been afraid to talk about himself. Has courted it.

As I'd asked the question, I'd kept my eyes on Lexi. She's a little calmer, her thumb finding her mouth again, her sobs reduced to a jagged intake of breath and a jerk of her shoulders. I raise my eyes to my husband. Wait for his answer.

'She said she didn't have time to see me. That she had a baby to look after.' He looks down at the top of Lexi's head. 'I don't remember what she said to me the next time I called round, or the next. I'd been her friend. Had been good to her. Loved her. I didn't understand what I'd done wrong and why she no longer wanted to see me.'

He hangs his head, and I see the awkward teenage boy he

must have been. But this is no time to feel sorry for him. At university, he took someone's life and over twenty years later shows no remorse.

He's also taken a child.

I look at Lexi, her pyjama top rucked up by Owen's arm to expose a centimetre of pale chubby flesh. Her face wet with tears.

'Of course she was busy, Owen. Looking after a child is time-consuming. You know that as we talked about it before the IVF... how our lives would change once we had a baby.'

Except I remember now it had been me who had done most of the talking. Owen had stood at the window, his hands behind his back. The thoughts in his head known only to himself. And, of course, we'd never found out the consequences of having a baby. Never even got close to it.

'It was lies.' Owen drags fingers through his hair. 'Fucking lies. She had time enough to see *him*.'

I'm confused. 'Him?'

'The kid's father, of course. The one who'd got her pregnant. The one she was still seeing... something she conveniently forgot to tell me. I still remember the moment when I found out. It was a bitter evening, the saddle cold under my arse, the wind chapping my lips as I rode to Pond Close. My mother had no idea I'd left the house, that I'd ridden over to Kayla's, and I'd had no intention of telling her.'

There's a sickness at the pit of my stomach. 'Why did you go?'

'Isn't it obvious? I thought I might talk some sense into her. Tell her I loved her and that, although she might not know it yet, knew she loved me too. Her parents' car wasn't in the drive, but the lights were on in the kitchen. I wanted to surprise her, not ring on the doorbell as I'd done so many times before. The garage door, the same one we have now, hadn't been closed properly, so I hooked my fingers under and pushed it up, closing it again behind me in case her parents came home unexpectedly. I let myself into the kitchen, had thought I'd find Kayla in there, but she wasn't. It was the kid, Maddie, sitting in a pile of wallpaper strips. There was blood on the wall. That writing you found. At first, I thought it was the kid's blood, but she was fine – smiling at me as though pleased to see me. It was then I heard the raised voices. Kayla and the guy who'd knocked her up. They were upstairs, I could hear the tap running in the bathroom and the guy was shouting at Kayla. Telling her to hold still while he bandaged her hand. That he couldn't believe she'd been so fucking careless and what was she doing anyway... stripping wallpaper when her parents could have done it? It was their house, after all.'

'So that was *Kayla's* blood we saw on the wall?'

Owen doesn't answer. Is too lost in the memories. 'She sounded like a harpy.' He blinks behind his glasses. 'To be honest, I was somewhat taken aback by it and by what she said next. The bastard had been shagging her best friend and as she'd stripped the paper, she'd been imagining it was his skin. *Why Phillipa?* She was shouting it, over and over. *Why fucking Phillipa?* It explained the writing on the wall, and I'd have liked to have heard more, but now the kid was getting up, strips of paper stuck to her dungarees. She was pleased to see me and wanted me to play, but I was worried they'd hear her, would come down and find me here. So I told Maddie I had a game of my own we could play. Someone had been clearing out the cupboard under the sink and the contents were on the worktop. There was a bowl of bits and pieces and I'd seen a packet of *Hello Kitty* stickers on the top. Taking it out, I peeled one off and stuck it to her dungarees. *It says Good Girl*, I told her. *If you get in the cupboard and stay quiet, you can have another.* I said I'd tell her mum to come and find her, that it would be a fun game. She couldn't have cared about the dark because, as I shut the cupboard door, I could hear her talking to herself. *Good girl, Maddie. Good girl.'*

My eyes fill with tears. That poor child. Poor innocent Maddie alone in the dark cupboard. Pressing a sticker to the back wall. Waiting for a game she was too young to understand. One that would have devastating consequences.

'What happened, Owen? What happened next?' I hold my breath. Wait for the truth. A truth I know I won't want to hear.

'When I listened again, the guy was yelling. Saying she was a mad bitch to use her own blood to make her stupid accusations. That she'd probably cut herself on purpose and that she'd better stop whining and clean it off before anyone saw.' He tuts. Shakes his head. 'Then it was Kayla's turn, screaming that he'd never have slept with Phillipa if he'd loved her. Would never have done it if he hadn't got her pregnant. If she hadn't had Maddie.' He gives me a straight look. 'You see it was the kid's fault Kayla was upset. She hadn't wanted that man's child. Had thought she was a nuisance.'

My breath shallows. It's hard to take it all in. 'People say things they don't mean when they're upset and angry. You should know that.'

But he doesn't. Owen's never seen things the way others do.

He shrugs. 'She said it... that's all that's important.'

Gooseflesh rises on my arms. All the time we've been living here, he's known about Phillipa and how she'd slept with her best friend's lover – Maddie's father. Owen had believed the child to be the cause of Kayla's unhappiness. He'd also believed he was the one who could make it right.

'So you took Maddie.'

Tears are streaming down my face as I see how it happened. Owen opening that cupboard door. Taking Maddie's hand and leading her through the hall where her mother's and her lover's raised voices could still be heard. Did he let the child walk to the pond or carry her? Did he glance back at that open front door, knowing they'd think someone hadn't shut it properly and the child had wandered out, or had he not even thought that far ahead? A voice in his head telling him this was what Kayla wanted? That it would make her love him.

Owen is pacing with Lexi in front of the lit patio doors.

'Kayla was an ungrateful bitch. Shut herself away and didn't want to see anyone. She didn't deserve to have a child any more than that cow next door. This one's so-called mother. Sluts both of them.' He jerks a thumb in the direction of their house. 'Not like us. Worthy. Deserving.' His eyes dip to my stomach. 'If the IVF had worked, that tiny egg, fertilised by my seed and growing in your womb, would have been my ultimate gift to you. The passing on of genes the greatest token of love a man can give. I can't tell you the number of times I pictured the headlines, *New Baby for* Sunday Times *Bestselling Author*. It wasn't to be, but no matter, God had other plans and he's made sure we've been given a second chance.' His eyes are bright with fervour. 'It was no coincidence Number 2 went on the market when we needed it. He brought us here to Pond Close. He brought us to *her*.'

Owen loosens his grip on Lexi. Puts her down and gives her a little push towards me. 'Here take her. She's yours.'

And in that moment, I realise how lucky we were that we didn't have a child, because something is seriously wrong with Owen. Dangerously wrong.

FORTY-NINE

RACHEL

I scoop Lexi up in my arms. Feel the wetness of her cheeks as she buries her face in my neck. The press of her knee against the soft flesh of my stomach. Thank God he's let her come to me.

Not wanting Owen out of my sight, I back away from him. I have to get to the hall. The front door. I have to take the poor little mite home to her family. The rest I can sort out later.

'What do you think you're doing?'

I stop. Force my body to stop trembling. 'I'm taking her home, Owen. This isn't right. When I get back, we can talk. Properly talk. We'll work this out.'

But what *is* there to work out? I feel sick to the core... My husband has confessed to murder, and it's only the feel of Lexi's little heartbeat against my chest that is stopping me from losing my head.

I have to stay in control for her.

'You don't want her?' Owen frowns. Head on one side. 'You don't want my gift?'

Panic claws at my throat. I don't know what to do. What to say. 'That's not what I said. I meant—'

'You don't want her?' Owen repeats, his jaw slack with disbelief. 'Give her back then.'

He takes a step forward and Lexi whimpers, her arms tightening around my neck.

I step back. 'No, Owen. You're frightening her.'

I should have run. Left the house while I had the chance. Or made something up. Said I was taking Lexi upstairs to put her to bed. Too late, I make a dash for the hall, but he's ready for it. Grabs Lexi under her arms and yanks her from my grasp.

She cries out, doubles over his forearms and reaches desperate arms to me, but there's nothing I can do. Not if I want to prevent him from hurting her.

Desperation strangles my voice. 'Please. Don't do anything stupid.'

'So I'm stupid now, am I? Stupid, cry-baby, two-pack Packard.'

He closes his eyes, and I know it's not my voice he's hearing but Kevin's.

'No, of course not. You're one of the cleverest men I know which is why you must see that this is crazy.'

Immediately, I wish I could take back that word too, but it's too late. Owen's face is taught with barely supressed anger.

'If you don't want her, I'll get rid of her in the pond like the other kid.'

My breath catches as the weight of his words hit me. He did it. He drowned the child. Has been living in the house where she lived, next to the grandparents who found her as though this is normal.

'Oh, my God, Owen.' I take a step away from him. Want him to tell me he's joking. That he didn't kill that little girl, that he won't do it again, but I know in my heart it's hopeless. It's no longer about me, how he wants to please me, keep me, but about himself.

He'll do it. I know he will.

Owen is no longer looking at me. His face has a look of concentration that I recognise. One he uses when he's worked out a tricky plot twist.

'I'll tell the police the whole thing was your idea.' He nods, satisfied. 'One you concocted with your lover.'

'Jesus Christ, I don't have a lover!'

'But you did. Don't tell me you've forgotten him already. James – the man who listens to you. Would do anything for you. If you need reminding, it's all there in my book.'

I see it all now. Owen is going to make out that his novel is my confession. Everything I've done to make Phillipa hate me is going to count against me. All that time with Lexi. The police report about Jade. He thinks he can put the blame on me because I have the motive, the means… even the lover I'd told Phillipa about. He'll carry Lexi to the pond. Hold her head under the water as he did Maddie. The evidence there in the book he thinks he'll publish. His new bestseller, *I Did It For You*.

Owen pushes past me, Lexi struggling in his arms, but I grab at him, my fingers gripping his sleeve.

'Owen, stop! You misunderstood. It's not that I don't want her, just that we shouldn't rush things. Need to take time to think how we could make it work.' I'm talking too quickly, saying anything to make him stop. 'What we need is a plan. A proper plan.'

He turns. Doubtful but with a glint of hope in his eyes. He looks at my hand on his sleeve. 'Really?'

I need to use that hope, that small indication that I *am* still important to him, and make it work for me.

'Of course. You know how much I wanted a baby. We'll keep Lexi. Find a place to hide her. Not your mother's house, as we need to take care of her, and we don't know when the estate agent will start showing people around, but somewhere else.'

His face brightens and he points to the ceiling. 'The attic. Yes, that would do very nicely.'

I force a smile. 'It would. We can put a cot up there and look after Lexi like our own, and when your book is published, when it makes the bestseller list like *Dead Air*, we can move away from here. Be a proper family like we've always wanted... you, me and Lexi. You were right, Owen. It will be your gift to me. The perfect gift.'

Owen smiles. Too caught up in his make-believe to see that what I'm suggesting is impossible. In the morning, the police will be back. They'll have made more enquiries, done some more digging and will have more questions to ask. They'd had a look round the house when they'd been round before, but this time they'll have a search warrant. It won't take long before Lexi is found, pale and tearful, in our attic.

I look at my husband, see the madness in his eyes, and am scared by it. Not because I'll have to play along with his fantasy, but because I know that once the adrenaline stops pumping around his body and he digests the situation, he'll see how it can never work. He'll become desperate and desperate people do desperate things.

I have to do something. And it has to be now.

FIFTY

RACHEL

'Lexi's tired. Let me go upstairs and get her a blanket. She can sleep down here while we talk.'

Owen still has her in his arms, and although my instinct is to take her, I'm not sure he completely trusts me. Is unlikely to give her to me. Also, for my plan to work, I will be better off without her.

He looks down at the child. She's exhausted by all that's happened, her eyes nearly closed. Too young to understand what's been going on. 'She's fine and we have a lot to organise. A lot of things to buy. We'll need a cot for the attic, nappies, whatever a kid of her age eats.'

My need to leave him, to go upstairs and do what needs doing is burning me up. 'We can do all that later. We'll make a list and think about how we'll get them without creating suspicion. Now, though, I have to get Lexi that blanket. The poor love is shivering, and we don't want her to get sick. Illness means doctors and questions.'

Owen smiles at me indulgently. 'I always knew you'd be a good mother. Go on then, be quick. But first, give me your phone.'

'Why do you need it?' He doesn't answer, but I know why. He still doesn't trust me. Not entirely. I don't need the phone, though. There's something I need more.

I hand it to him, and he nods, satisfied. 'Go on then.'

As I hurry up the stairs, I blank my mind to everything except what needs to be done. I don't go into the spare bedroom where the blankets are kept but go straight into Owen's study. If he's not to suspect what I'm doing, I'll have to act quickly. The only weapon I can use to get Lexi away from him and to a place of safety is his precious novel. I have to make him believe I'll destroy it.

I drop to my knees by his desk, grabbing at the pages I dropped in my haste to go downstairs, not caring that they're now out of order. When I have them all, I go back onto the landing, then stop, fingers gripping the newel post at the top of the stairs. How can I be so stupid? What I have in my hand is only the hard copy. The digital copy is on his computer, locked in a folder to which I have no access. What use will it be destroying one without the other?

I run back, put his manuscript on the desk and wake up the computer. For this to work, I have to get into that file. I sit in Owen's chair, find the file and click on it. The box for the password comes up, and I watch the curser flash as it did before. This time, I *have* to make it work.

Think. Think.

I type in *Pond Close*, my heart sinking as the inevitable message pops up. *Incorrect password*. I try again with *Maddie*, then the names of all his novels. None of them are right. I glance at the door.

Shit. Shit. Shit.

I press the heels of my hands to my forehead. Focus. Focus. This is not the time to fall apart. Pulling open the drawer of his desk, I shove my hand into it and drag out his notebooks and flick through them. Searching for anything that could give me a clue. But it's like looking for a needle in a haystack. Everyone knows the best, most secure, passwords are the ones that contain numbers, capitals, special digits. How could I think I'd ever guess it?

I thump my fists on the desk in frustration.

'Rachel.' Owen's voice comes to me from downstairs, and I freeze, my fingers hovering above the keys. He sounds irritable.

'I won't be a moment.'

His voice comes back. 'What's taking you so long?'

I don't answer. Panic has taken hold, and my mind won't work properly. What would have been in Owen's head when he'd made up the password? I can't think. Can hardly breathe. Soon he'll come up the stairs to find me.

My eyes scan the room in desperation. Beside me is Owen's bookcase, his thrillers neatly arranged in date order. I've already tried all of their names, so they're no help. My eyes stop at *Dead Air*, the one that took off in a way the others hadn't, bringing him the respect and recognition he craved. I look at it. Look at the file. Is it possible? Might Owen's ego have dulled his common sense. Made him use something as simple as the word that is running through in my head?

My fingers begin to type. Below, I can hear Owen moving around our house.

Soon he'll be up here.

I may be wrong, but it's my only chance.

FIFTY-ONE

RACHEL

Owen is looking up at me from the hallway.

'What took you so long and where's the blanket?'

He's no longer holding Lexi. Maybe he's put her down on the settee. Is waiting for the blanket to cover her.

I steel myself. Know I can't put it off. I wave the manuscript over the edge of the banister. 'I didn't come up for the blanket, Owen. I came up for this.'

'What do you mean?' He frowns, confusion etched in the lines of his brow. Squints up at me through his glasses. 'What are you holding?'

I swallow. This is no time to crack.

'It's your manuscript.'

Owen takes a step closer, the hall light shining through his thinning hair. 'What the hell are you doing with it? I said I didn't want you to read it until it was published. Until it was a bestseller.'

My hands are shaking, and I steady them on the wooden stair rail. Look down at him. Behind me is the open door of Owen's study. The file unlocked. The digital copy of his manuscript deleted.

I hold out the sheaf of papers into the empty space, see how his mouth drops open. 'This is the only copy left, Owen. I deleted the rest.'

He looks aghast. 'What game is this you're playing?'

'It's no game. Every word is true.'

'But how? That file was password protected.'

'You thought the word *Bestseller* was enough, did you?'

His usually pale cheeks are mottled red. The muscle that moves at the base of his jaw and the white-knuckled fingers that grip the newel post, telling me I'm right. He had thought it enough. I can just imagine the smile of self-importance on his lips as he'd created the word that he believed would keep me out.

He puts a foot on the first step, reaches out a hand. 'Give it to me, Rachel. You have no need of it.'

I draw my hand in, hold it behind my back. 'Oh, but I have. I will destroy this copy too if you don't let me take Lexi home. This has gone far enough.'

'You wouldn't dare.'

'Wouldn't I?'

In my pocket is the lighter I use to light scented candles at Christmas. I'd put it there before coming upstairs and now my trembling fingers drag it out. As Owen watches, wide-eyed, I press in the ignition button, strike the spark wheel.

The flame dances. I don't let it touch the paper but hold it near enough for Owen to wince.

He holds out his hand. Palm towards me. Eyes pained. 'Stop!'

I release the button and the flame disappears. 'Then give me back my phone. Let me call the police.' I think of my mobile. Still on the table where Owen put it. 'Let them take Lexi back to her mother.'

Owen runs a hand through his hair. Then, without warn-ing, his face changes. He smiles at me. 'You look tired, Rachel.

This has all been very stressful for you. Why don't you let me run you a bath? A nice deep bath like my mother used to run for me.'

He closes his eyes, nods to himself as though remembering something. I've no idea why he's suggested it, but instinct tells me it's something to fear.

'I don't want a bath. I want to take Lexi home.'

Owen takes one step up. 'It will make you feel better. I promise you. My little sister loved her baths too. *Used* to love them.'

'Stay where you are!' I hold the lighter to the manuscript, fear making my hand shake. The flames dance at the edge of the paper. 'I mean it, Owen. I'll do it.'

But he's not listening. He's coming up the stairs now, taking them two at a time.

As he reaches me, the flame licks the first page, curling the edges. Devouring it and catching the ones underneath. The pages are too hot to hold, and I have no choice but to release them, jumping back as the blazing manuscript falls at my feet. I watch in horror as some of the burning pages float down the stairwell and onto the hall floor.

The smell of burning paper grows stronger. It's joined by the acrid stench of singed wool as the carpet catches. Owen gives the cry of an animal in pain. He throws himself onto the floor, his outstretched fingers reaching for the charred pages. The flat of his hand striking ineffectually at the licking flames.

Smoke rises, setting off the smoke alarm at the top of the stairs. Its shrill, incessant beep pulses through my head.

It seems so quick, but the flames are already spreading, the heat intensifying. Fear roots me to the spot as the stair rods catch, their paint peeling and bubbling. Wood charring. Only the thought of Lexi, alone downstairs, stops me from giving into the panic that threatens to overwhelm me. I press my back against the landing wall. I have to get downstairs to her, but

Owen is on his knees between me and the first step. Grasping at bits of paper. Flames licking at his clothes. His eyes wide with panic.

My eyes are stinging, and I can no longer see clearly. The air is being swallowed by the smoke, and each breath I take is laboured. The stairs have caught now, casting a strange orange light on the bare walls. Embers rise and dance.

How quickly the fire is spreading. I can't just stand here watching it. I have to get downstairs. Call for help. Blinking through the smoke, I feel my way to the bathroom, soak a towel under the bath tap and place it over my head. By the time I come out again, I can see nothing but flame and black smoke. Have no idea where Owen is.

I can't see where the landing ends and the stairs start and my head hurts from the incessant beeping of the smoke alarm that competes with the crackling of the fire.

There's the crash of burnt wood dropping to the hall floor below, then something else. A cry. It's coming from the direction of the living room, and I know it must be Lexi. I've got to save her. Got to get her out of the house.

Keeping close to the wall, I pull my sleeves over my hands and push through the smoke. Water from the wet towel drips down my face as I feel my way to the stairs. I have no idea where Owen is or what he's doing. All I know is I have to get to Lexi before the fire spreads to the downstairs rooms.

I cough, but the sound is feeble. Not strong enough to release the smoke that's been sucked into my lungs. I'm at the stairs now, terrified that at any moment I'll feel Owen's fingers around my ankle, that he'll drag me back into the flames and the smoke, but thank God I don't. Fighting for breath, I lean against the wall, arms outstretched, palms pressed against the paintwork. One step at a time I descend until I'm in the smoke-filled hall.

'Lexi! Lexi! It's all right. I'm here.'

I throw myself into the living room, the floorboards above my head creaking and groaning as the fire consumes them. I run over to the settee, but the little girl's not there. She must be hiding.

'Lexi, don't be frightened. Where are you?'

With rising panic, I look behind the settee, then under the table. When I don't find her, I check the patio doors, but they're shut.

Where is she? Where is Lexi?

I stand in the middle of the living room not knowing what to do. The hall is already filling with smoke. It billows into the sitting room, on a draught. Black and acrid. A strange orange glow is behind it as though the flames are being fanned. I hadn't noticed it on my way down, but the front door must be open. It has to be Owen who opened it.

I'm flooded with fresh terror. He's got Lexi, and I know where he's taking her.

Tears of desperation run down my cheeks. I have to save her, but I've left it too late. As I attempt to push through the door, the smoke and heat forces me back and when I try to breathe, each inhalation is more painful, more lacking in oxygen, than the one before.

Knowing the patio doors are my best chance of getting out of the house alive, I drop to my hands and knees. I manage a few feet, but it's so hot, the room so black with smoke, I can no longer see. I curl into a ball, coughs wracking my chest, and close my eyes, the flicker of orange flame playing against the back of my lids strangely comforting. *Is this how it will end*, I think. *For me and Lexi?*

As consciousness leaves me, I don't see the man who forces open the patio doors. Who runs into the room and lifts me in his arms. Don't hear him call to his wife.

'It's okay, Phillipa. I've got her.'

No, I don't see Carl or any of the other neighbours who

stand in their nightwear, terrified faces breaking into relief as I'm carried out onto the green. The last image I'd had in my head, before the blackness descended, had been one from my imagination. Lexi with her small hand in Owen's.

A second ribbon tied around the trunk of the birch tree. Waving in the breeze.

FIFTY-TWO

OWEN

Owen stumbles through the night, looking back only once to watch the orange flames that rise behind the upper storey windows of their house.

The kid is squirming in his arms, and he holds her tighter. Runs again, though it's hard when his lungs are full of smoke. Beneath his feet, the grass is damp, and as he hurries on towards the gate in the iron fence, wind whips his hair across his face. Perhaps Rachel was right, and he should have it cut. He'll do it before his next talk... the next interview. A change of image. That's what he needs.

There's a shout up ahead and Owen hesitates, not knowing if he can be seen. Steve is running out of his front door, one arm through his jacket. His mobile to his ear. He runs to his neighbours' house, thumps on Simone's door. His boy, the lairy one, is outside too now. He shouts something to Steve and runs, head down, across the green. Not looking Owen's way. Not seeing him.

Owen turns to look in the direction the boy is running. Phillipa is outside their house, her turquoise kimono belted tightly around her waist. Silhouetted against the orange. She's screaming Carl's name, Rachel's too.

Charlie has reached the front door. Aaron as well. They're looking for a way in, but the smoke is too thick. Pam is coming out of her front door. She runs to the end of the cul-de-sac and waits, hands on hips, for the fire service they must have called. Above the roar of the fire, Owen thinks he can hear the siren. Or maybe it's his imagination.

Phillipa's older children are with her now. They press into her, but the woman just stands there, hand to her mouth, watching the flames as though she's never seen fire before. Owen scoffs. If she'd read *Tight Spaces,* as she'd said she had at the book group, she'd know what a real fire looked like. Watching the scene in front of him, he can see that he'd written that chapter rather well. Vividly one might say. God knows why it hadn't sold well.

The bitter taste of disappointment is with him again. Has never left him, if he's honest. His mother's words too. *Get out of my sight, Owen. You're nothing but a waste of space.* But he must look forward to the future, not look back. *I Did It For You,* won't meet the same fate... he knows it in the very soul of him.

But then he remembers. The book no longer exists.

The child in his arms is kicking him with her cold, bare feet. Twisting and stretching away from him, but he holds her fast. The fire engine's wail is closer now, and he turns again, his attention drawn to the group gathered outside the burning building. Phillipa has broken away from her children, is running towards their house, her kimono flapping. Hair escaping from its bun. Now it's not his wife's name she's calling but Lexi's. Has she guessed? Is it possible?

Whether she has or hasn't, time is running out. Holding Lexi's foot against his stomach to stop it from kicking, he stumbles on, his only thought to get to the pond. The police mustn't find him with her. Must believe it was Rachel's doing.

It's hard to lift the latch on the gate with one hand, but Owen manages it, slips inside and closes the gate behind him. He hasn't brought a torch, but he doesn't need one because the moon is bright tonight, turning the birch's trunk a fairy-tale silver. As it had over twenty-five years ago.

He looks around. It's the first time he's been here since that day. The house where Kayla and Maddie had lived, with its sad aura, had drawn him to it. Given him inspiration. But this place is different – he'd been scared that if he looked down at the pond, he might see Maddie's face looking back at him from beneath the surface of the water. The memories of that night too strong. Crushing his creativity. Allowing doubt to creep in.

The wind blows, sending a ridge of ripples across the pond's surface, each one edged with moonlight. Owen sets Lexi down. Points. 'See that?' His lips are pressed to Lexi's ear. The words he speaks, ones he's said before. 'It's where the fairies live. Would you like to see them?'

Lexi nods through her tears as Maddie had and Owen smiles to himself.

'Then we'll need to get closer.'

He takes her hand. Leads her nearer to the pond's edge. Behind them the fire roars and cracks. Voices shout. Momentarily, he wonders what has happened to Rachel. What has become of her? But he pushes the thought away. Kayla. Anna. Now Rachel. They didn't want what he'd offered them, and he won't waste time thinking about them. He will move on from this. Find someone more deserving of his love.

But first, he must take care of matters here.

'The water's beautiful. See how the moonlight shines on its surface. It's where the fairies bathe. Rachel told me how you like your baths. Let's see if they will let you join them.'

They're in the reeds now, the ground beneath their feet wet and muddy. Lexi pulls back. Shakes her head violently. 'No bath.'

'But you must.' He bends. Scoops her up in his arms. She starts to cry, but he isn't worried. No one will hear her this night.

As he carries her closer to the water, the wail of the siren stops. He turns. Sees that over the top of the railings, the orange sky is strobed with pulsing blue. He needs to be quick.

Owen wades in, careful to keep his footing on the slippery bank. The water is cold, and he shivers. In front of him, the moon is a perfect silver disk on the pond's surface. He reaches down. Lowers Lexi into the centre of it, one hand on the back of her head. The other on the centre of her chest.

Lexi struggles, but she's small. Easy to hold. He slides his hand from under her head. Presses down, watching the water close over her face as it had with Maddie and his baby sister.

He thinks of his wife in their burning house. *I did it for you, Rachel*, he says under his breath. *You are to blame.*

FIFTY-THREE

RACHEL

I feel as though my chest will burst, every breath excruciating. I can hear voices, some I recognise, others I don't.

'Can you hear me, Rachel?' My eyes are prised open, first one then the other, and all I can see is the bright light that's shining at them.

Someone's holding my hand. Its warmth is comforting, and I squeeze it.

'I think she's awake.' It's Simone's voice and I'm glad.

The grass is cold and wet beneath my back, and when I open my eyes a crack, I see the green overalls of the paramedic who's crouching over me. 'You're going to be fine, Rachel. We've put a sterile dressing on the burns on your arm, but we need to get you to hospital. Let me slip this over your head... it's something to help you breathe more easily.'

I let her put the oxygen mask over my nose and mouth, then lift it again as the enormity of what happened tonight hits me. I try to sit up.

'Oh my God. Lexi!' I grip hold of the paramedic's arm. I have to tell them. They have to know. 'My husband... he's taken her to the pond.' I point in the direction of the green. 'He'll kill her. Drown her like he did Maddie. You have to stop him. You have to tell someone.'

Something passes between Simone and the paramedic. Is there something I don't know?

'What's happened? There's something you're not telling me, isn't there? Oh, Jesus. Please don't say she's dead?'

Simone squeezes my hand. Swallows.

'You don't have to worry about Lexi. She's not been harmed. You must think about yourself now. Let them get you to hospital and do some more checks. The important thing is you concentrate on getting better. You've had a terrible shock, and the doctors need to make sure you haven't inhaled too much smoke.' She stops, looks away, a tear running down her cheek. 'I'm sorry we argued, Rach. Sorry I wasn't a better friend.'

But I'm not listening. I need to be sure they're not lying to me. Covering up the truth until I'm fully recovered.

'Where is Lexi? I need to see her.' My voice comes out as a croak.

'She's there. Like I said, she's fine.'

She points behind her, and I see Phillipa. She's sitting on the kerb, her child in her arms, her little body swamped by a blue blanket. As I watch, Lexi reaches up a hand to her mother's face, and Phillipa bursts into a fresh wave of tears.

'My baby. My baby,' she croons, and my heart bursts with relief.

'It was Geoff who found her,' Simone continues. 'He pulled her out of the pond and the paramedics checked her over. He'd been woken by your smoke detector and had phoned the fire brigade. As he'd come out of his house, he'd seen Owen crossing the green with Lexi in his arms. They were heading for the pond – an odd thing to do, seeing as the fire had already taken hold of the upstairs of your house. All the other men, the younger ones, Steve, Carl and the two lads, well they presumed you were still in there. They were trying to get into your house, but the fire had caught hold by the front door, and when they smashed a window, the fire was too fierce to climb through. There was nothing Geoff could do to help, so he made the decision to go after Owen. Find out what was going on.'

Another paramedic has joined the first. They lift me onto a stretcher and wheel me to the waiting ambulance. It's then I see the police car outside Pam and Geoff's house. I turn my head to see better, expect Owen to be in the back seat, but the car's empty.

Simone is walking beside me, still holding my hand, the other supporting her bump. I look at her. 'Where is he? Where's Owen?'

My eyes are still stinging from the smoke and the ointment the paramedics put in. All I want to do is sleep, but I have to keep myself awake. Her answer is important.

Simone looks across to the paramedic, a question in her eyes. Receives a small nod of affirmation in return. She holds my hand tighter.

They've given me medication to keep me relaxed, to dull the pain, and I can barely keep my eyes open. Simone's lips are moving. She's telling me something about my husband, but her voice dips in and out of my consciousness.

As I'm wheeled into the ambulance, I see people crossing the green. Police with torches that slice through the night. The gate is open, and, through it, the pond lies mirror-flat in the moonlight. There are people kneeling beside it. More ambulance crew, I think.

Beside me, Simone is crying softly, but I must have misheard her answer because what she's said is impossible. The words unthinkable as though lifted from one of Owen's own novels.

He's dead, Rachel. Her words fill my head. *Your husband is dead.*

FIFTY-FOUR

Eight Months Later

Phillipa picks up a pair of metal tongs and captures a barbequed chicken breast between its prongs. She puts one on her plate and one on mine.

'Salad with it? New potatoes?'

I nod and accept the plate from her. Balance it on my lap.

'It was good of you to do this, Phillipa.'

'I wanted to.' She looks away. Pats her hair, still unused to the shorter style. 'Do you think I did the right thing cutting it?'

'I think it looks lovely. It suits you. What do you think, Lexi? Do you like Mummy's hair?'

'Yes.' The little girl wraps her arms around her mother's legs. 'You look pretty, Mummy.'

Phillipa laughs and rests her hand on her daughter's curls. 'You do too, sweetie. Now if you've had enough to eat, why don't you go and play? Jo Jo's in the dinosaur tent and you could join her. The tyrannosaurus and triceratops could have a battle. What do you think?'

Lexi laughs. She runs over to the small nylon tent, a land of dinosaurs printed on its sides, and lifts the flap. Soon we hear the sound of giggling. A dinosaur's roar.

Phillipa takes the garden seat next to me. 'I never did thank you.'

I look at her. 'What for?'

'For everything you did for me and Lexi. The time you gave us.'

'It was my job.'

'I know, but Lexi loved you being there, and I couldn't have done without you.' She looks embarrassed. 'I know I treated you like shit, and I also know I've never apologised either. But I'm doing it now. I was a cow, and do you know why? It was because I was jealous of you... of your friendship with Simone. After Kayla, I'd never been good at friendships, and it's because I couldn't trust myself after what had happened. You see, Kayla never forgave me for sleeping with Maddie's dad, Stuart, and I never forgave myself either. I hated that I'd hurt her. Blamed myself for my part in Maddie's death because if I hadn't done what I did, the two of them wouldn't have argued. Wouldn't have left their little girl alone downstairs. I missed her friendship so much, and when Kayla moved away, I never heard from her again. It was Geoff who told me she'd had another child... a boy called Aaron. Geoff who told me she'd taken her own life.' She reaches inside her sleeve for a tissue and blows her nose. 'Things became a little better when Simone moved into the close. We became friends and when, a few years later, you and Owen moved in, I couldn't bear the thought of you spoiling it. I'm so sorry.'

I turn to her, knowing how difficult it must have been for her to say all this.

'You don't need to be sorry. It was Owen who spoilt my friendship with Simone, not you. As for you and Kayla... it must have been hard for her, and I understand why you feel guilty, but you were just teenagers. These things happen and you couldn't have known how it was all going to end. You have to put it behind you.'

Phillipa looks down at her hands. 'That's kind of you, but it doesn't excuse how badly I treated you. After having had Lexi, my self-esteem was at zero. I made the mistake of telling Carl about me and Stuart, and he used it as an excuse to do whatever the hell he liked. What's sauce for the goose is sauce for the gander was his motto. You're a beautiful girl and he's always had a roving eye. I felt threatened. Not that I had any need... I see that now. You're a lovely person, Rachel, and I should have known that.'

She looks over at Carl. He's playing football with Steve and the teenage boys. When he sees us looking, he waves. On the other side of the makeshift goal, Chantelle is lying on a blanket, top rolled up to expose her toned midriff to the early summer sun. Long legs clothed in the usual tiny denim shorts. I'm no longer sure that Phillipa knew about her and Carl, and I certainly won't be the one to tell her because, since Owen took Lexi, Carl's been a doting father. An attentive husband. Also, it's been months since I've seen him cross the green when Steve's car's been missing from the drive.

I smile. 'You don't need to apologise.'

Phillipa looks down at her plate of food, stabs half-heartedly at a cocktail sausage. 'But I do. I'm ashamed of how I behaved and what you must have thought of me. Lexi's pregnancy wasn't planned, and I found it hard having another child at a time the other two were older and I'd just got my independence back. I became controlling: bedtimes, food lists, you name it. It was my way of coping. It's no excuse, though, and I should never have taken it out on you when you had troubles of your own.'

I feel colour rise to my cheeks. 'I'm sorry too. Not only for what Owen did but for everything. At the garden party, I overheard you say you'd smack Lexi and that set me on a path I should never have gone on.'

'I know I said it, but I'd never have carried it out, Rachel. I've never smacked Lexi. Never.'

'I know that now and should never have reacted the way I did. I should never have presumed that what you said meant you didn't love or care for her. It's no excuse but after the failed IVF, I became depressed and started to question other women's ability to be a mother. I took it too far and began to imagine I was the only one who could do that job.'

I think of Jade. How my fixation on keeping her safe had begun and how I'd started to think of her as my own child. I see now why her mother hadn't been happy with me, but on the night she'd found me and Jade by the pond, there had been an innocent explanation. I'd been reading Jade a poem from the *Flower Fairies* book and through the window had seen the moonlight reflected in the water of our garden pond. *It's where the fairies bathe,* I told her. *Do you want to see?*

Something Owen had once said when the moon was full. I'd thought it romantic then.

I know now how Owen had made the situation worse. Hinted to the police that I was unstable. It had been another way to keep control of me. To keep me from leaving.

Phillipa looks at me with sympathy. 'We've both struggled in our own ways.' She looks over at the *For Sale* sign on the other side of the road. 'Another move. Another family living in Pond Close. It makes me nervous after everything that's happened. How do you feel about it?'

'Sad, of course, but excited too. I don't think you should worry. The new owners have two children, and I'm sure they'll fit in very well. It will be another excuse for you to throw a garden party... or should I say a green party.'

We both laugh, but Phillipa's eyes are sad.

'I know, but I'm sorry to have to say goodbye.'

'Me too.'

I take a bite of the chicken. It's delicious. Phillipa has done us all proud. It's hard to believe that only last year she was throwing us our welcoming party. Now the banner inside the small marquee says, *Sorry you're leaving*.

Simone wanders over, Ethan in her arms. 'Ouch,' she says as she takes the deckchair beside me and gently prises open her baby's little fingers. 'Let go of Mummy's hair. How are you doing, Rach?'

'I'm good.' Without thinking, my fingers stray to the shiny pink skin that runs down the side of my arm. It took a while to heal, but now I hardly feel it. 'What about you?'

It's a question we've asked each other many times since they found Kevin, the divers pulling his lifeless body from the reeds below the weir. We'll never know for sure what happened the night Kevin disappeared, but I have my suspicions. The lake with its weir was the place where I'd sat with James, the place where Lexi's coat had been found – placed there by Owen to put the police off the scent. He's the common denominator between the two things, but he's no longer alive to give his defence.

'I'm doing all right. Today's a better day.' Simone reaches across and squeezes my hand, knowing I understand. Knowing I have experience of how awful the bad days can be. 'Would you mind holding Ethan for me while I get some food? Sorry he's a bit soggy. He's teething again.'

I say I don't mind and Simone hands him to me. She's right. The bib he wears around his neck is soaked, his dribble darkening the letter M that's embroidered on it to a deep red. It's nice that he's wearing it as, even though Geoff and Pam have never liked to talk about it, between us, in small ways, we try to keep Maddie's memory alive. I think of the *Hello Kitty* sticker pressed to the wall of the kitchen cupboard. The room was one of the few that escaped the worst of the smoke, and I've left the sticker there.

Lexi's back and pulling at Phillipa's arm. 'I need a wee, Mum.'

Phillipa sighs. 'No rest for the wicked. You don't mind me leaving you?'

'Of course not.'

She gets up and leads Lexi across the green in the direction of their house. The shock of almost losing her daughter has changed her, and their relationship is now stronger than it's ever been. I'm glad for her.

I settle in my chair, enjoying the rest of my lunch. On the other side of the marquee, Pam and Geoff are talking to Steve, glasses of Prosecco in their hands. Like Phillipa and Simone, they've never blamed me for what Owen did and have chosen not to hate me because I'm his wife. *Was* his wife. Of course, Owen's death has made that easier, but I'll always be grateful to them for their understanding because, in one way or another, what happened to Maddie left a fingerprint on all our lives.

I look over at the wild area in the centre of the green. The railings have been taken down and there's a yellow bulldozer next to where the pond once was. It's been filled in, and they're turning the area into a wildlife garden with plants that will attract the butterflies and bees. A bench, with Maddie's name on it, has already been erected beside the silver birch and, although it ought to be a place of sadness, strangely it isn't. In years to come, when the pond is just a memory, people will wonder how our close got its name, but it was the right thing to do. It's something on which we all agreed at the last residents' meeting.

Geoff is only half listening to Steve, and I see he's looking at me. He raises his glass and I pick mine up from the ground by my feet and do the same. I'm sad he and Pam are moving, but I understand why. They'd never managed to make a true break before, had only moved as far as the house next door to the one they owned. Not wanting to live at Number 2 with its memories, but unable to tear themselves away from the road where their granddaughter had lived her short little life. I know that Maddie hadn't shared Geoff's blood, but Pam had told me he'd felt the weight of her death as keenly as she had.

He'd blamed himself for not keeping the little girl safe. Should have seen what was under his nose and believed the stories Aaron had told him when the boy had moved in with them after his mother's suicide three years earlier. Stories Kayla had told him when she was high on something or other about a teenage paperboy she'd befriended when she was expecting Maddie. A boy who couldn't tell the difference between friendship and love. One who pestered her so much she'd started to fear him.

Owen someone.

The association between that paperboy and the man who'd moved into Number 2 had only come to light the night of Owen's talk to the book group. When he'd mentioned that he'd once lived in the area, had dreamt of becoming an author back when he was a paperboy, Pam had felt as though someone had walked over her grave. She'd left early and told Geoff. That teenage boy who had stalked their daughter... it had to be him. It *had* to be.

No wonder I hadn't seen Geoff around. That punch must have left its mark on his hand as well as on Owen's side.

I look at the freshly painted windows of my house. At the new tiles on the roof. Geoff had only known a part of it, of course. Would have had no idea that Owen had been at the house on the night of Maddie's death. After all, no one had seen him and, for all the years after, Geoff had believed *he'd* been the one to leave the front door open.

That he didn't, will be of little comfort to him now he knows the truth.

People ask how I can continue living in Pond Close after everything that's happened, and it's a difficult question to answer. In the aftermath of the fire, when the terrible things Owen had done had been in all the papers, I'd thought a lot about moving. But out of the tragedy, something wonderful happened. The whole close came together, wrapped me in its collective arms and supported me through the months to come. Simone offered me her spare room while the insurance claim was going through and the fire damage repaired. Thankfully, the worst of the damage was confined to the top floor, but it's only recently I've moved back in. Without Owen in it, the house is different. I've grown to like it and feel I owe it to Maddie to make it a happy place.

Owen's notoriety means that his books have started to sell again – *Tight Spaces* finally making the bestseller list. The irony isn't wasted on me, but I'd be lying if I said the money from the royalties hasn't been useful. I haven't kept it all though... a proportion has gone to The Fertility Foundation.

'Penny for them.' Simone places a hand on my shoulder.

I cover her hand with my own. 'Oh, nothing you'd want to hear, and I don't want to bring the mood down. It was just thoughts about the house. The close. You know.'

'I do.' She drops a kiss on the top of my head. 'You're doing great. You know that, don't you?'

I smile up at her. 'Thank you. You too.'

Ethan has fallen asleep on my lap, so she takes him from me and puts him in his pushchair. I bend, set my paper plate on the grass.

'I hope you don't mind, but I need a leg stretch. I've been sitting too long.'

'Of course not. Want some company?'

I shake my head. 'I'm all right. I won't be long. I'll be back before Phillipa brings out her famous pavlova.'

Simone laughs. She knows there are times when I like to be by myself and doesn't question it as she needs that too – private time to process everything that's happened. To grieve for what k is best. I'm staying too. Even after

t I'll miss seeing your little one

ch his arm. 'You and Pam will

at, don't you?'

be back. Not when there are so

own his face. 'He would have

er. He puts it on his lap and

blanket and hands it to me.

e it.'

hreads that make up the

by Pam for her grand-

er his shoulder.

before tomor-

he place

see his

ght he

for

When I was at primary school.
cul-de-sac of identical houses. I u
lot when I was nine or ten an
community came back to me
next piece of work. I wanted
hidden behind the houses' s
delve into the lives and secrets

So that's what I did, and T

I hope you enjoyed *The*
would be very grateful if yo
hear what you think, and i
new readers to discover one

I enjoy hearing from r
my Facebook page, throu
website.

Thanks,

Wendy x

EDGEMENTS

onderful editor at Bookouture,
nd invaluable insights bring
make them the best that they
    unwavering support since
e, all those years ago, has
    I am immensely grateful

            ture, your collective
                ly appreciated.
                tegral role in
                ders. And I
                vers whose
                are instru-
                audience.

                    Tracy
                    experi-
                    ation.
                    ns of

                        da
                        k

we've lost. It's what makes her such
rub my chest. Recently, I've been
small price to pay for the joy t
weeks.

As I walk towards the wildl
my hand on my growing sto
happened that day in the woo
the trees of the clearing, and
whelm me, I tell myself that
That this baby's father i
James... the better side of hir

It's something I must n

I reach the bench and
play patterns on my le
warmth of the sun.

My eyelids da
cleared.

'Mind if I

I open

'Of cc

He si
across th

I s

the tea

'I'

H

no r

r.

e thank you to everyone who
hardly believe that this is my
ut readers, an author would
u enjoyed reading my book

and want to keep up-to-
on up at the following
ared, and you can

me – places
ke District
s Hidden
eetheart.
adition
might

ested
ies
ts

many nights I've lain awake wor
night of the fire when Geoff pull
Owen slipped and drowned. No

My husband's words are in 1
him a helping hand, he woul
anyway. It was a mercy for ever

He wouldn't have known i
A life for a life.

I get up and go to the t
that's been there for the las
pocket... will give it to Geof
me to know. *Needed* me to

With a last look at t
others, forcing my mind t
my baby. My friends a
that Phillipa offers
hand in hand t
take them to a
I'm happy fo

I'm glad
with Geoff.

My si
years ago
We'

created. Thanks also to my family who always read m[y] books... hopefully not just because they feel they ought to!

Finally, the biggest thank you of all must go to my husba[nd], Ian, for his constant faith in my ability to produce good b[ooks], his support and understanding during the countless hou[rs] are dedicated to writing them and for being my rock.

PUBLISHING TEAM

...g a manuscript into a book requires the
...f many people. The publishing team at
...re would like to acknowledge everyone
...o contributed to this publication.

Audio
Alba Proko
Sinead O'Connor
Melissa Tran

Commercial
Lauren Morrissette
Jil Thielen
Imogen Allport

Cover design
Aaron Munday

Data and analysis
Mark Alder
Mohamed Bussuri

Editorial
Jennifer Hunt
Sinead O'Connor

Copyeditor
Jane Eastgate

Proofreader
Catherine Lenderi

Marketing
Alex Crow
Melanie Price
Occy Carr
Ciara Rosney

Operations and distribution
Marina Valles
Stephanie Straub

Production
Hannah Snetsinger
Mandy Kullar
Jen Shannon

Publicity
Kim Nash
Noelle Holten
Myrto Kalavrezou
Jess Readett
Sarah Hardy

Rights and contracts
Peta Nightingale
Richard King
Saidah Graham

Made in the USA
Columbia, SC
April 2024

34105967R00186